Only The Thunder Knows

Gord Rollo

JournalStone's DoubleDown Series, Book I

Gord Rollo (signature)

LIMITED EDITION HARDCOVER
__6__ OF 100 COPIES

JOURNALSTONE PUBLISHING

Only the Thunder Knows

By
Gord Rollo

JournalStone
San Francisco

Copyright © 2013 by Gord Rollo

All rights reserved. No part of this book may be used or reproduced by any means, graphic, electronic, or mechanical, including photocopying, recording, taping or by any information storage retrieval system without the written permission of the publisher except in the case of brief quotations embodied in critical articles and reviews.

This is a work of fiction. All of the characters, names, incidents, organizations, and dialogue in this novel are either the products of the author's imagination or are used fictitiously.

JournalStone books may be ordered through booksellers or by contacting:

JournalStone
www.journalstone.com
www.journal-store.com

The views expressed in this work are solely those of the authors and do not necessarily reflect the views of the publisher, and the publisher hereby disclaims any responsibility for them.

ISBN: 978-1-936564-82-8   (sc)
ISBN: 978-1-940161-16-7   (hc – limited edition)
ISBN: 978-1-936564-79-8   (ebook)

Library of Congress Control Number: 2013935628

Printed in the United States of America
JournalStone rev. date: June 7, 2013

Cover Design: Denis Daniel
Cover Art: Alan M. Clark

Edited By: Norman Rubenstein

Dedication

I'd like to give a shout out to my friend and fellow author Steve Savile. He's a brilliant writer and a huge inspiration for me. More importantly for the project you're holding in your hands, it was Steve who originally suggested the idea for a dark tale about the grave robbers turned serial killers, Burke and Hare. For years we talked about writing something together and I'd hoped this book might eventually be the one. Unfortunately, Steve is so incredibly busy (not that there is anything unfortunate about that—he's earned every bit of his success) we just couldn't find the time to make it happen this time around. When this opportunity came along for me, and I heard that Rena Mason was writing a historical horror tale set in Great Britain, I knew I wanted to write something in a similar historical vein as well. Burke and Hare fit that theme perfectly. I asked Steve if he minded if I wrote the story myself and he graciously told me to go ahead. I still hope we get the chance to work together sometime soon, but for now I'll be content if Steve reads my book and doesn't think I screwed it up too badly.

Endorsements

"*Only the Thunder Knows* is a wonderfully written story by Gord Rollo, possibly his very best writing (which is saying quite a bit). The story starts with two grave robbers but it moves into unexpected territory as it continues and by the end I was totally enthralled. I was amazed at the skill Rollo brings to the table to be able to pull this off. Very highly recommended!" – **John R. Little**

"Readers who enjoy toying with alternate-historical hypotheses and can endure gore should find these lively accounts appealing." – **Publishers Weekly**

A Little Knowledge
Is
A Dangerous Thing

An Introduction by Alan M. Clark

This volume marks the beginning of the new Double Down series of books to be released by JournalStone Publishing. The unusual *tête-bêche* books are inspired by the Ace Doubles from the 1950s to the 1970s.

Part of what draws the two novellas in this book into one volume is that each of the authors has chosen to give their story a well-known historical setting. Both take place in Great Britain; Gord Rollo's, "Only the Thunder Knows," in Edinburgh in the late Georgian era of the resurrectionists, particularly Burke and Hare, and Rena Mason's, "East End Girls," in Victorian London during the time of Jack the Ripper.

I love a good historical fiction or alternate history tale, one that helps me do a bit of time-travel, and these stories transport me to fascinating periods. Nearly everyone enjoys looking back in history and considering a simpler time. Some of that pleasure comes from trying to imagine how the world might be today if events had unfolded differently in the past. For me, much of the enjoyment comes from knowing that the people of the past had something to look forward to; some of the advances in science and medicine that we enjoy today. Those people had hope of a better world, and we know they had the guts and the drive to get there, for here we are. When casually considering the past, however, we often don't think about what it took to turn those hopes for a better world into reality; the struggles, the growing pains, the unintended consequences of trying something new.

Both the late Georgian and Victorian eras saw enormous advancements in science in Great Britain. With the science came new technologies in medicine and industry. Of course there were those who capitalized on the economic growth that ensued, and they had their share of hubris, their ofttimes heedless and single-minded efforts to drive the technologies into the future resulting in unintended consequences that caused their fellow man no end of trouble and harm. Of course we are always on the cusp of knowing more, but frequently, even when we have only a little knowledge, we tend to have big ideas—sometimes dangerous ideas—of what we could do with it. But then, this is in part how we learn. We make mistakes. It's messy, but there seems to be an inevitability about the process and no good way around it.

What's fascinating to me is that when looking back on such eras we are strangely nostalgic about our naiveté. Some even lament the loss of those *simpler times*. What these periods provide for the writer is settings for great tragic drama.

And Mason and Rollo have employed them for just that.

"East End Girls" takes place in the 1880s when the industrial revolution had made Great Britain the richest nation in the world. That same revolution, however, had put so many of the British people out of work that the East End of London experienced some of the worst poverty known anywhere at the time. The poor and vulnerable were the prey of Jack the Ripper. Perhaps nothing could have stopped the first murder, but with better law enforcement techniques the subsequent murders might have been prevented. The repeated loss of life becomes more poignant when considering that fingerprinting, a technology that might have helped catch the killer, was introduced to the London police and rejected by shortsighted officials in 1886, 2 years before the Ripper. In this case, the *lack* of action in taking up a technology caused unintended harm. Yes, I think it even as I tap the keys to write this—they were *simpler times*. Jack the Ripper may have had little fear of being caught. Because the history of the Ripper has many such wellsprings of collective human regret, I have always been fascinated with stories of the murderer and have explored the history in my own writing. Mason's tale has wonderful new twists and turns to add to the growing body of speculation about Jack the Ripper.

Gord Rollo's story is centered around the most notorious characters from the dark history of bodysnatching, William Burke and William Hare. To this day, the best way to study anatomy is to dissect a human being. In modern times we tend to have plenty of people willing to hand over their bodies after death to this purpose, but that's not how it's always been. In the past, due to religious beliefs and other scruples throughout most of the developing world, we have not been consistently willing to give up our dead for dissection sufficient to the need of every one striving to become a physician.

Whenever we've failed to meet that need, a market for stolen dead bodies has emerged. My grandfather, Dr. Sam Lillard Clark (1898 to 1961), was head of the Anatomy Department at Vanderbilt University in Nashville, and was on the Tennessee Anatomical Board (he called it the Board Stiff), charged with the task of securing cadavers for all the medical students in Tennessee. When there were not enough to go around, he employed a body snatcher. I have long loved the history of bodysnatching, ever since reading my grandfather's paper, "Medical Education from the Ground Up," that he wrote and delivered to his gentleman's club in the 1940s. Part of the paper are the words of his body snatcher—originally recorded on Dictaphone® (wax cylinder dictation machine), then transcribed by my grandfather into the paper—telling of his exploits in the Nashville area, the city where I grew up.

Rollo's novella puts a shovel in my hand and pays me handsomely to dig for corpses alongside his characters, and I'm right there with them when they make an incredible discovery that turns the reader's expectations inside out.

When I was asked to paint the cover art for this Double Down book, I was excited by the subject matter. Reading the beautifully crafted stories I became immersed in long lost, gritty worlds of British history, both realistically and fantastically portrayed by Rollo and Mason. Then I was offered the honor of writing this introduction! Rarely have I been presented with a project that so well suits my own interests. I hope you enjoy this book as much as I have.

Only the Thunder Knows

By
Gord Rollo

Chapter 1

Edinburgh, Scotland
October, 1828

Other than the incessant rain, which is pretty much a given this far north, the Gaffer had told Charlie Mawson hot wax burns would be what he'd hate most about igniting the gaslights along the narrow cobbled streets of Westport. *The Warden's Curse* he'd called it, but the Gaffer had been wrong. Naturally, Charlie cursed every time he held his pole aloft and scalding drops of melted candle rained down on him, but the skin on his hands had toughened up – burnt into insensitivity most likely – and for the last week he had taken to wearing a wide-brimmed felt hat which he fancied made him look like a Spaniard out to fence his way across some pirate's galleon. Besides, practice had taught him ways to avoid most of the spills. The burns he could cope with.

No, it was the fog he truly despised, the thick Edinburgh pea-soupers that left the cobbles invisible beneath his feet as he trudged along the empty streets.

Charlie loathed being alone when the fog descended on the city. And he hated the way his mind conjured up all kinds of demons and phantoms – always just out of sight and reach but only just so – hovering ominously on the periphery of his vision, masked by the swirling mist. And when the fog rolled in extra thick, as it had tonight, blanketing Westport in its eerie shroud, Charlie's palms would grow sweaty and chills danced up and down his back as iron bands of dread tightened slowly around his chest, squeezing the very breath from his lungs.

Charlie had thought it a stroke of genius on his part to apply for a job as a Warden with the gasworks – instead of being cooped up in some rat-infested factory along the Firth of Forth all day long, he'd be working outside, no one watching over his every move. And it was good money besides. He couldn't believe how many folks on the route paid him an extra ha'penny a week to knock them awake come sunrise. Easy money, he'd thought, knocking on a few windows after he'd doused the gaslights for the day to come. Thirty days into his employment, and the fog had convinced Charlie that a factory job wasn't the 'evil to end all evils' after all.

Ah, to Hell and buggery, just get on with it, yer fool, Charlie thought, chastising himself. *Once the blasted lights are burnin' you'll feel better.*

A Hackney cab ghosted by in the distance; or perhaps it was one of those fancy new two-wheeled hansom cabs he'd been hearing about lately, its iron-rimmed wheels striking sparks on the uneven cobbles. Though in truth he might never have known it was there without the clop of the horse's shoes and the clatter of the wheel rims on the broken stones. The fog smudged out its black shape until it simply ceased to be.

Charlie shivered, thinking of ghoulies and ghosties and other nasty things that went bump in the night.

Fear is peculiar like that, Charlie knew. You struggled through with clenched teeth like you were lugging a bloody great bag of coal on your back. You've just got to get on with it or it will drop you in your tracks. And right enough, once he'd ignited most of the gaslights along the High Street he felt more in control. The flames burned off some of the fog and pushed the darkness back to a safer distance. Charlie knew it was all in his head but nevertheless he felt the bands around his chest slowly ease their grip. He took several deep breaths, doing his best to relax.

Then he heard the footsteps.

Slow and measured.

Heavy, confident strides.

Assuredly male. Not the leggy gait of a whore out working the streets or the nervous tap-tap-scuffle of a more refined lady – no self-respecting woman would be out this late, he reasoned, certainly not in this part of town – definitely a man.

He felt his chest tightening again.

The footsteps approached out of the fog, coming from some still unlit section of the city but with the all-encompassing white mist it was impossible to judge if they came from behind him, ahead of him or from either side. That was another thing Charlie hated about the fog; it rendered direction meaningless. He strained to peer through the gloom but there was nothing to see except a calico cat sheltered under the eaves of the local bakery, enjoying the lingering aromas of cinnamon and saffron that were drifting out from the air vents.

Suddenly, like one of the wraiths that plagued his imagination, a tall figure dressed in black strode purposefully out of the night, the curtain of fog torn asunder and scattered by his appearance. Charlie stared at the shape coalescing out of the mist. The fragment of jaundiced light from the gaslight gave the man's face a deathlike pallor, as though his bone-white skull showed through the folds of skin drawn over it. The newcomer was like something that might walk out of Dante's Hell. Tails fluttered like the wings of black birds around his legs.

The footsteps slowed.

Stopped.

Charlie very nearly screamed but he bit down on it hard enough to draw blood from his bottom lip.

The newcomer was big, well over six feet and easily fifteen stone, though his bulky overcoat and top hat made him appear both wider and taller. Their eyes met for a moment but Charlie quickly broke the contact and looked away, pretending to fumble with the glass casing on the light above him despite the fact that it was already lit and closed. Fear tied anxious knots deep in his belly.

Sweet Mary, Mother of All Things Good and Holy!

He had thought, for no more than a heartbeat, that the tall man had no eyes. Good Catholic boy that he was, Charlie moved instinctively to make the sign of the cross on his chest but he stopped himself. He didn't want the stranger thinking he was some simpleton fresh out from the asylum.

Just keep yer head down an' let him walk by, Charlie, my old son. Just let him walk by…

"A word with you, young sir?" a deep, gravelly voice asked. Then silence and Charlie had no choice but to look up and face its owner.

A small measure of relief washed over him: The man wasn't some mystical Speaker of the Dead; he did in fact have eyes and not cold round shillings, albeit the strangest eyes Charlie had ever seen. Twin blanks; the whole eye the same ice white as the stranger's long hair and slightly ragged beard – an exact match for the shifting banks of fog. A shiver wormed its way down the length of Charlie's back.

"Can I help you, Gov'nor?"

"That depends. I'm looking for Tanner's Close," White Eyes said. "I was told I might find a lodging house there. It is, after all, deep into the dead of night and even the most restless souls must sleep."

Directions. All he wants is a place to kip down. Thank Christ for that. For all that Charlie still couldn't look the stranger square in the eye.

"Aye sir…'tis." Charlie turned and pointed along the street in the direction of the Quayside. "Down that way toward the water, Tanner's is the fourth turning you'll come to, you can't miss it. Go into the crescent and you'll see Log's Lodging House right on the corner. Big building. Bit rundown, but then what isn't around here? Anyway, like I said, you can't miss it."

He was rambling.

White Eyes made no response. His inspection was invasive. It made Charlie feel dirty, violated, as though the tall man wasn't staring *at* him, but rather *into* him. Perhaps, Charlie thought wildly, he could see into his soul and was actually reading it then to see if he spoke the truth or not. Charlie shook his head blaming the crazy notion on the wee dram of whiskey he'd knocked back before coming out. Apparently satisfied, he gave Charlie a slight nod then moved off down the street without so much as another word.

Would a thank you 'ave killed you, you upper- class git? Oh no, too good to be thankin' the likes of a simple Warden. Bleedin' Toff.

The stranger stopped in midstride, inclining his head ever so slightly as though listening to some sound only he could hear, and then walked on. Over his shoulder, he called: "My thanks, young man. You'll find your reward, I am sure, in Heaven. Ah… and speaking of the good Lord's house, the old lady on Princess Street won't wake up come sunrise, so save your banging, Charlie Mawson. She's sleeping the good sleep."

Charlie could only stare, unwilling, *unable* to turn his back on this mysterious man. *How the bloody buggerin' Hell does he know my name?*

Chilled bone deep, Charlie watched the stranger walk away. One by one, each gaslight along the High Street dulled, flickered, and then went out as he passed it.

Charlie dropped his candle and fumbled for the flask of whiskey he kept hidden in the depths of his coat pockets, not nearly as afraid of the fog now as he was of the darker things that walked within it. Shaking, he uncapped the silver stopper and drank deeply. The whiskey burned on its way down but it didn't even begin to touch the chill in his rapidly beating heart.

* * *

Maggie Hare answered the door almost before the first knock had sounded. She threw it wide open and braced herself there in the doorway like some common fishwife, ready to give her miserable excuse for a husband a mouthful for coming home in the middle of the night stinking of beer and smoke.

She'd kept a faithful vigil at the downstairs window for hours with only the ticking of the grandfather clock in the common room for company. Not that she could see anything of the streets outside. A fog had crept in off Colston Hill and the peaks of the Highlands beyond, smothering the city in mist so thick she had trouble seeing the end of her nose much less the road and the workhouses and factories beyond her front stoop. William, her husband, was a good for nothing drunk. *Worthless as a human being, worth even less as a husband*, Maggie thought bitterly. Given his usual state of inebriation she was constantly surprised when he found his way home, but then even the mangiest of mongrels seem to have the knack for finding their beds and a softie to feed them come morning.

"Damn you, William Hare! If you've been out pokin' some damned whore–" Maggie launched into her tirade but the familiar invective had barely left her tongue before she saw the stranger waiting on the doorstep.

She wasn't sure who the tall dark-clothed man was, but he definitely wasn't her William.

"Ah, my sincerest apologies, Good Wife. I appear to have come at a bad time," the stranger said, no hint of the Scottish burr to his voice; nor Irish for that matter. An English Gentleman maybe, out in the dead of night. "I was hoping to rent a room but I can return in the morning, or perhaps you know of somewhere else nearby?"

"Goodness me, no, sir. Come in, come in. It's colder 'n a witches tit out there… you must be frozen. We've got a nice warm fire stoked and I can heat up a bowl of broth for you no trouble… get some heat into your old bones, eh?" Maggie graced him with her most winning of smiles, pretending that it was a common thing for complete strangers to come calling this late at night. It was nothing short of magic the way the thought of getting her hands on the stranger's money dampened her anger with her husband.

"How long will you be with us, mister…?"

"Black… Ambrosious Black," he said, smiling. "I know, quite a mouthful, but you get used to it by the time you get to my age. I was thinking something along the lines of a couple of months, perhaps even more. It all depends on the work I have to do here really, so it's hard to say exactly."

"A basic room is two 'n eight a night, nothing fancy mind, just good plain home cooking and a warm bed." Her eyes took on a far away quality as she wrestled with the arithmetic in her head. Two shillings, eight pennies a day, for at least sixty days was almost ten guineas. "Half up front, of course," she added hurriedly.

"Of course," Black said, reaching into his top coat pocket for his leather purse.

"Black with the white eyes." Maggie found herself saying.

"Pardon?" Black said, his smile spreading.

"Black. Funny name for a fella with white hair and white eyes...oh my, you ain't blind are you? Can't be giving you something upstairs if you's blind...oh do listen to me prattling on like a fool."

"I'm not blind, dear lady. Though a downstairs room, perhaps out of the way of your other guests would be appreciated. I'll be working during my stay."

"Well," she said doubtfully, "We have got a room out back, William uses it for his workshop, not that he ever does any work, mind."

"Marvelous."

"I think William's got a cot in there."

"Even better." He palmed five guineas into Maggie's hand, more than he even owed. "I can see we are going to get along like a house on fire, Mrs. Hare."

"Do call me Maggie, everyone else does," she said, without so much as wondering how he had come to call her Hare and not Log, in the first place – old Mrs. Log had been dead a good twenty years now and they'd just never bothered changing the name. Most likely someone had told him so.

"Of course, Maggie... now about that broth?"

Maggie Hare bustled her new guest through to the pantry where she set a pan of yesterday's rabbit stew to cooking and settled down for however much small talk it would take for her William to come rolling home.

Ambrosious Black was the perfect gentleman, taking an interest in her ceaseless blather and making her feel almost beautiful with his gentle manner and his pretty way of talking – and it had been a long time since Maggie had felt beautiful. A life with William Hare had beaten it out of her.

The old grandfather clock in the corner chimed half past and then the hour, without any sign of the master of the house. Maggie was fed up with making excuses for his behavior – the truth, him being out all night tomcatting around with whores and doxies down by the Cattle Market and Gallows Gate didn't make for endearing anecdotes to be shared with strangers. Instead, she dismissed his absence with seven words: "William? He's a drunk and a fool."

There was little more to be said on the subject.

"Well, if you'll excuse my rudeness, Mr. Black, I'm afraid I'm going to have to turn in. A girl needs her beauty sleep, you know."

"Surely not, Maggie. A natural beauty like yourself?"

"Aye, that's me that is, a diamond in the rough. Well, goodnight."

Black watched her go, content to just sit there for a while longer in the flickering gaslight, thinking.

Sometime later he snuffed out the gaslight and wandered through the downstairs of Log's Lodging House in the dark, familiarizing himself with the lie of the land. The privy was right beside his 'room' and it stank to high heaven. Mrs. Hare, he decided, was not a fastidious cleaner.

His room wasn't locked. There was no point, there was nothing to steal in there, not even the mattress from the bed, which was a wooden pallet softened by mildewed straw and a single moth-eaten blanket. There was a large double window at the rear end of the room, held together by a simple latch, and a bare wooden table that was fit for firewood if nothing else.

The room was pitiful for the money – the Hare woman had played him for a fool with her two-and-eight a night for a crib in a pigsty – but it wasn't important. It would suit him just fine. All his too long life he'd shied away from excess and luxury. Excess led to weakness of body and mind. Weakness was for fools like William Hare.

Black unlatched the window and threw it open, letting the fresh air in and the stale reek of urine out.

The fog, he noticed, was already lifting. Come sunrise it would be as though the rows of houses with their slate rooftops had never been away. That was how he liked to think of it – not that the fog came and hid the houses but that it took them away to some distant land where if the sleepers awoke they would see wonders aplenty through their shuttered windows. It was a fine sentiment but hardly likely. These fogs were not the same fogs that had gathered over the Island of Apples so long ago. Now, perhaps in those mists miracles might have flourished, but not in the choking factory smog of this filth-ridden city.

He settled down on the cot, drawing the blanket over his body, content to sleep in his clothes. But sleep offered Black no solace. He tossed and turned fitfully, plagued by dreams of ancient deaths and treachery – familiar dreams peopled by familiar faces, still alive with hope and the need to believe in all things good, the same naïveté that would lead them inevitably into Hell.

And one face, most beloved of them all, with red eyes, weeping blood.

* * *

Black started awake, looking instinctively at his hands for the telltale blood and where once he might have scrubbed them, over and over until his frantic actions actually produced some of the blood of his dreams, he ignored the guilt and lowered them.

While he'd slept an owl had perched on the windowsill. It flapped its powerful wings several times, banging them against the frame, its five-foot wingspan larger than the window allowed. The creature watched him now, curiously. Behind the great white bird, the first rays of dawn were creeping into the room, chasing the shadows away to wherever it is that darkness hides.

Waking to find a menacing bird of prey in their room would shock most people, fearful of its long curved claws and deadly hooked beak, yet it didn't faze Black in the least. Instead, it brought a contented smile to the old man's weathered face.

"A late night, my friend. I trust you found him?"

Seemingly affronted that the old man had to ask, the large owl rotated its head toward the window and closed its eyes without feeling the need to dignify the question with a response. Ambrosious Black roared with laughter, climbing stiffly out of his less than luxurious bed.

"I'll just go see for myself then, shall I?"

The owl had nothing to say. It was already fast asleep.

Chapter 2

With the sun barely over the horizon, Black presumed he'd find the common room of the lodge dark and empty, everyone still tucked away in their beds. He was pleasantly surprised to see a warm fire already burning in the hearth and Maggie Hare bustling around preparing breakfast. Her dark hair was tied up in a tight bun but strands stuck out in all directions, making it look like someone had glued a bird's nest to the top of her head while she'd been sleeping. Black stifled a laugh. Perhaps her beauty sleep hadn't gone quite as well as she'd hoped. Still, Ambrosious gave her top marks for being up and at it, and tired as she must have been she still greeted him with an enthusiasm he found honest and refreshing.

"Top of the morning, sir," Maggie said. "Had a feeling you'd be an early riser, I did. Thought I'd get the fire lit...nip the chill out of the room for ya."

"Many thanks, ma'am. You shouldn't have bothered so. Still, I could get used to a woman who knows how to treat a man like a king. Now if only I were a few years younger..."

"Oh, go on!" Maggie said, blushing as red as the coals in the fire, unconsciously fiddling with her hair, trying to straighten out the tangles. "I'm not much of a sleeper... never was. May as well be getting 'bout my business, right? Besides...someone has to keep wee Donny company. He's *always* up at the crack of dawn."

Black was confused. "Donny?"

"Behind you, in the corner there. He's easy to miss."

Black spun on his heel to see that the room did indeed have another occupant. Over by the window, tucked in beside the grandfather clock, a tiny wisp of a man with a shiny bald head and a salt-and-pepper-colored beard sat hunched over a chess board. He was oblivious to their conversation, intently studying the intricately carved game pieces, his round spectacles hanging so low on the tip of his nose the slightest movement would surely cause them to fall.

"I see why you call him wee Donny," Black said. "Not a dwarf, is he?"

"No. Just a strange little old man. Been living here for years. Before I met William. Before I took over from Mrs. Log, even. Plays his chess all morning, sleeps most of the rest of the day. Why don't you go say hi while I fix you up a plate?"

"Sounds good. I'm famished."

"Then I hope you like hard- boiled eggs, 'cause our chickens are still learnin' how to lay kippers and bacon?"

Black smiled at Maggie's joke, one he was sure she'd used a great many times. "Eggs are fine."

* * *

What wee Donny perhaps lacked in physical stature, he appeared to make up for intellectually. Standing watching him play a chess match was one of the most astonishing things Black had witnessed in quite a long time. Donny was playing himself – simultaneously in charge of both black's and white's moves – and he did so with such a ferocious speed that Black was sure there was no thought behind his decisions, that he was just shuffling the pieces around at random. Not so. The more he watched, Black was sure the tiny old man was playing textbook- perfect chess, setting up classic attack and defensive strategies in the blink of an eye.

The strange little man even seemed to take on a different, distinct personality depending on which side he was currently playing. His black side – the side that was clearly winning – showed itself with a big toothy grin and larger eyes than white, who would squint, grind his teeth, and grumble obscenities under his breath. Black almost expected Donny to reach over to shake his own hand, after the match ended. Instead, he just cleared the board and immediately began to set the pieces back into position for the start of the next game.

Black decided not to bother him, moving over to the window to have a look outside. As he'd predicted, the thick fog of last night was but a memory now, replaced by a drab grey sky filled with sickly dark clouds ready to burst with rain at any moment.

Another lovely morning in Edinburgh! Black thought. *God how I miss being back home in...*

"What opening do you prefer?" Wee Donny asked, interrupting his thoughts.

"Pardon?"

Donny pushed his spectacles back into place, and squinted up at Black. "Chess openings, of course! Which one do you prefer using?"

"Oh...well I've always been a fan of the Gambits. King's Gambit more than Queen's, but I like them both."

The little man hunched over the chessboard screwed up his face as if he'd bitten into something sour. "King's Gambit! Are you daft, man? No one falls for that move anymore. You'll never see me give up control of the center of the board just because you dangle a pawn in my face; I can assure you that!"

"You'd decline the gambit, then?" Black asked, amused by the old man's passion for the game.

"Decline it! I'd hammer it right back down your gob! Check mate in twelve or thirteen moves."

"I see...well we wouldn't want that now, would we? What opening would you suggest?"

Wee Donny scratched his bearded chin for a moment, considering the question seriously. "Seeing as you're obviously no' a master, like myself, I think you'd be better off using a sound defensive opening like the Knight's Sacrifice. Protect your king at all times, right? That's the way to win!"

The smile vanished from Black's face, gone as if his face had never known how. Unwanted visions flashed in his mind, rapid-fire images of men screaming in agony on a field of emerald-green grass. Of men writhing in pain, futilely reaching out for help as they lay dying in puddles of their own blood. And once again of the great man who wept crimson tears—

"...chance to attack your opponent's weak side," Donny said, but Black had been lost in his dark memories.

"Sorry...what were you saying?" Black apologized.

"The sacrifice, mate! Aren't you listening? The Knight's Sacrifice? Have you ever used it?"

"That I have, old-timer...a long, *long* time ago." There was a somber quality to Black's voice, a tone filled with heavy burden and dark regret. Donny didn't notice, happy that he had found a worthy playing partner.

"Wonderful! Have a seat and let's see how you fare."

"Me? Play chess?" Black asked, shaking his head. "God, no. I studied the moves for years, sure, but I've never actually played the damn game. Always thought it a bit silly, truth be told."

Wee Donny was confused. "Never played? But you said—"

A loud crash in the hallway, followed closely by the slamming of the front door stopped the little man in mid-sentence. Both he and Black turned quickly to investigate. Entering the room – or rather, stumbling into it– was a tall stocky man with greasy black hair dressed in a pair of soot-stained dungarees and a threadbare wool sweater. He had a thin face, wild bloodshot eyes, and the aroma of someone who'd either been out drinking all night or had recently had the misfortune of falling headfirst into a giant keg of whiskey.

"The master of the house?" Black bent down to quietly ask Donny. Fear was shining in the little man's eyes, telling Black everything he needed to know.

Donny nodded once, then quickly hunched back over the chessboard, trying his best to disappear into his chair. From the look on his face, if he'd been able to jump right into the chessboard, hide among the pawns and rooks in the only world that made any sense to him anymore, Black was sure he would have gladly done so.

"Maggie?" the new arrival shouted. "Where the hell's my meal, woman?"

Black looked over just as Maggie had been entering the room with a plate full of eggs. *His* eggs, presumably. The smile slid from her face, seeing that her husband had finally returned home. However it wasn't replaced by the angry scowl Black had expected, hearing the harsh way she'd talked about Mr. Hare last night. She was angry all right, but being careful not to let it show. What her face *did* show was a look remarkably similar to that of Wee Donny's. For all her brash talk, Maggie was obviously frightened of her man.

"William. I didn't know you were home," Maggie said. "Umm...these eggs are for—"

"For who...?" Hare asked, his voice rising, his dark eyes swiveling to take in Wee Donny and Mr. Black. Maggie didn't know what to do. Her eyes found Black, silently pleading. Black nodded in her husband's direction, understanding perfectly.

"They're for you William, of course," Maggie answered, placing the eggs down in front of him. "Eat up, while they're hot."

Hare grumbled something incoherent then greedily started shoveling food down his throat. Maggie started to head back to the pantry, but turned to meekly ask, "What took you so long, William?

You…you promised me you wouldn't be staying out all night like this anymore."

Hare glared at her, a line of yellow yolk running down his chin, dripping onto the plate. "None of your god damned business, woman! Mind your tongue and just be thankful I bother coming back to this dump at all. Hear?"

"Yes, William. Sorry…it's just that—"

"If you really need to know," Hare interrupted, "I was chased around all bloody night by a muckle big bird. Everywhere I went this beast followed me. Scared me, it did. I'm man enough to admit that. I stayed in the pub until the sun was up and I was sure it was gone."

"Oh, come on now, William. Surely you can come up with a better lie than that?" Maggie said, some of her fire rekindled by her husband's outlandish story. "A big brute like you scared of a sparrow!"

"This wasn't some stupid wee sparrow, Maggie. It was a great white monster: big yellow eyes with huge black claws and a curved beak. You should 'ave seen it Maggie! I tell ya, there was something 'no natural about it!"

"Blimey! What kind of bird was it?"

"How the blooming hell should I know, Maggie? My mate, Burke, thought it was maybe an albatross. He said they're evil, bringing disease and bad luck to whoever sees them."

"Your friend's been reading too much Coleridge," Black butted into their conversation, helping himself to a seat at Hare's table. "It wasn't an albatross…it was an owl. A Snowy Owl to be precise. Quite rare in these parts."

"My friend doesn't read, Mr… Who the hell are you, anyway?" Hare asked, ignoring Black and looking toward Maggie for the answer.

"Sorry, dear. I meant to introduce you. This is Mr. Black. He'll be staying with us for a few months or more, using your old workshop out back. Paid half up front he did too, so mind your manners."

A light went on in Hare's eyes, a greedy gleam that made his tired, bloodshot eyes look even worse. Suddenly, he was cheery and all smiles, Black's new best friend whether he wanted one or not.

"Pleasure to meet you, sir," Hare said, reaching across the table, extending his large sweaty hand for Black to shake. "Maggie been treatin' you fairly?"

"Oh yes. Like a King! I was hoping for some eggs, though."

"You heard the man, Maggie. Make yourself bloody useful and get the man some eggs. Do I have to think of everything around here for ya?"

"No, William. You don't. Eggs will be right out, Mr. Black. Sorry for the wait."

Maggie shuffled off to make more eggs, leaving Black and Hare alone at the table, each silently sizing the other up. It was Hare who spoke first.

"You've seen it, then? The white bird?"

"Now and then, yes, but let's talk about something else. Something important. I have a proposition for you."

"A propo… what? What does that mean?"

Black smiled, "It means that if you're up for a little hard work, and can keep your mouth shut, you're about to make a whole lot of money. Understand?"

Hare was smiling now, too. "Perfectly, Mr. Black. Perfectly! What would you have me do?"

"Two things. First, meet me at the docks tonight at eight o'clock. I have some crates arriving by ship that I'll need you to bring back here to my room. They'll be heavy and I don't want them broken, so you might want to bring someone along to help. Your nonreading friend, perhaps?"

"Done. What's the second thing?"

"We'll talk about that later." Black rose from his chair. "Depends if you bungle the delivery, or not." He turned and headed for the front door.

"What about your eggs?" Hare asked.

Black paused but didn't turn around. "You eat them, William. If things go as planned, you'll need all the strength you can get."

Chapter 3

William (Billy) Burke was a burly man with sandy brown hair and overgrown bushy sideburns running down his cheeks all the way to his chin. He was a morose chap, silent and brooding throughout the day but quick to become foulmouthed and mean tempered whenever the booze started flowing at night. He saw nothing wrong with – and in fact took great pleasure in punching, kicking, stealing, lying, and generally whoring his way through life. In short, he was a rotten, nasty man; as close to a true friend as William Hare was ever likely to get.

Besides sharing the same proper name, both men had left their native Ireland to find work on the Union Canals in Scotland, but neither felt the need to demean himself with such arduous manual labor – both too damn lazy to work for their money. It was no surprise then, both men leeched onto weak women who provided a roof over their heads, food in their bellies, and enough money in their pockets to meet one another in one of the sleazy, run-down pubs Westport had to offer. Through a blur of whisky, ale, prostitutes, gambling, and barroom brawls – sometimes all on the same night – Burke and Hare became best friends and partners in crime. Rarely was one found without the other. Theirs was a symbiotic union of excess, greed, and violence that would soon lead to infamy. Not tonight, though. Tonight they had work to do.

* * *

"Move yer arse, ya muckle big lump," Hare urged. "We can't be late."

Burke wasn't sure what to make of his friend tonight. William sure was acting strange. Either worried about something, or perhaps excited? He couldn't decide which, yet. Naturally, they were at a pub, The Gown and Gavel, which was already full with a wide assortment of local rabble. Despite the early hour, there were dirty factory workers and haggard merchants on their way home from work; dolled up whores and fast-talking con men just heading there; young toughies in looking for a fight; older women in heavy make-up in looking for the young toughies; and numerous drunks not bothering anyone, just swaying on their barstools or already lying face down on the sawdust-covered floor. A *wonderful* crowd, as far as Billy was concerned. The makings of yet another fun-filled night, and hell, William wasn't even drinking! God only knew what that meant. Couldn't be good, though.

"What's so special about tonight?" Burke asked, taking another slurp from his pint of bitter. "You don't even know how much this bloody lodger of yours is gonna pay us yet."

"It'll be enough. No worries. I got a good feeling about this bloke. He's up to something. Something he needs a couple fella's with strong arms and closed lips. Hear? Tonight's only a drop in the bucket, Billy, long as we don't blow it being late."

"So move yer arse," Burke muttered, slamming his empty glass on the table and heading for the door.

"Now why didn't I think of that?" Hare laughed, turning to follow his friend.

Outside, a light drizzle fell from a black swirling sky. It was more of a mist than a real rain, and Burke and Hare barely noticed its presence, thankful it was milder tonight and the incessant fog had so far been held at bay. Hopefully the weather would hold at least until they'd finished and were comfortably back in the pub. After that, the fog and rain could do as it pleased.

The Gown and Gavel was on Bishop's Row, one of the better streets of Westport – if in fact, *any* street in this filthy section of the city could be described in that manner. Still, as run-down and low-class an area as Bishop's Row was, it may as well have been Princess Street outside Edinburgh Castle compared to where Burke and Hare were headed.

The harbor of Westport, commonly known simply as The Docks, was a terrible place, a four-block area on the shores of the Firth of Forth, an estuary of the frigid North Sea. It was the worst of the worst; an enter-at-your-own-risk no man's land if ever there had been one. After dark, the only people who considered visiting were sailors, thieves, murderers, and fools. Even the police, prostitutes, and rats seemed to steer clear. No one would bother Burke and Hare, though. Men like them tended to blend right in.

Turning onto Canal Road, the dimly lit street curved slowly to the right as it descended toward Ferry Street and the water. It was normally dead quiet by this time, the streets deserted by people with enough sense to lie low and let the shadows of the night pass them by. Tonight though, there was some sort of commotion going on outside the Ripley Theatre, with people milling around on the steps and in front of the old building. Burke and Hare picked up their pace, anxious to see if there was trouble afoot. Unfortunately, it was only a group of traveling actors moving some of their props and stage sets from the back of several wagons inside of the storied theatre.

The Ripley had been popular with the privileged and artsy crowds years ago, before the riff-raff took over, but the affluent members of society didn't feel comfortable coming to this seedy area of Edinburgh anymore and the massive brick building that once entertained royalty had been empty for the better part of five years. Apparently, that was about to change.

Not that Burke and Hare gave a rat's turd about a bunch of silly toffs parading around in silk tights and ridiculous pancake make-up, spewing words that barely seemed human – never mind English – at the top of their lungs to a room full of rich snobs. No thanks, definitely not for *real* men like them. Only wankers would be caught dead in a theatre. Heads high, snickering openly at the men these thugs considered girly and far below them on the societal food chain, Burke and Hare would've happily passed by forgetting the actors and their asinine play, but the sound of a pair of working horses pulling to a stop behind them caused the two friends to stop and look. Few, if any people living in this area could afford a cab ride so they were naturally curious as to who might climb out.

Their interest was piqued further once the driver stepped down to open the door and a heavenly set of sexy long legs appeared from within. Attached to the legs soon followed a woman so stunningly beautiful the men's jaws nearly hit the cobbled street. She wore a dark green dress hanging low off her shoulders and slit high up her thigh. Her hair was raven black, shiny as silk, and hung halfway down her exquisite uncovered back. When she turned their way, Burke and Hare gasped as her dress was nearly as low cut on the front, brazenly exposing the woman's large full breasts, barely contained within a black leather corset. Everything about this women said money; years of pampered living and classy refinement, but there was also a subtle, dark, dangerous way she moved that screamed sex; a street-hardened erotic temptress rather than the product of high society.

"Look at that, Billy!" Hare said.

"I see her, William," Burke answered, his words slurred, dripping with drunken lust. "Do you think I'm blind? How could I miss a strumpet like that?"

"Not the woman, dullard…quick, up there on the roof. Look!"

Burke reluctantly tore his eyes away from the lady in green, following Hare's shaky extended finger skyward. At the peak of the theatre's roof, wings spread fully out at its sides like a stone gargoyle protecting its chosen sanctuary, was the massive white bird that had scared them last night, anticipating their every move, forcing them to cower indoors until the break of dawn.

"Blimey!" Burke shouted, causing others in the crowd to look up and notice the strange albino animal. "It's that great bloody beast again! What's it doing, William?"

"I don't—" Hare began to answer.

"You've seen that bird before?" A strong female voice interrupted him. Burke and Hare nearly gave themselves whiplash snapping their heads down to see who it was speaking. It was the woman from the cab. Up close, she was even more impressive. Her jade eyes perfectly matched the shade of her dress; so large and alluring they actually managed to capture both men, holding their stare away from the tempting pleasures exposed below. For a few seconds, at least.

"Seen it?" Burke replied. "Bloody thing chased us across half the city last night, it did. Kept swooping down on us, claws ready to have a go at our eyes."

"Really...?" She said, taking a step closer. "How fascinating."

"We think it might be an albatross. Evil, cursed birds, I'm told. Tell the lady, William?"

Those strange jade-colored eyes turned Hare's way, boring into him with an intensity that made him uneasy for some reason. The woman was strikingly beautiful, the sexiest woman he'd ever stood this close to, but there was something about her – a hunger, perhaps – that made him distrust her.

"Aye. I mean, no. It's not an albatross. I forgot to tell you, Billy. I was told it was an...ahh...hell I can't—"

"An owl," the woman said. "A Snowy Owl, perhaps?"

"That's right. That's exactly what he said it was."

"What *who* said it was?" she asked, stepping even closer – too close – a quiet desperation in her tone that set Hare's alarm bells ringing again. Maybe it was all in his head, her intoxicating flowery perfume playing tricks with his simple mind. Regardless, he wasn't about to expose his employer to anyone, even someone as stunning as this.

"Oh...I can't remember. Just one of the local lads down at the pub. He'd seen a bird like it in one of those fancy picture books."

"I see," she said, stepping back and dropping her eyes to the ground. "Well...it's been a pleasure, gentlemen. Good evening." She started to walk away, the men's eyes unconsciously drawn to her backside and the magnificent sway of her hips, but she surprised them by turning back. "Forgive me for not introducing myself. My name's Magenta. Magenta Da Vine. A stage name, of course, but it has a certain ring to it, don't you think?"

"Definitely," Burke answered, "I take it you're part of the play, then?"

"Aye. We're doing *The Scottish Play*, naturally." When neither Burke nor Hare showed any sign of knowing what she was talking about, she explained further. "It's called *Macbeth*. Shakespeare's best, in my opinion." It was clear neither man still had any idea what she was talking about, so she dropped the subject.

"What were your names, again?"

She was looking at Hare, obviously asking him but Burke decided to jump into the conversation, anything to get her to pay some

~ 37 ~

attention to him. He couldn't let William get all the bragging rights in the pub later.

"I'm William Burke, at your service ma'am, and this big lump is my mate, William Hare. Our friends call me Billy, just to keep it simple. You can do the same."

A seductive smile flashed across Da Vine's face. "William Hare and Billy Burke…two fine strong Irish names. I like that! Maybe I'll see you around sometime."

With those promising words, she winked and walked off into the front doors of the Ripley.

Both men watched her until she disappeared into the theatre, neither managing to breathe until she was gone from view. Facing each other, they had a good laugh.

"It isn't everyday you meet a woman like that, my friend," Burke said, puffing out his barrel chest. "Think she fancied me?"

"How could she not, Billy?" Hare smiled.

He slapped his friend on the back and shoved him in the direction of the bottom of the hill. They'd wasted enough time here. Miss Da Vine was certainly a delicious distraction but a fine woman like that would never have anything to do with a couple of common blokes like them. Foolish to imagine any different; not that it stopped either one of them from doing a little wishful thinking as they walked on.

And who could blame them?

The smile stayed on Hare's face until he remembered the bird. *The Snowy Owl*, he corrected himself. Glancing back up at the roof of the theatre, the owl was now gone, silently slipped away into the approaching night almost as if it had never been there at all.

Maybe it's some kind of ghost, he thought. Nonsense of course, but the notion stuck in his mind.

"Come on, Billy. Let's go."

Chapter 4

With the theatre behind them, Burke and Hare walked down the rest of Canal Road, turning onto Ferry Street at the bottom of the hill just as the echo of the bells at St. Giles' Cathedral reached them, chiming eight times across the city, indicating the hour. They were going to be a few minutes late but neither acknowledged the fact or hurried their pace. They walked in silence, both men increasingly wary of their surroundings, instinctively on guard even though there was no obvious sign of danger. In this area of urban decay and degradation, caution wasn't recommended; it was demanded.

The fog was thicker here, rolling in from the frigid sea, an eerie moving carpet of darkness that covered the filthy street, blotting out the sight of their feet as they moved forward. They didn't need to see where they were heading to find the docks – all they had to do was follow the putrid stench of rendered whale blubber, salt water, and rotting fish guts. Within minutes, they were there.

"Where's your new pal, then?" Billy asked. "Tells us to be on time, but he'll get here whenever he damn well pleases, I suppose."

"No idea, but I'm sure he's here somewhere. Let's go back toward Canal Road and see if we can—"

When William stopped and turned, Ambrosious Black was standing right behind them, touching distance away, monstrously large in a black overcoat and top hat. He was leaning on a wooden walking stick, glancing casually at an expensive silver pocket watch.

"Christ almighty!" Hare said, shocked such a large man could sneak up on them so stealthily. "Nearly stopped my heart, ya did! Where did you come from?"

"You're late, William," was all Black said, a smoldering anger in the tone of his voice. "You wouldn't have me thinking you were unreliable now, would you?"

"Course not. We were held up outside the Ridley, sir. Some artsy group is opening the theatre again. Won't happen again, gov, on my word."

Black's white eyes bored into Hare for several more seconds then slid away to examine the other man beside him. "And who's your equally inept mate?"

"My name's Burke, sir. You can call me Billy."

"Billy it is," Black said, "You lads follow me. I've wasted enough time here."

Slipping his pocket watch out of sight, Black strode off into the swirling fog and Burke and Hare had to practically run to keep up with the older, yet unpredictably spry white-haired man. Black led the two thugs past the busier commercial docks and down toward the far end of the boardwalk where a fancy private ship named *Garfield's Galleon* was moored. It was a splendid sailing vessel – one of the newer Yankee Clipper cargo ships, its circular wheel of paddles powered by steam engine rather than the wind.

"This is it, men," Black said, pretending not to notice the look on his workers' faces. They were suitably impressed with the ship, naturally, but it was greed that shone most brightly in their eyes. Black could almost hear their thoughts, calculating what a fine ship like this must be worth and wondering how deep their employer's pockets might actually be. More importantly, they were wondering how much coin was in this enterprise for them.

Beside the dock, in a pyramid stack of 2' x 2' wooden crates waited Black's offloaded cargo. It was a smaller pile of goods than

Burke and Hare had been expecting, but once they lifted the first container and realized how heavy the crates were, they began to realize that indeed, they'd be earning their pay this night.

"Blimey, Gov'nor!" William said. "What have you got in these crates...rocks?"

"Actually, yes," the white-haired stranger said. "Well, stones to be exact. Blocks of corundum stone from the Emerald Isle. I'm a sculptor, you see, and it's up to you and your mate to get these crates back to my room at Tanner's Close without damaging them. I've rented a pull cart for you. It's over there beside the wall."

"How'd they get on the dock?" Billy asked, seeing no work crew or block and tackle assembly anywhere in sight.

"Not that it's any of your business, but the rather handsome gent there, standing on the aft deck of the Clipper offloaded them for me. His name's Nickolas Garfield, a colleague of mine from the United States."

Burke and Hare peered through the fog and light rain to catch a glimpse of Mr. Black's friend but all they could make out was a tall well-built man wearing black dress slacks and a navy blue knit sweater, his white captain's hat pulled down low to conceal his clean shaven features.

"By himself?" William asked, clearly astonished.

"Let's just say Mr. Garfield is a very special man and leave it at that, shall we? If he can handle the blocks, surely you two strapping young men can get them the rest of the way with no worries. Right?"

"I guess so, sir," Billy said. "We'll do our best."

"You'll do better than that, Billy Boy. Deliver them intact and I'll pay you handsomely. So much as crack or chip one of them...trust me, I won't be pleased."

There was clearly a threat in Mr. Black's words, and ordinarily that would have set Burke and Hare off in a rage, but tonight neither of them was in the mood for a fight. They wanted to be paid for this job, sure, but there was something unsettling and uniquely dangerous about their mysterious employer and neither friend wanted to do anything that might upset him.

"Are we clear, gentlemen?" Black asked, his tone lighter, friendlier.

"Yes, sir," William said. "Perfectly."

Chapter 5

Taking turns – one man pushing, one pulling – it took two full hours for Burke and Hare to lug the heavily weighted cart back to the lodging house, and another half hour to carefully unload the wooden crates into the back storage room that Mr. Black was using as his bedroom and workshop.

Although the two toughies were too stubborn to admit it, both were secretly relieved to have the job behind them without damaging any of Black's important stones. The task complete, their collectively dull minds quickly turned to the night ahead – a night filled with drinking, fighting, and whoring – now that they'd have extra money in their pockets. By 11:00 p.m. they were on their way out the door, more than ready to hit the pub but a high-pitched scream up on the second floor stopped them in their tracks.

"That's my Maggie!" William said. "Come on!"

They ran up the stairs two at a time only to find Mrs. Hare sitting numbly on a chair outside of room number 6.

"What in blazes are you yelping about, woman?" William asked, his concern turning to anger seeing his wife unharmed and wasting their valuable drinking time.

"It's Mr. Murdock," she said. "I just walked in and found him dead on the floor of his room. See for yourself. I can't believe it. We were having a nice chat downstairs less than an hour ago. Now he's gone!"

William and Billy pushed past Maggie and peered into room 6. Sure enough, an old heavyset bald man in a frayed brown suit lay sprawled just inside the door, eyes wide open but not seeing anything in this world anymore.

"So what?" William asked, sympathetic as usual. "The old bugger snuffed it. Was he paid up?"

"You're a cruel man, William. How can you ask such a thing with poor Mr. Murdock not even cold yet?"

William just shrugged, slapped Billy on the shoulder and started back down the stairs. "Well, we're off for a few pints, love. Don't wait up."

"Oh no you're *not*," Maggie shouted, chasing her good-for-nothing husband to the front door. "You're not leaving me here like this. Not with him just lying there in the doorway!"

"What do you want me to do with him? Take him to the pub with us?"

"I don't care what you do with him, but he's not staying here. Take him to the hospital or something."

William was about to tell her it was a bit late for that, but knew from the look on her face she wasn't in the mood for jokes. "Okay, Maggie. You win. Come on, Billy. We'll drop him off on our way."

* * *

Using the same pull cart they'd used earlier to transport the wooden crates, Burke and Hare once again found themselves out transporting a load; only this time one not made of heavy stone. Maggie had found them a tattered blanket to cover Murdock's body with, but they were still getting some unusual stares from the people they walked past on the street.

"Let's just dump him here," Billy said for the third time since they'd left the lodging house. He was tired, thirsty and in a foul mood.

"We can't, fool, but I'll tell you this. I'm no' taking him all the way to the Edinburgh morgue either."

"Oh yeah?" Billy asked, interested. "Where's he going then?"

"Bristo Port. Jimmy Mack told me about a doctor there that gets the dead bodies delivered to him from the jail after they swing on the gallows."

"Christ! What's he do with them?"

"The hell do we care? All I know, he's a lot closer than the city morgue."

"Can we find him? What's his name?"

"Pretty sure it's Knox."

* * *

Dr. Robert Knox was a rake-thin man with a pallid tone to his flesh not far removed from the men he usually operated on. Knox did indeed accept the deceased bodies of convicted criminals. He ran a small school for newly graduated doctors in the rapidly advancing study of dissection, providing surgeons with vital hands-on training to study human anatomy and improve their operating techniques. It was a thriving, respected school, but impossible to keep running steady; the demand for freshly deceased bodies being far greater than the prison's limited execution schedule – their only legitimate source of donated cadavers. So it was when Burke and Hare stumbled to his door, he was more than pleased to take the body of Mr. Murdock off their hands.

"Thanks lads," Dr. Knox said, excitedly twirling the ends of his handlebar mustache, seemingly unconcerned that what he was about to do was highly illegal. "This is completely unexpected but a *huge* help to me."

"No worries," William said. "Helps us too. We'll be off, then. Night, gov."

"Wait a second," Knox said as Burke and Hare were turning to leave. "I haven't paid you yet!"

"Paid?" Billy said, his eyes widening at the notion.

Dr. Knox went into his office, returning a moment later to count seven one-pound notes into Billy's slightly shaking hand. When Knox was finished, he bid them good night and thanked them again for their service. Burke and Hare were both too stunned to even speak so they nodded and shuffled away as fast as they could.

"Seven pounds, William!" Billy said once they were out of earshot. "Can you believe it?"

"Bloody Hell!" William said, overwhelmed. It was an outrageous sum of money – more cash than either of them regularly earned in months. "We're on a roll, mate!"

"Aye. Between this toff with the silly mustache and the white-haired old git at your lodge, we'll be rich in no time!"

They both started to laugh, but their jovial mood was cut short when a familiar, large-winged bird suddenly swooped out of the fog like a disembodied wraith causing them to drop to the street, hands frantically covering their heads in case of attack. The Snowy Owl landed on a nearby fence post, swiveled its head to look back at them cowering, and screeched out a series of loud hoots. As if this was some sort of arranged signal, Ambrosious Black strode out of the darkness in the bird's wake, appearing just as suddenly as he had down by the docks, towering over the fallen men.

"Not unless you learn some respect, you won't!" Black said. "Follow me before I change my mind…"

With that, Black turned and walked off into the night, forcing Burke and Hare to jump up and follow, less they be left alone with the bird of prey.

"How in blazes did he hear me?" Billy asked, whispering.

"No idea, mate, but do as he says, hear? And keep that muckle big trap of yours shut next time!"

* * *

Burke and Hare skulked along behind Mr. Black keeping a respectable distance behind their mysterious employer. In the fog, sometimes it was difficult to see where they were going and to keep pace, but the phantom owl flew close on their heels, ensuring they didn't lag too far behind.

Eventually, Black crossed Main Street and walked through the high steel gates of a place neither man following would have guessed in a hundred years would be their destination – Calton Cemetery.

"Why's he taking us here," Burke asked. "He's not going to snuff us, is he?"

"Not likely. Steady, Billy. I smell money in this. Black's obviously a man of secrets, right? Well, he'll pay handsomely to a couple of strong blokes like us that know how to keep them."

Deeper into the old cemetery Black took them, finally stopping on a grassy hill and waiting for his cohorts to walk closer. Once they were standing face to face, Black chose to remain silent, staring at both men with a strange look of either amusement or disgust; it was impossible to tell which. The silence unnerved Billy first, and he blurted out something, anything, just to break the tension hanging in the chilly air.

"Ah…is that beastly bird following us with you? Is it your pet?"

"My pet?" Black repeated, laughing at the absurd assumption. "Of course not, dolt. Nazza is my eyes…and my friend. We've traveled together many, many years."

William was tired of this senseless chitchat and butted in to say, "No offense, sir, but bugger the bird! I want to know what your plans are for us? Why did you bring us out here to this terrible place?"

"Fair enough," Black said. "The second job I mentioned. Remember? Good. Look around, then. Tell me what you gentlemen see."

"Easy," Billy said. "I see dead people."

"Do you now?" Black chuckled. "Where? I don't see any wandering around. Are you sure?"

"They're in the ground, obviously. Where God intended them to be."

"Precisely. Look down then, lads. See where you're standing."

Burke and Hare looked down to see their shoes covered in soft brown dirt that looked and smelled like it has been recently turned.

They were standing on a freshly dug grave. "Oh hell!" William shouted and jumped to the side, eager to get back onto the damp grass.

"What do you see now, Billy?" Black asked.

"Umm…nothing. Just some poor bugger's grave. They must have buried him in the last day or two."

"And how about you, William? Is that what you see too?" Black asked. "Just a pauper's grave?"

Hare thought it over for a minute, piecing the events of the day together and remembering where they'd just come from. Then it dawned on him and he smiled coldly. "No, Mr. Black. That's not what I see at all."

"What is it, then?"

"Opportunity, sir. I see opportunity!"

Black smiled darkly, a great unnerving feral grin spreading across his bearded face. "Excellent. Now we're getting somewhere."

Chapter 6

"What in blazes is that bloody racket?" William shouted for the second time, staggering down the stairs to confront his trembling wife.

It was only six o'clock in the morning, but Maggie Hare had been up and cleaning for nearly an hour already. She enjoyed these first few peaceful hours each day before everyone else at the lodge woke up and started ordering her around again. The last thing she needed was William roused from his brief inebriated slumber. He hadn't wandered home until the wee hours of the morning, and Maggie could tell from the tone of his voice he was still half drunk and in a murderous mood. Never a good sign – for her, or the unfortunate person who'd unwittingly woken him.

"Shush William...you'll wake the whole house."

"Bugger them all. What in hell is making that infernal clanging noise? It feels like someone is driving a nail through my skull with every bang! If that wee bastard Donny is up making that row I'll—"

"It's no' Donny, William. He's by the fire playing his chess, as usual. It's Mr. Black. He told us he'd be starting his work this mornin', remember?"

Maggie expected her husband to fly into a rage, cursing his way to the back workshop to put a stop, once and for all, to their recent arrival's banging, but she was surprised by his reaction. Amazed, in fact. Instead of anger clouding William's unshaven face, another emotion altogether surfaced. Was it *fear*? Couldn't be.

"Oh. Mr. Black. His...his statue. Right. Maybe I'll just pop in and see how he's making out."

"Don't you hurt him, William," Maggie said, still convinced her husband would return at any moment to the nasty man she knew. "He's our best paying guest and we can't afford to lose him."

"No worries, hen. I just want to see if he needs anything." William started toward the back room, but paused halfway down the hall, almost as if he was hesitant to carry on. Turning back, he asked, "Go wake up Billy for me. He's kipping up in Mr. Murdock's empty room. And put a cuppa on for us, luv."

With that said, William headed for the workshop, leaving his wife open-mouthed and wondering what was wrong with her husband this morning. Having no answer but happy William was at least no longer shouting, Maggie headed for the kitchen to put on a pot of tea and go wake up her least favorite person in the world.

* * *

William knocked lightly on the door and nervously waited until his guest bid him enter. Ambrosious Black was immersed in his work over by the open window, the early morning sun cutting through the gloom to give the large man excellent light to guide his clearly skilled hands. Before him on a raised dais, a stone bust was taking shape, the head and shoulders of a man with piercing eyes peering out from within an ornate armored helmet. The work was nowhere near finished but was already intricately detailed enough that it took William's uncultured breath away.

"My God, Mr. Black. It's stunning!" William took a few steps closer but a noise to his left stopped him. It was the bird. The owl, perched on the bed frame as still as the statue its master was chiseling. Only its eyes moved, riveting Hare to his spot just inside the door, the sight of its immense body and razor-sharp talons deterrent enough that William approached no further.

"Well?" Black asked without looking away from the bust. "Did you find anything last night?"

"No sir. We didn't."

"Then why bother me? Can't you see I'm busy?"

"Sorry. I just wanted you to know Billy and I dug up three more, after you left. It was hard work and—"

"Your pay is on the table. Take it and get out."

"No, it's not the pay, sir, it's where you 'ave us digging. Everything in the old part of the cemetery is, well…old. Dusty boxes filled with chalky bones and threadbare rags teeming with spiders. We were hoping to have a go at some of the, shall we say, *fresher* graves."

"You'll dig where I damn well showed you. Grab a recent corpse for your doctor friend on your own time if you want, but best do it sparingly or you'll attract unwanted attention. Your work for me comes first. Let me know when you find it."

"Find what, sir? That's just it. Billy and I have no bloomin' idea what we're looking for. Perhaps if you—"

"Trust me; you'll know when you see it. It's *impossible* to miss. Take your money and get out. I'm trying to concentrate."

Dismissed, and despite having other questions for his employer, William had no choice but to bite his tongue and walk over to the wooden table to gather his pay. There was a pile of shiny guineas on the board, much more than Black owed, and for a moment William considered taking more than his do. When he looked over his shoulder though, the white beast was still intently watching his every move and he thought better of stealing anything from this odd, mysterious man.

William gathered his coins and left without another word.

* * *

Burke was awake, or to be more precise, half awake, sitting droopy-eyed and hung over at one of the tables in the common room. He looked up, bleary-eyed and miserable, when William entered the room to sit across from him. Mind you, after his frustrating visit with Ambrosious Black, Hare wasn't in the best of moods either. He was a man not used to being intimidated, and being afraid of a crazy old man wasn't sitting well in his belly. There just wasn't a lot he could do about.

Not yet anyway.

"So did our *boss* tell us what we're supposed to be looking for?" Burke asked. "Or is it still some bloody big secret?"

"He said we'd know when we see it...whatever *that* means? I'm of a mind to march right back in there and tell him to stuff his job up his holier-than-thou arse! I mean who does he think he is?"

"Don't know, mate, but his coins are all that matter. I don't give a fiddler's fart about him as long as he keeps paying us."

"I suppose."

"And speaking of pay...what happened to the seven pounds we got from Doctor what's his face?"

"We spent it already. Well, actually *you* spent it already."

"What? That's impossible. How could I go through that much money in one bloody night?"

"You couldn't, but the five whores you were sniffin' around sure could. Pissed away all our stash without even getting in their britches. Nice work!"

Burke only had vague memories of the night before but enough snippets to know his friend was probably right. He'd been buying everyone in sight a pint and a dram for a while there. "Well, good thing we know how to make more, right?"

"Right you are, Billy Boy. Right you are."

Chapter 7

True to their word, Burke and Hare knew how to make more money and although neither of their unfortunate women would agree, they were more than capable of doing hard manual labor if they wanted to. Over the next four weeks they really put their backs into their new job, digging up enough old graves to keep Mr. Black happy while he sculpted his statue, as well as keeping Dr. Knox well stocked in fresh cadavers for his anatomical dissection course. No, their biggest problem wasn't working hard.

It was having restraint.

Ambrosious Black had warned William that digging too many fresh graves would attract unwanted attention but they hadn't listened. The pound notes offered by the surgeon were far more tempting than the sculptor's coins. But whereas no one really cared who rooted around in the ancient cemetery grounds, *everyone* in Edinburgh wanted to know the identity of the ghouls who were unearthing the recent dead. Within days, Burke and Hare had angered some of the local residents, furious their dearly departed had gone missing from their holes, and from there the cemetery authorities had taken a keen interest in their nocturnal visits as well. By the time mid-November rolled around, the powers that be had started to set up on-duty guards to prowl the property at night and had also gone to the police for help.

In due time, many other enterprising men and women would eventually take to grave robbing to earn their unsavory livings, and it would become so much of a problem the cemeteries of this fine city (and many others) would have to have walls and fences built around them to protect the newly interred. Medical research and surgical training schools would eventually become thriving businesses in Scotland and England, and the underground purchasing of fresh cadavers would become such an issue history would soon remember this strange period as the "Resurrectionist" time. For now though, there was only Burke and Hare, two crude uneducated men slightly ahead of the other lawbreakers of their day.

Fate, more so than the police, was catching up to them though.

William and Billy were oblivious to all of these behind-the-scenes security happenings, of course, caught up in the joy and freedom their newfound wealth offered them. Never in their entire pitiful lives had they drank and whored and feasted and partied and lived everything to excess the way they were doing, and the sad part was that neither one of the men thought the gravy train would ever end. They were wrong, but the police and cemetery guards weren't the only people they needed to worry about.

There were far more dangerous individuals starting to pay attention to their dastardly deeds.

Chapter 8

Stuart Tattersall felt like his heart might burst out of his frilly shirt with unabashed joy as he watched the stunning raven-haired beauty rehearse on his stage. The tall, skeletal-thin director at the newly reopened Ripley Theatre was, like everyone else who saw Magenta Da Vine perform, instantly in love with his leading lady. Simply put, Da Vine *was* Lady Macbeth – no other woman could possibly do justice to the role. Simultaneously graceful, sophisticated, and charming, delivering her lines in a powerful yet passionately feminine way that would have stirred Stuart's masculine side if he'd had one. Instead he just stood offstage in awe and giggled like a schoolgirl as Magenta finished practicing an important scene from Act 3.

"*Nought's had, all's spent,*
where our desire is got without content;
'Tis safer to be that which we destroy,
than by destruction dwell in doubtful joy."

There was a brief moment of silence, and then Stuart hollered, "Wonderful!"

The small gathering of cast and crew broke into cheers and everyone rushed onstage to congratulate Magenta. They were all bit players and castoffs from other, more successful theatre groups in Britain and they all knew that Miss Da Vine was their best (and maybe *only*) chance at ever playing to a full house night after night. If all went as expected, it could be the start of something big for a lot of them so a little well deserved ass-kissing went a long way.

Magenta happily accepted their adoration, never once showing her utter distain for the lot of them, or letting on that she had no plans whatsoever to help any of them with their pitiful careers and lives. It wasn't her fault they were terrible actors and sadly inadequate human beings. They had themselves to blame for that. No, she was only here in Edinburgh to help one person and one person only – herself. The rest of these vermin could do the world a favor and go drown themselves in the North Sea as far as she was concerned. But she played her part in this little charade perfectly; smiling and joking with the other cast members friendly as could be, until she looked to the rear of the house and noticed Angus and Big Josh enter the theatre.

Finally, she thought, pointing to the new arrivals and gesturing them toward her dressing room with her perfectly manicured nails.

"Stuart, my dear," Magenta said, taking a few steps toward the ghastly man who'd been chosen to mold this untalented riff-raff into shape before opening night. "Let's take a little break, okay? I need to have a word with these good men. Won't take but a moment...I promise."

"Anything you say, Magenta my love. Take your time." To the other cast members, Stuart shouted in a much harsher tone of voice, "Take ten people. Use them to try and learn your bloody lines!"

Magenta made her way offstage, still smiling and encouraging her co-workers until she reached the side curtain and left them all behind. She left the sweet smile and happy demeanor onstage as well, scowling through the backstage passage that led to her change room and her two associates who had better have some good news for her. She'd met Angus Brooks her first night here in the city and it had been him who'd introduced her to Big Josh McDaniel. Both were common variety thugs, ignorant and uneducated, a step or two out of the gutter. But Magenta knew she'd need a little muscle in the weeks to come and Angus had been the biggest bloke in the pub at the time. Turned out, his mate Josh was even bigger – but whereas Angus was broad shouldered and muscular, Josh was tall, baldheaded, and fat as a cow. Neither man was good for much to be honest, but they were eager to please and for the time being they'd have to do.

Angus and Josh were waiting inside the dressing room, the nervous looks on their dirty faces telling Magenta everything she needed to know before they even opened their big mouths. The fools had failed again.

"So what's your excuse this time?" she asked, the venom in her voice making the much larger men cringe in her presence.

Neither man would ever admit to being afraid of the sexy actress, but neither were they bold enough to look her in the eye. There was something intimidating about her, something powerful and savage that simmered below the surface, hidden deep within her flawless beauty that both men somehow sensed and understood on a more primitive level. They kidded themselves into thinking they were only here for the money, but the truth was they were both mesmerized by the voluptuous Miss Da Vine and would have done her bidding for naught if she'd commanded it.

"Sorry ma'am," Angus said, "but it's no' for a lack of trying. We just don't know what we're looking for. We've been digging out the graves like you said but there's nothing in the bloomin' boxes but skin and bones."

"Aye," Big Josh said. "And the bodies be stinking to high heavens too."

"Stinking? They shouldn't have any smell left to them by now. What cemetery are you digging in?"

"Highland Park, last night," Angus said. It's a big one over by the castle."

"Idiots!" Magenta screamed. "I told you to dig in the Calton Burial Grounds. It's the oldest cemetery in Edinburgh."

"Well, Highland is pretty old too, I think, and it was a lot closer to where—"

"I don't give a rat's arse how far away Calton is. Do what you're told or I'll find someone who will. Understand?"

"Umm...perfectly ma'am," Josh stammered, "but you see, that's part of the problem. Someone else digging, I mean. There was a guard posted outside two of the places we walked by last night. Angus thought one might even 'ave been a policeman."

"Policeman? At the cemeteries? Whatever are you on about? Why would they post guards at a graveyard?"

"Have you no' read the papers lately? Their calling them Resurrectionists. Sneaky buggers too."

"I haven't heard a thing."

"Let's just say Angus and me are no' the only blokes out creeping around where the dead sleep. That's why we didn't dig at Calton Cemetery yet...it's awful close to the police station. A wee bit *too* close for comfort, if you know what I mean?"

"Are you telling me that someone else is *digging* in the same cemeteries we are?"

"Aye. And whoever they are, they've been at it longer than we 'ave. Been starting to stir up a whole heap of trouble, they 'ave."

Magenta was stunned by the news; shocked into silence for a moment as her mind raced to figure out exactly what this all meant, and more importantly, what she could do about it. *Who are these people? What do they want? Could they possibly be looking for the same thing that I am? Impossible. Or is it? What if...*

"Oh *shite*," she said, almost under her breath but loud enough that both her burly guests heard her.

"There a problem, ma'am?" Angus asked.

"Maybe. Maybe not. Only one way to find out, though."

"And what's that?"

"Change of plans, boys. Forget the digging for a few nights. I want you to go on a hunting trip for me instead."

"Hunting?" Big Josh asked, his flabby jowls flapping as he looked in confusion back and forth between Angus and their mysterious boss. "I don't understand, my lady. Hunting what?"

"Not what, you dolt. Who! These Resurrectionists, of course. I want you to find the people we're in direct competition with. Find them and bring them here to me. Rough them up if you please but I want them relatively undamaged when they get here. Think you can do that without screwing it up?"

"Yes ma'am. Won't be a problem."

"Good. Get it done then, gentleman, or don't bother coming back."

Chapter 9

The fire blazed in the hearth, covering the room in a comfortable blanket of heat. Ambrosious Black was taking a break from his stone work and enjoying the quiet of the lodging house's common room for a moment. Burke and Hare were out doing his bidding in the graveyard (or they certainly had better be), Maggie was in the kitchen washing up the mess from supper, and Wee Donnie was in his usual spot over in the corner, lost in his chessboard and not bothering a soul. It was the first real moment of peace Black had enjoyed in days, what with his precious statue nearing completion and requiring his total concentration and effort lately. It felt wonderful to just clear his troubled mind and sit back and relax for a few minutes. Too wonderful, as it turned out; within a few minutes the exhausted sculptor was fast asleep.

He didn't wake up fifteen minutes later when Maggie came back into the room to stoke the fire, or even in thirty minutes when Wee Donnie finally put away his board and hobbled off to bed for the night. So profound was Black's weariness tonight, that he even slept through the noisy arrival of Burke and Hare, making a pit stop home before heading back to the pubs. Billy and William were drunk already of course, and wouldn't have thought twice about waking up the old man in a normal situation but just as they walked into the common room to warm themselves by the fire, Black spoke one word in his sleep. He said, "…gold."

It was only the first of many things the sculptor would say this night. You see, when Ambrosious Black fell into a deep, bone-weary sleep, he wasn't a snorer like a lot of people. No, but he did talk in his sleep. By day he was rigidly in control of his every action and word, everything carefully calculated and thought out, but when he drifted off into the Land of Nod some guarded part of his subconscious mind sometimes broke free of its chains and found an outlet in his willing tongue.

"...too many men have died for the gold...too much blood spilled," he said to whoever he was speaking to in his dreams. In reality, he was speaking to Burke and Hare, who had suddenly taken a great interest in what the old man had to say. They sat down at the table and waited to hear more.

And more they did.

Much of what Black muttered was beyond their understanding, but certainly not all. Black spoke in fractured sentences, with William and Billy piecing things together, holding in their laughter as their intimidating boss told them bewildering stories of mythical beasts and magic swords, armored horses and skies darkened by flying arrows, and something about a man Black referred to as the Forever King dying on a bed of emerald green grass. Twice he clearly said the words, "Knights Templar" and shivered in his slumber, saying, "Death of the carpenter... Blood of the traitor."

A door slammed shut somewhere upstairs in the house, making both William and Billy jump. When they looked back at their mysterious storyteller, Black's eyes were open, his haunted white eyes gazing at them in silent accusation.

"What are you fools looking at?" Black said. "When did you get home? You're supposed to be out earning your keep."

"We're just on our way back to the graveyard," Burke said, the lie easily slipping from his mouth. "We just stopped by for a cuppa to warm us up and we heard you in here talking. Figured you were speaking to—"

"Talking about what?" All signs of exhaustion gone from the sculptor now; Black leaping to his feet and demanding an answer.

"Nothin'," Hare quickly jumped into the conversation, not trusting his dimwitted mate to keep his mouth shut. "We just heard you muttering gibberish. Something about horses and kings and such. Children's stories. You were asleep but woke up before we could slip out and leave you in peace. Sorry we woke you."

Black wanted to say more but stopped himself short, realizing he'd probably said far too much already. He desperately wanted to know what he might have accidentally said in front of these oafs, but exhaustion had loosened his tongue too much already and anything he said now would only be making it worse.

"I've got work to do…and so do you. Good night."

With that, Black stormed out and back to his room at the rear of the house.

"What in blazes was a' that about?" Burke asked.

"I have no idea, mate, but I'm startin' to have a bad feeling about this."

"Why? Because of a bad dream? You should hear some of the rubbish you say in *your* sleep. He's just an old man who's gone off his nut!"

"Aye…maybe. That or he has demons in his head. There's something no' quite right about that man, Billy."

"Forget the bugger, William. Let's go get us a pint or two."

"Fine, but after that I think we should go dig a bit more. If Black *is* a loony, I wanna be sure to keep on his good side. At least for now, hear?"

From the back room, the steady din of Black pounding violently on his chisel again could be heard. In many ways, the loud ringing noise was preferable to the silence in the house. William made the sign of the cross on his chest and headed for the front door. Billy just smiled and fell into step behind him.

"You worry too much, William. I mean…what could possibly go wrong?"

Chapter 10

The Gown and Gavel was packed to bursting tonight, filled with drunken rowdy men and a wide assortment of lewd and lascivious women. Some of the ladies were young, some were old, some were thin, and some were fat; some girls were blondes, some were brunettes, a few were beautiful and most were ugly as sin but each and every last one of them had something in common – they were all perfectly willing to help Burke and Hare spend their secret stash of money. Despite William's best intentions, Billy and he never made it out of the pub and over to the Calton burial grounds until they'd drank enough beer and whiskey to kill a horse.

"Can't we just go home?" Burke said, his head buried in a bush from where he'd just emptied his stomach. "It's too late for shovelin'. And too cold. I hate this time of the bloody year."

"Quit your sniveling, Billy. I'm no' asking you to help. Just stand guard while I dig up one real quick. He's watching us…I know he is."

"Who? Black?"

"No. His beast." Hare's eyes scanned the sky above but there was nothing in sight, not that he could see much in the foggy gloom. "He's up there somewhere. I can feel his muckle big eyes on me back."

"The bird? You serious. You're scared of the Albatross?"

"It's an *owl* you stupid git. And you're scared too. You nearly peed your pants last time you saw it."

Burke's stomach was still in knots and he was in no mood to argue. "Whatever, William. Just hurry it up, okay. I want to go home to bed."

"Aye, me too. Just keep your eyes open and your gob shut. I can't dig and keep watch at the same time."

"Sure, sure. No problem. Get to it."

Hare put his back into his work and twenty minutes later he'd uncovered the rotted wooden lid of an old coffin less than three feet below the surface of the grass. A rush of excitement sobered him up even more than the hard labor had done, and he pried open the lid hoping this would be the grave the old sculptor was waiting for.

It wasn't.

It was dark and hard to see clearly but by the meager light of the barely visible moon and the soft glow of the gaslights on the nearby street, William could see just enough to know there was nothing hidden within the hole he'd just dug other than a broken skull and a few rags of tartan clothing clinging to the rack of dry bones attached below it. Just another old grave; nothing unique or special about it, and certainly nothing hidden among the bones that would interest their white-eyed benefactor.

"Dammit to Hell!" Hare swore under his breath. "Another bloody waste of time." There was no response from his longtime friend, and William turned to see where he'd gone. "Billy?"

Burke was fast asleep, his head buried in the bush he'd spilled his guts in, snoring peacefully as if he hadn't a care in the world. Hare laughed at his mate and climbed out of the hole to go wake him up. "Good for nothin' lump!"

William walked over and was just about to wallop his friend with the business end of his shovel but as he was about to strike, a bright light flared off to his right and the sound of approaching footsteps made his heart race.

The Police! William thought, sure their grave-robbing days were over. He fell to his knees and quickly slithered back into the hole in the ground he'd just climbed out of, far happier to lie with the desiccated corpse than meet whoever it was that wandered around in the cemetery. If he could have reached Billy and pulled him into the hole as well, he would have, but he didn't want to risk waking him and having him start hollering the way he probably would. It was safer to just let him sleep and hope the strangers would walk on by without knowing they were there.

The footsteps came closer and all William could do was lie down in the old coffin and pray they wouldn't spot Billy and come investigate. Out of the darkness, the glow of a portable gas lamp illuminated the night, chasing away the shadows as well as any lingering hope William had of them not being caught.

Shite, he thought. *We're buggered now!*

William was sure he'd see the familiar dark blue cap of an Edinburgh police constable peek over the rim of his hole but the man who walked into sight turned out to be a huge baldheaded giant. Whoever he was, he looked down at William and smiled with a mouth filled with rotten black teeth.

"Who in blazes are you?" William asked. He knew that wasn't the smile of a policeman but that thought only made him feel mildly better.

"A friend," the giant said. "Get out of the hole, if you please."

William didn't see what other choice he had. He sat up and climbed out onto solid ground, his mind spinning as he tried to figure out what was going on. "Look here," he started to say, but from behind him someone stepped in close and clobbered him across the back of the head with something hard. He landed face first beside Billy, who was somehow still sleeping through this and William's last thought before he blacked out was that he'd kill his incompetent mate with his bare hands if he ever got the chance. It was as comforting a thought as any as he spiraled down into a deep, dark sleep.

* * *

"I'll wake the bugger up and you can ask 'im yourself," someone said in the darkness. There was a smelly burlap bag over William's head and he couldn't see who was speaking even if he'd wanted to. His hands were tied tightly behind his back as well.

Hare's head was still ringing from the blow to the back of his skull but he was with it enough to hear the man's gravelly voice clear as a bell and know that Billy and he were in trouble.

Check that...they were in *big* trouble.

Then the bag was roughly yanked away and the same fat giant who'd smiled at him at the cemetery slapped him roughly across the face. He'd seen that William was already awake but he'd slapped him anyway, just for the sheer fun of it.

"Wake up, princess," the big man said. "The lady would like a little chat with you...and you'd do well to mind your manners, hear?"

Lady? William thought.

When the giant stepped out of the way, the last person Hare expected to see standing in the doorway was a beautiful woman. Not just any beautiful woman, either. With her jade-colored eyes, her raven hair, and the plunging neckline of her expensive red dress, William immediately knew this was the highbrow actress Billy and he had met outside of the Ripley several weeks ago. She hadn't spoken a word yet, but he was sure of it – he'd recognize those eyes and that scrumptious cleavage anywhere.

What was her name again? It was a color, wasn't it?

He wasn't the only one with a good memory; the woman smiled as she stepped forward to speak.

"Well, well, well...look at who we have here! Let me think...William wasn't it. Yes. Both of you were named that. What's your last name again?"

"Hare, ah...ma'am. And Billy's name is Burke."

"That's right. William Hare and Billy Burke. My big strong Irishmen come back to visit me again. How sweet is that?"

As hard as it was to look away from the woman's brazen beauty, Hare took a moment to look around the room he was in. It was a warehouse office by the looks of it, with a beat up old desk and a few chairs surrounded by boxes and wooden crates. From the salty smell of the stale air William could tell they were somewhere down by the docks but couldn't tell exactly where. Standing in the small rectangular room was the woman (whose name he still couldn't remember – *was it Violet?*) the big fat man with the terrible smile, and another huge muscular man who'd presumably been the bloke who'd rapped him across the head earlier. Billy was nowhere in sight.

"Do you remember me?" the woman asked.

"Aye, but I can't remember your name just now. Getting walloped in the nut by your goons might have something to do with that."

"It might at that, yes. Regardless, my name is Magenta Da Vine and I'm very happy to see you again."

"Pardon me for no' being quite as enthused. Where's my mate? Is he dead?"

This caused the actress to laugh. "Dead? Good heavens no. What sort of lady do you take me for? He's sleeping in the other room, tied up like you but right as rain. Angus and Big Josh didn't even need to clout him with the shovel like they did you. Right Angus?"

"Aye, ma'am," the more muscular of the two big men said. "We just pulled him to his feet and he stumbled along beside us. He threw up in the cab but otherwise gave us no worries."

Lovely! William thought. *That's Billy all right. My hero!*

"So what do you want, huh? There's easier ways to get a hold of me than bashing my brains out."

"I'm sure. I didn't know it was you I was looking for, though. All in all, I'd say you got off lucky. I was expecting whoever the lads brought back to be in a lot worse shape than you are to be honest. Do I need to have them knock you around a wee bit more? It's up to you, really."

She smiled at William again, showing her perfect white teeth, but there was no warmth in her face or in the way she loomed above him. Pretty or not, there was a cold menace to this woman that William found threatening despite her petite size and outward demeanor. He knew deep down that this wasn't the type of person to cross, and at the moment feared for his life more than he ever had in any of the knife fights and all out brawls Billy and he had been in over the years.

"No, ma'am. I'll help you with whatever you need, if I can 'course."

"Good lad. I knew you were a smart one, right from the first second I saw you. Okay, we'll keep this nice and simple then. What are you doing running around the city cemeteries in the middle of the night?"

Miss Da Vine's smile was still in place but it was as if the temperature in the room had dropped ten degrees. An icy silence descended on the room and William knew he had better not lie to the woman. Trouble was; he was also smart enough to not want her to know the truth either. He'd better be careful here.

"Well…I should think it was obvious. We were digging up graves. Have been for a while now. Why? What's the problem?"

"What are you looking for?"

That was the big question, wasn't it? As much as William was afraid of the actress and her goons, he was just as afraid of Ambrosious Black back at home. There was no way he was about to tell Da Vine about their dealings with the sculptor. He had to tell her something though, so chose the lesser of two evils.

"Dead bodies, of course. What else would you find in a bloomin' cemetery?"

The actress took a step back, hands on her curvaceous hips, contemplating his answer. It didn't seem to be the one she'd been expecting but William kept his face blank and his mouth shut. Let her make the next move.

"Why would you want to dig up dead bodies? Lots of them, from what I've been reading in the papers."

This was an easy one.

"For the money. Easiest pound note we've ever made." William wasn't about to tell her they actually made a lot more than that. He wanted to keep this as simple as possible so he wouldn't trip himself up and be caught in a lie.

"A pound? Wait…someone pays you to do the body snatching? Who?"

The feral look was back on her face, and again William refused to tell her about the deal he had cut with Mr. Black.

"His name's Knox. He's a doctor. Well, actually a surgeon who teaches doctors. We dig the graves and take the fresh bodies to him. If it's an old bag of bones in the hole, we check to see if there's any jewelry or pocket watches or what have you, but for the most part we make our cash bringing him the ones who don't stink too badly yet."

"What does he do with them?"

"I didn't really know, or care for that matter, but Billy says he runs a school to teach new doctors how to do surgery. Learn where all the body parts are and such. I think he's quite busy."

"I still don't understand. Why would he *hire* you fools to dig up corpses?"

"Well ma'am, it's no' exactly on the up and up, if you catch my meaning. The only legal bodies his school can use are the criminals who end up swinging on the end of a rope and the prison's no' pumping enough of those poor buggers out to meet his demands I guess. I don't know…go ask him yourself. All I know is he pays us a king's ransom and asks no questions."

Magenta Da Vine took a step back and started laughing, a genuine happy emotion this time, and the tension that had been in the air evaporated as if it had never been. The actress was back to being her charming, flirtatious self, ready to treat William like a long lost friend rather than someone who'd been beaten and brought here against his will.

"Well that's a wonderful little arrangement you and Billy have worked out for yourselves. Easy pickings by the sound of it." To the man she'd referred to as Angus earlier, she turned and said, "See, I told you, I knew he was a smart one, I did. Get him untied and help the gentleman to his feet."

"Certainly, my lady," the muscular man said, and quickly came over and cut the knot on the rope that bound William's hands. Angus pulled him to his feet and dragged him over to sit down in one of the desk chairs.

"Sorry about the confusion, William," Magenta said, taking one of the other seats across the desk from him. "A bit of a mix-up is all. I was thinking you might be…well, let's just say I thought you were doing something else in the graveyards. I like the way you and your mate operate though. I like it a *lot*."

William said nothing. He couldn't think of anything that seemed appropriate and wasn't about to say something stupid to make her mad now that she seemed to be about to let them walk away.

"I've got a grand idea," she said, a touch of that feral animal gaze creeping into her eyes again. "How about from now on you and Billy work for me?"

The way she said it, it didn't exactly sound like a question.

"Doing what?"

"That's the easy part. Doing exactly what you're already doing."

Now it was William's turn to look confused.

"You want us to look for dead bodies for you?"

"No, not quite. I want you to look for something else. Something *special!*"

Chapter 11

"You're kidding me, right?"

It was 10:00 a.m. the next day and it was Billy speaking. Even though William had already explained the entire chain of events to him twice already, he still couldn't wrap his simple mind around things. They were back in the common room at the Lodging House, resting by the fire after their long and strange night.

"The strumpet from the theatre wants to hire us to search in the graveyards too, same as old man Black?"

"That's what she said, yeah. You'd have heard her yourself if you didn't hold your booze like a wee girlie."

"But none of this makes sense," Billy said, ignoring the jab his mate had thrown at him. "She didn't tell you what we're supposed to be looking for either?"

"Nope. Same as Black. Just told me she was after something *special*, whatever the bloomin' hell that means?"

"Think they're both after the same thing?"

"Almost for sure, mate. Has to be."

"And they don't know we're being paid twice for the same dig?"

"Neither knows the other person even exists. Black just thinks we're greedy buggers, which we *are*…and the woman thinks we're working for Dr. Knox. 'Tis a thing of beauty, huh?"

"Sure is, William. Unless of course they find out what we're up to. That might no' go so well for us…hear?"

The thought had occurred to Hare already, but it was a risk he was more than willing to take. They'd made more money in the last month than in the entire last year – and there was a lot more to be made where that had come from. Besides, he wasn't convinced they'd *ever* find anything other than dust and bones in the old graves so what did it matter?

"That won't happen as long as you keep your big gob shut from here on out. We also need to stop tossing around money at the pubs, hear? Some folks are already starting to ask questions about where we suddenly struck it rich and if the right people start looking our way we might be—"

A loud banging noise echoed down the hall, cutting off William's speech midsentence. The noise had come from the sculptor's room and seconds later they heard the old man's door swing open and the approach of his footsteps.

In a whisper, William said, "Quiet…he's coming. Not a word now, hear?"

Billy nodded his head, his lips sealed.

Ambrosious Black entered the common room dressed to the nines in a brand new black suit, wool overcoat, and a matching top hat that made him look incredibly tall. He wore a huge smile on his face and seemed to be in a wonderful mood, especially for this early in the day. He removed his hat and bowed to the men sitting in front of the fire.

"Morning, gents…so glad you both could make it on time. Today's an important day for us and there's no time to waste."

"What's so bloody important about today?" Burke asked. "Why you dressed up so fancy like?"

"I'm dressed this way, Billy, because today's the day we unveil my statue to the city council. The Right Honorable Mr. Walter Brown, the Lord Provost of Edinburgh himself will be there for the reveal."

"You mean it's finished?" Hare asked, partly happy to be nearly done dealing with the frightening Mr. Black and his beastly bird but equally sad that one of their deep-pocketed benefactors might soon be leaving.

"Certainly is, William, and I think you boys are going to love it as much as the people of Edinburgh surely will. Come…we have to get moving."

"Where we going?" Burke asked.

"To the cemetery, of course. We can't build it here, dolt! The council paid handsomely for a statue of Robert the Bruce to stand guard over Calton Burial Grounds and by sundown tonight they'll damn well have one. I've rented a block and tackle and some scaffolding that should already be there waiting for us but I hope you lads got yourselves a good night's sleep. You're in for a long day."

William was remembering how heavy the stones were when they'd first moved them from the docks to the back room and wasn't exactly looking forward to that kind of strenuous activity today, not after everything he'd been through last night.

"Well, at least the stones should be lighter than last time, now that you've chipped away at them and such."

"Very true, William. Only some of them will be much more fragile now and I pray to all that's holy you and Billy Boy understand how important it is to me that you get those stones there without any damage."

"You mean we won't get any bonus wages if we break something?" Billy said, only half joking, trying to be funny. Black's mood instantly went darker than his name, the smile vanishing from his pallid face. He bent down close to the men before speaking in a quiet voice.

"I mean I'll rip the hearts out of your bone cages if you so much as chip one of the stones. Understand?"

Both burly men gulped down a healthy mouthful of fear.

"Yes sir," they answered together.

"Excellent! Now let's get to work."

* * *

The day crawled by agonizingly slow for Burke and Hare, the physical labor of moving and positioning the intricately sculpted stones not nearly as taxing on the exhausted men as the prolonged mental stress of not dropping or damaging the statue was. The pressure of having not only Black supervising their every move, but also half the city council who were slowly gathering as the sculpture got closer to completion, was intense and at times nearly overwhelming. Any other day, on any other job, William and Billy would have walked away and quit without a second look back but both men knew leaving wasn't an option so they kept their mouths shut and worked harder than either lazy man had worked in his life.

At least they'd had help.

The scaffolding Black rented had indeed been waiting for them, fully assembled and miraculously built in the proper place for them to get straight to work. William still hadn't held out much hope they could construct a large statue in one day but waiting beside the scaffolding, block and tackle equipment in hand, had been a tall muscular man in a wool pea coat and white captain's hat. Something had been familiar about him but neither Billy nor he had been able to place him until Black introduced the man as Nicholas Garfield, the friend of his from America who'd unloaded the original crates of stone from his Yankee Clipper steamship onto the docks for them.

Mr. Garfield hadn't been much of a conversationalist. In fact, he barely said a word other than muttering obscenities to urge Burke and Hare to hurry up several times; but what he lacked in small talk he'd more than made up for in sheer brute strength. Blocks of stone that Billy could barely push an inch along the grass, Garfield moved with one huge calloused hand as if it were a child's play toy. William could remember wondering how one man could have possibly unloaded Black's crates that fog-shrouded night they'd first met, but after watching the strongman work throughout the day he would never doubt him again; and nor would he ever want to cross paths with the American in a less agreeable situation. The man was a walking monstrosity, a physical freak of nature and William wondered who some of Black's other friends might be, but quickly decided he'd rather not know – and definitely didn't want to meet any of them.

The less he knew about his employer and his social circle, the better.

The hours passed. By hook or by crook, by brute strength or incredible skill, by stubborn hard work or perhaps simply good luck the statue slowly took shape. Black himself took charge near the end for the finishing touches; disappearing with a wire brush and a bucket of some awful smelling liquid beneath the massive tarp he'd had them conceal the sculpture within to hide the finished product from the gathering crowd's eyes. He was out of sight for over half an hour, but just as the last of the sun's rays were fading in the coal-polluted western sky Black appeared with an empty bucket and a huge smile on his sweaty face.

His statue was finished.

Burke and Hare were grinning nearly as much as the sculptor, never being more thankful that a day's work was finally over. They moved off to the side and happily stayed out of the way as Black quickly cleaned himself up and then launched into a brief but passionate speech about his sculpture.

"History remembers how King Robert made his last stand against the English hordes outside the nearby town of Bannockburn, June the twenty-fourth, in the year of our Lord thirteen hundred and fourteen, but what many Scots don't recall was that many of those brave souls who died defending the flag that day came from Edinburgh and their bodies were brought back and buried right here in Calton Cemetery."

There was a smattering of applause, and then Black continued.

"It's my fervent hope that this statue remain in this hallowed place for hundreds of years, reminding all who stand in the Bruce's mighty shadow exactly how high a price this nation paid for its independence and the brave men and women of this great city paid for the freedom you enjoy today."

When he was done, the small gathering of city officials and onlookers politely applauded and Black stepped to the side to allow Mr. Brown, the Lord Provost to begin his own speech about how excited the city council was to bring this statue to fruition after years of planning and how he hoped the people of Edinburgh would appreciate this tribute to the great man every proud Scotsman owed a massive debt to.

There was more applause followed by a round of handshaking; none of which interested Burke or Hare in the least. As Irishmen, it was all just useless political talk; they didn't give the slightest damn about Robert the Bruce or any of these fancy toffs' boring history lessons. They just wanted to get this ceremony over with, get paid, and make their way to the nearest pub for a stiff drink or two. As far as they were concerned, they'd earned it.

The chairman of the council thanked Black for all his efforts (naturally failing to make mention of all the back-breaking work William and Billy had just done) and signaled for the tarp to be removed. With great fanfare, several members of the crowd grabbed hold of the edge of the canvas and began to pull. Inch by inch the cover slid off the wooden scaffolding and soon dropped to their feet on the grass. Even William gasped when he saw what was revealed.

"Look at *that*, Billy!" he said.

Both men stood to their feet, suddenly just as interested in the statue as the rest of the excited crowd obviously was. Everyone was clapping and yelling and slapping Black on the back, congratulating him for his incredible work. The statue of King

Robert stood close to twelve feet tall to the tips of his crown, the details in his handsome face, intricate armor, and the huge sword strapped to his hip all so realistic it nearly took the uncultured workers' (along with everyone else's) breaths away. Burke and Hare had known the sculptor's skill was top-notch and without equal as they'd watched the statue slowly take shape today, but the stones had still been covered in dust and grime and even they'd been unprepared for the beauty of this final product.

"How'd he get it so shiny?" Billy asked, but William wasn't much help.

"Don't know, mate. Had to be whatever that stinky liquid was in the bucket. Looks like he's been polishing it for months. That's no' possible...is it?"

Billy could only shrug.

They had to wait around for another half an hour, waiting for the crowd to disperse but eventually the excitement died down and the members of the city council took their leave, more than pleased with the magnificent statue they'd commissioned. Black eventually came over to speak with them, handing William a heavy stack of coins.

"You lads did good work today. Better than expected, truth be told."

"Are we getting that bonus, then?" Billy said, always the clown.

Black looked at him sternly for a moment but then burst into laughter. "Why in blazes not, huh? You've caught me in a rare mood, Billy. Here you go." The sculptor dropped another few coins in Burke's outstretched filthy hand. "Now get out of my sight. I want to have a few moments of peace with King Robert if you don't mind."

"Of course not, sir," William said. "Just one question, gov'nor. What was in the bucket that made the stone polish up like that?"

The smile on Ambrosious Black's face faltered a little at the question but he recovered quickly and said, "Just soap and warm water and some good ol' fashioned elbow grease."

"Soap and water? That's it? Impossible!"

"Nothing's impossible, William. You'd be surprised what can be accomplished with hard work. And speaking of which...you lads need to get crackin' on your *other* job for me. Time is short and I'm expecting results, not excuses, hear?"

William said the only thing he could.

"Yes sir."

Chapter 12

"Soap and water, my arse!" William said, his teeth clenched in anger.

It was the following night, and although both Burke and Hare were still exhausted from the previous day's strenuous work helping build the statue (not to mention several hours of drunken foolery in the pub after) the men were back in Calton Cemetery trying to keep both of their mutually impatient employers happy. It was cold and rainy tonight, the fog so thick the grave robbers could almost reach out and comb through layers of it with their bare hands. The ground they were digging in was much harder than usual, not frozen but not far off it either. It didn't snow too often here in Edinburgh, what with the city's proximity to the water, but it wouldn't have surprised William or Billy in the least to see some of the white flakes flying soon. Making things worse, the wind howled in from the North Sea and cut straight through their clothes, chilling them to their bones even though they'd each worn an extra sweater. It was a terrible night to be outside even for a moment, much less standing exposed to the elements out in these open fields.

It was no wonder Hare was in such a foul mood.

"No way could soap shine up those stones like that. I'm telling you, Billy, he's lying to us. I mean, did you smell that bucket for God's sake? Smelled worse than your sweaty socks after no' changing them for a fortnight."

"For the tenth time...I hear you," Billy said, pausing his digging for a moment to blow in his hands to try and warm them. "I just don't know why you keep going on and on about it? Why do you care?"

"'Cause I don't like being bloody lied to, that's why. I've about had enough. Who in blazes does the old git think he is?"

"Careful, mate..." Billy said, his eyes looking skyward. "That horrible beast of his might be listening. I told you I saw it following me earlier today. It was—"

"I don't care about the blasted owl. I'm getting sick and tired of letting these people order us around. Bollocks to Black and double bollocks to that bitch down at the theatre. Neither of them will give us a straight answer and they expect us to freeze our cocks off digging though ground as hard as bloody rock. I've a good mind to–"

"Shhh...quiet!" Billy said, tugging on William's arm to try and get him to duck down out of sight. "Did you hear that?"

"Hear what? I didn't hear—"

"Shhh...there it is again. I think someone's coming!"

Now that Hare focused he could hear it too. Footsteps – heavy ones too, not someone who was trying to stay quiet – were approaching from the south. With the fog and the rain, it was impossible to tell who it might be or if perhaps it was more than one person headed their way. The visit the other night from Magenta Da Vine's goons was still fresh in Hare's mind, so he grabbed the spare shovel and whispered in Burke's ear, "Keep low and out of sight. I'm gonna circle 'round behind the buggers."

Before he could argue, William disappeared into the miserable night, leaving Billy standing there all alone inside a half dug grave. Billy crawled out of the hole and crouched down behind a small blackthorn bush. The ground was semi-frozen but was still saturated enough to soak through his pants. He was already drenched to the skin anyway, so what did it matter? Hopefully whoever was in the cemetery with them would go away and leave them alone. The sooner they could get out of here tonight, the better.

A dim glow shattered the gloom, and a short, stocky older man with a grey beard pushed his way through the fog and headed straight for the grave Billy had been digging.

"Hey you!" the man said, easily spotting Billy's muddy boots sticking out from behind the bush. "What's your game then, mate?"

There was no reason for Billy to stay in hiding anymore so he climbed to his feet, (just now noticing the new arrival had a pistol aimed his way) and tried to come up with a believable excuse for why he'd be here digging on a dismal night such as this.

"Hello pops. I work for the cemetery, you see, so relax. Been way behind lately so I just thought I'd try and get caught up on—"

"Don't you *'ello pops* me. I know exactly what you're up to, mister, so *shut* it. I told Mr. Farris I'd catch the rotter stealing a' the bodies and now I've gone and done it. You'll rot in prison for this, you will. Just wait and see."

"Easy now, old-timer," Billy said, stalling for time. "This isn't what it looks like...I can promise you that."

"Save yer lies for the police. Now drop that shovel and slowly put—"

CLANG!

William's shovel rang off the cemetery guard's skull, forcibly driving the old man head first into the frozen ground and shutting him up in a hurry. The potentially dangerous confrontation was over as easily as that.

"Take your time, why don't ya?" Billy said, rushing over to toss away the fallen man's handgun and make sure he didn't try to get back up. "The old bugger could have shot me dead!"

"Aye, and done the world a favor. Stop your whining and let's tie him up."

"Umm...don't think that's gonna be needed. I think he's snuffed it!"

"What?"

"He's dead. Check 'im yourself if you don't believe me."

William did just that, but sure enough the old guard was no longer breathing. Whether it had been the vicious blow to the back of his head that had killed him, or the way he'd been pile-driven face first into the hard earth, it really didn't matter. The long and short of it was that Burke and Hare were suddenly in a heap of trouble. Getting caught and brought to justice for grave robbing was bad enough, but getting charged with murder was a whole lot worse.

As in swinging from the gallows worse!

"What did you wallop him so hard for?" Billy said, a touch of panic in his voice. "What are we supposed to do now?"

William was way ahead of his less imaginative friend, already calculating the odds of their next move in his head. "We've got two choices, Billy. Either we finish digging that hole and bury the old bugger alongside whoever we find there or…we go pay Dr. Knox a visit and turn this little setback into a win-win for everyone."

"What? You mean sell him? We can't do that?"

"Why not? Knox likes his bodies fresh, right? You don't get much fresher than this. We'll smear a little dirt on his face and clothes and the doc will think we just dug him up, same as always. Who's to ever know?"

Burke thought hard about that for a few seconds but then a big smile spread across his face. "I like the way you think, mate. Makes me wonder why we've been busting our hump for a' those other bodies though? Why bother going to a' that trouble, right? Especially this time of the year. I mean, I know we still have to dig the old graves for Black and Da Vine, but why do we need to keep freezing our arses off and risking getting caught digging up the fresh ones?"

Hare was smiling now too, patting his friend on the back.

"It's a good question, Billy. A good question indeed!"

Chapter 13

The transition from clueless bodysnatching to ruthless cold-blooded murder was seamless and relatively easy for the two Irish freeloaders. Killing a man or woman in an alleyway or dark doorway was much quicker and cleaner than dragging a stiff corpse out of some smelly hole in the ground. It required a whole lot less effort too. They needed to refine their methods of course; bashing someone in the head with a shovel inflicted considerable damage to the body and left incriminating evidence behind that a heinous crime had been committed.

To remedy that problem, the fledgling killers soon learned to suffocate their targets so it would appear to anyone who might examine the bodies that they'd somehow died of natural causes. Hare would hold his hand over the victim's nose and mouth while Burke put the full weight of his body across the chest of the victim, not allowing them to breathe. They still worried about the dire consequences of being caught by the police but as the calendar turned over into the month of December, and as the body count (as well as their stash of money) started to build, so too did their cockiness and blatant disregard for the law. As far as Burke and Hare were concerned, they could do anything they damn well pleased.

Unfortunately, they still had to put on a convincing show of trying to please both Ambrosious Black and the equally intimidating Magenta Da Vine. Although Burke and Hare had no real need for their mysterious benefactors' paltry stipends anymore, earning a far better payday for their secret deliveries to Dr. Knox, they were determined not to unnecessarily anger the sculptor or the actress if they could avoid it. Quite simply, and perhaps shockingly, the hard-nosed serial killers were still afraid of them both – even though they'd be hard pressed to give a reason as to why. It was just a gut feeling they had; a strong sense of hidden menace that even dangerous men such as they could not ignore. Therefore it was easier to risk the occasional foray into the guarded graveyards than it was to face the consequences of not doing so.

And so the rainy days and cold fog-shrouded nights slowly passed...

* * *

"Come on Billy...put your back into it, man!" William said, tired from another pointless night of digging in the older section of the Calton burial grounds. "You work like an old woman."

"Oh piss off, why don't ya? My fingers are freezing off and I'm digging as fast as I can. We shouldn't even be out here and you bloody well know it."

"You worry too much, mate. We're pretty safe way back here. The guards and the coppers are only watching the fresh holes out by the road. They're only interested in nabbing grave robbers, no' honest blokes like us."

"What are we doing here, if it's no' called grave robbing?"

"Well...wasting our drinking time for one thing!"

"Right you are there, William. Truest thing you've said a' night. Let's get out of here, then. I've had my fill of shoveling."

"Me too, but look...you're practically standing on the lid. Let's just finish this one and be done with it."

"I'm too tired. You want to see another box of old crumblin' bones, 'ave at it then." Billy climbed out of the waist-deep hole in the ground and handed the shovel over to William. "I'm done!"

"See, you even *complain* like an old woman," William said with a smile on his dirty face, not really angry with his friend. It was his turn to dig anyway. "At least keep an eye out for anyone headed our way, right?"

"Aye, I'm watching. Just hurry it up."

William began to dig and sure enough, within twenty shovelfuls he'd scraped the top of the wooden box buried below his feet. Five minutes later he had the entire lid uncovered and was surprised to see it didn't look as old and rotted as all the other cheaply made coffins normally looked. In fact, it still looked quite solid.

"Well, well, well...what do we 'ave here?"

Billy, despite what he'd promised only a few minutes ago, was stretched out on the grass with his eyes closed and was nearly fast asleep. "Huh?"

"Come look at this, mate. Something's *different* about this one."

"Different how?" Billy said crawling over to look down in the hole.

"The wood and the construction's old but look how good of shape it's in. Almost looks new but that's no' possible way out here. Is it?"

"How should I know? Open the blasted thing and let's have a look."

William nodded his head and went back to work. Most of the old boxes were crumbling to bits under their feet, but with this one he had to use the edge of the shovel to pry up the corners of the lid. There were twice as many nails holding this lid in place than in any other coffin they'd opened, and even though they didn't think it possible, William and Billy found themselves getting excited about what they might be about to find. Billy jumped into the hole too, and by getting both their hands in under the lid, they were able to finally loosen the wooden top enough to heave it up and out of the hole.

What they saw within the coffin nearly took their breath away.

The dead man lying inside the box was huge, a hulking muscular man wearing a soldier's wool tunic and leather boots, whose broad shoulders barely squeezed inside the confines of the wooden walls. His size was impressive, but what shocked the body snatchers most was that his skin and hair were still intact. Every other body they'd checked in this part of the cemetery had been nothing but dust and bones, but this man, this unknown warrior, was almost perfectly preserved. From his clothing and the location where they were digging in the ancient burial grounds, he surely had to have been buried in this hole hundreds of years ago, but he looked as if he'd breathed his last breath only a week or two ago. Impossible, but nonetheless true.

"He's a Templar," William said, still in awe at what he was seeing.

"Huh?"

"A Templar Knight, Billy. See the red cross on his tunic?"

"Aye. He's wearing a sword too. Look!"

"I see it."

"Something's no' right though, William. No' *natural*. I mean, Templar or no'...why hasn't the big bugger rotted away like a' the rest?"

"No idea...but didn't Mr. Black say something about the Knights when he was yammerin' in his sleep the other night?"

"Aye, he did. Think this is the bloke he was talking about?"

"Could be. One of them at least."

"He also mentioned something about gold, right?"

"That he did, Billy. That he most *certainly* did. Let's have a look..."

William knelt down and began to search around the soldier's legs and along his sides. All traces of weariness or worry about being caught by the police were gone now, the excitement building by the second as he felt around for the possible treasure.

"Maybe Black is after the sword?" Billy said. "Something like that's gotta be worth a pretty penny, right?"

"Probably is, yeah, but my gut's telling me he's after something..." William started to say but the breath was sucked from his lungs at what he'd caught a glimpse of. The soldier's arms were bent and his gloved hands were clasped above the center of his chest. When William had nudged the dead man's left arm it had moved his hand enough that a glimmer of something shiny was revealed beneath. With a trembling hand, William reached over and pried open the Knight's gloved hands.

"Sweet Mary, mother of God!" he whispered. "Look at *that*, Billy!"

There was a golden chalice hidden under the man's gloves, resting above the Templar's burly chest. The cup wasn't fancy or adorned with jewels; it didn't even have any carvings or written engravings on its smooth curved sides but it was impressive nonetheless. It practically glowed in the meager moonlight filtering through the fog, a magical golden heart hidden in this place of death.

"We've found it!" William said.

"What is it?"

"Don't know, mate, but I've got a good guess. Do you remember what else Black was muttering about that night by the fire...the part about blood and the death of the carpenter? Something about a traitor too, right?"

"Something like that, yeah. It was just a dream."

"Don't be so sure. I didn't think so that night and I'm even more sure of it now. Think about it: The death of a carpenter, the Knights Templar, and a golden chalice. Even a brainless lump like you can put those things together."

"You don't mean the Grail, I hope? The *Holy bloody Grail*! Have you lost your marbles, William? That's just make-believe, a children's bedtime story."

"You sure? Maybe that's why this bloke in the hole hasn't rotted to bones. He's protecting the carpenter's cup...or maybe its protecting him."

"So it's magic now, is it? Come off it, mate. Do you hear yourself?"

"I'm no' saying that I believe in the Grail, Billy, but I'll bet you Black and Da Vine do. Guaranteed. This is what they've both been looking for."

"What do we do now, then?"

"We take it, obviously. Are you simple?"

"That's no' what I mean, William. 'Course we take it. I mean, who do we give it to? The sculptor or the actress?"

Now that was a good question.

William briefly considered keeping it for themselves but again, his fear of Ambrosious Black and Magenta Da Vine ruled that option out in a hurry. He was a simple man with simple needs and the chance that he might be in possession of the priceless cornerstone of countless myths and legends – hell, the very foundation of a worldwide religion – never really entered his mind. In this one instant, William decided honesty was probably the best policy. As soon as this chalice (fabled or not) was delivered, Billy and he could stop all this blasted digging and concentrate on more important matters for Dr. Knox. Just having the sculptor and the actress out of their lives for good was treasure enough, as far as William was concerned. Not that this made their choice any easier.

Who would get the prize?

"We're going to have to think on this for a few days, Billy. I never thought we'd actually find the bloody thing, right?"

"We don't tell *either* of them, then? We keep it a secret?"

"Aye...for now. Just until I can figure out who'll pay us more. No one's getting this cup for free, that's for sure!"

"Now you're talkin', mate. Can I keep the sword too?"

"Don't think that's a good idea, Billy. Best not. Fewer ties we have to this grave the better, hear? We've got to fill in this hole like we were never here. Can't have anyone finding out about our big friend...or his sword. Come on, grab your shovel."

Chapter 14

All good things must eventually come to an end.

Immersed in the nefarious underworld of bodysnatching and murder in an attempt to supply the surgeons with their cadavers – not to mention the daunting task of keeping their golden secret hidden from Black and Da Vine – it was only a matter of time before Burke and Hare were brought to justice to answer for their heinous crimes.

No matter how clever Billy and William believed they were, or how careful they thought they were being, the net was slowly closing in on them. Despite it being the Christmas season, public outrage was at an all-time high, and there were eyes and ears in every graveyard and on every street corner anxious to lay claim to the rewards the police offered for information leading to the arrest of the *'resurrectionists.'* Ironically, it wouldn't be the cemetery guards or the police constables who would ultimately trigger their undoing – it would be a roomful of student doctors.

Burke and Hare let their greed get the better of them and they ended up killing an eighteen-year-old young man by the name of James Wilson. Wilson was a simpleton with a deformed foot but he was well liked by the locals for telling riddles and jokes to the neighborhood children. Daft Jamie, as he was called, was well known throughout the Westport area, and when his dead body turned up on Dr. Knox's dissection table a few nights later, several doctors and members of the student audience immediately recognized the poor boy.

It didn't take long for the police to become involved, and once they got their hands on Robert Knox, he was happy to explain to them who it was that had been supplying his surgical school with Daft Jamie and the other bodies. Naturally the good doctor claimed he had no idea where the corpses had come from or any knowledge of wrongdoing and promised to help their investigation all he could. The police may or may not have believed Knox, but in the end they didn't care – they finally had their men.

And Burke and Hare were suddenly in big, big trouble…

* * *

Edinburgh Prison near the top of Calton Hill was a terrible place. It was old and crumbling, with most of the stone cell walls covered in mold or moss from the constant moisture in the air. There were heavy iron bars on the windows, of course, but no glass to keep the howling wind and rain outside where it belonged, the fog rolling into the tiny rooms thick enough that the prisoners needed to feel their way around some nights just to find their cot.

The police had separated Burke from Hare the minute they'd been dragged here from the pub, kicking and screaming their innocence all the way, and William had no idea which cell his friend was being kept in. He'd tried calling out to Billy several times that first night, but the only responses he'd gotten were from other prisoners telling him to shut his gob and go to sleep. It had been two full days and nights since William had seen anyone other than the same foul-mouthed fat man who brought him a bowl of cold porridge each morning and a stale sandwich made from some kind of greasy grey meat for supper. Eventually he'd have to see a lawyer or judge, he supposed, but for the time being the powers that be seemed content to just let him rot.

On the third morning of his incarceration, William's nasty guard forgot to bring his gruel altogether, instead showing up hours later with the first bit of information shared with Hare since his arrival. Unfortunately, the news was grim.

"Hey, Cockbreath?" the jailer said, "Just heard they're gonna give yer neck a bit of a stretching, they are! Soon as they can get the gallows ready, I'm told."

"Hang me? Without even having a trial? They can't do that...can they?"

"They can do any damn thing they want, mate. Who in blazes do you Irish bastards think you are, anyway? The rope's too good for the likes of you two animals, they ask me. I'd just slit yer throats and be done with it."

William knew he wasn't going to get anywhere by talking with this brute so he decided to try and change the conversation.

"When can I speak to a lawyer? Surely I'll be allowed to—"

"A lawyer? For a senseless prick like you? Everyone already knows you're guilty. Why would they give you a lawyer?"

While William tried to come up with a suitable answer to that, the guard started to laugh, slapping his dirty palms on the wooden part of the door and grunting like he'd never said anything so funny.

"Just pulling yer leg, you silly toff. 'Course you'll get to see a lawyer, for a' the good it'll do. Before that, though, you've got a visitor."

"Who?" William asked.

"Some woman. Probably your wife comin' to say good riddance. Don't know. Don't care. I was just told to come and get ya."

The guard unlocked the door and stepped into the room carrying a pair of rusty shackles to put on William's ankles and wrists.

"Try anything funny and I'll bash yer brains out right here and now and save a'body the bother of a fancy trial, hear?"

William nodded and let the boorish guard do his work, the whole time trying to understand why Maggie would be coming here to see him. With all the trouble Billy and he were in, he'd thought she was probably the last person to ever willingly come for a visit. People might start wondering how much she knew about the bodysnatching and the murders, and if maybe she was involved in the crimes and deserved to be sitting in a jail cell alongside him.

"Right then," The jailer said. "Steady as she goes..."

William hobbled out the cell and moved down the damp stone corridor as quickly as his shackles allowed. The guard poked and prodded him from behind through what seemed like a maze of tunnels, but eventually William was herded into a clean, wooden-floored room with a desk and two chairs. Sunlight and a refreshing cool breeze blew in through the open window set high on the outside wall. He was roughly shoved into one of the chairs and left in irons for whatever was about to happen.

"Sit there and keep yer trap shut. Someone will bring her in soon."

William ended up having to wait nearly half an hour for his visitor, but that was fine. He still wasn't sure what he was going to say to Maggie and it was far nicer here in this room than in his cold, dark cell. When the meeting room door finally creaked open, William turned expecting to see Maggie's angry face, furious with him for what he'd done, but he was wrong. It wasn't his wife sitting down across from him after all.

It was Magenta Da Vine.

Out of the frying pan...into the fire, William thought, his heart leaping into his throat. *Why would she be here?*

Da Vine sat in silence, a slight smile on her ruby-red lips, but her eyes were dark and brooding, perfectly relaying her mood to William without having to say a word. Outwardly she appeared calm and in control, but inside she was mad as hell. The actress had toned down her sexuality for today's visit, wearing only a touch of makeup and a simple brown dress buttoned all the way up to her collar. She was still a beautiful, full-figured woman, but just not as boldly stunning and noticeable as usual. William tried his best to meet her gaze but found it nearly impossible to do. Instead, he asked the question he'd had on his mind.

"What are you doing here, ma'am? Not exactly the kind of place for a refined lady such as yourself."

"I could ask you the same, William. What are *you* doing here?"

"Well...it's not like the coppers gave me much of a choice, did they?"

"How could you have been so bloody stupid? Even I had heard about Daft Jamie...did you really think he wouldn't be missed?"

William didn't see any reason to lie or make up stories around Da Vine so he answered her honestly. "The simpleton was Billy's fault, no' mine. He was dead before I even got home. I just helped take him to the surgeon."

"You were *supposed* to be out digging in Calton Cemetery for me, or had you forgotten about that?"

"'Course not. We didn't..." *need to* William nearly said, but caught himself. "We just didn't want to, I guess. Dr. Knox was paying us a lot more than you, see, and I had a sore back from a' the digging and umm..." He was rambling and couldn't think of anything else to say so he stopped right there, unable to look at the actress' face.

She gasped, seeing through his lie in an instant.

"You found it, didn't you?"

This time he did look up. "Found what? We didn't even know what we we're supposed to be looking for."

"But you found it anyway. Where is it?"

"I don't know what you're on about, lady. Billy and I haven't found anything but old dried-up bones. That's a' there is in those fields."

Da Vine looked at William long and hard. "Well then...I suppose there's no sense in us continuing this relationship, is there? Consider yourself fired. I can always find other men who know how to work a shovel."

William couldn't help but to laugh at that one.

"Fired? Ha! If you hadn't noticed, being unemployed isn't exactly my biggest worry these days."

"That's true, but seeing as you've no interest in digging for me anymore I've really got no reason to stop them from taking you to the gallows. Enjoy your day, Mr. Hare. Sorry things didn't work out between us. I had such high hopes…"

The actress stood up and started heading for the door.

"Hold on…don't be running off like that. You're saying you can help Billy and me? You can stop them from hanging us?"

"No…not both of you. Someone has to pay for what you fools have done; the crown will demand it, but I've always thought you had more brains than the rather vile Mr. Burke, so I'm giving you the option. One of you can walk away from here, William. Who's it going to be?"

Billy had been the best friend he'd ever had, but William didn't even feel the need to answer that last question. It was obvious who he was going to choose.

"How can you get me out of here? It's impossible."

"Do you honestly doubt me? If I say I can do something, it will be done."

"Yeah…for a price."

"Of course. There's *always* a price to pay, silly. Give me what I want and you'll get your life back. Simple as that."

"But I don't know what you want? I already told you—"

"You're wasting my time," Magenta said, taking another two steps toward the door. "You and your mate can rot in Hell together. Goodbye, William."

"*WAIT!* Don't leave. I…I might be able to help you."

"Might's not good enough. Do you have what I want? Yes or no?"

"Yes."

"Prove it. Tell me what it is?"

"It's a cup, but not just any cup, right? The carpenter's cup. The golden chalice. The Holy Grail!"

Da Vine looked shocked. "How do you know about the Grail?"

"I may be a fool, ma'am, but I'm no' an idiot. Mr. Black mentioned the Templars in his sleep one night. He also mentioned the death of the carpenter. When Billy and I found the golden cup cradled in the arms of a Templar Knight I put it all together. The blood of Jesus was supposedly collected in a golden cup, and the Templars are the protectors of the Grail so what else could it be?"

"Oh you're a smart one, William. At least you *think* you are. One question though. Who's Mr. Black?"

William knew he'd slipped up by mentioning the sculptor but what did it matter now? Things couldn't get much worse than they already were. "Ambrosious Black. He rents a room off Maggie and me. He's looking for the Grail too."

"Ahh…and what does this Mr. Black look like?"

"He's an old man but strong as a bull. White hair, white beard. Hell, even white eyes on the bugger. For a while Billy and I were afraid of him and his beastly white owl."

"As you should be," Da Vine said. "He's a dangerous man. I knew it! I just *knew* he was here. So that's what he's calling himself these days, huh? Interesting."

"You know him?"

"Trust me, Mr...*Black* and I go back a long ways together. Never mind him, though. Where is it?"

"Where's what?"

The smile was back on the actress' face, but the hunger in her eyes had never burned brighter. In a hushed voice she said, "Don't toy with me, boy. My patience is at an end. Where's the Carpenter's Cup?"

"Hidden somewhere you'll never find. Get me out of here and it's yours. My life for your precious Grail…deal?"

The raven-haired actress looked William up and down, trying to determine if there was any way he was lying to her. Satisfied he had to be telling the truth, she walked back to the table and sat down.

"Deal. Okay…a lawyer is coming to see you later today. He works for the crown but he'll be on our side. He'll say they don't have the evidence to pin the murders on both of you so he's coming to make you an offer: Freedom in exchange for your testimony in court saying that Billy Burke was the mastermind behind all these crimes. You provide King's evidence against your mate in exchange for a full pardon. It'll take a few weeks before the hearings and the trial but you'll manage. Billy hangs…you walk away. Understand?"

"Yes."

"And you're okay with that?"

"Perfectly."

The actress began to laugh. "You're a right cold bastard, William."

"Coming from you, Miss Da Vine…I'll take that as a compliment."

Chapter 15

January 28, 1829.

An icy rain had fallen from the black, stormy sky for most of the night, soaking the members of the gathering crowd who were angry enough—or perhaps foolish enough—to brave the wintery chill in order to get the best available viewing spots in the market square. Naturally, the very best seats were indoors, watching from the dozens of windows in the neighbouring buildings, but those warm and dry vantage points were reserved for upper-class people with money to spend, and had been reserved weeks in advance. The commoners on street level had to make do as best they could: huddled together, hands tucked deep into pockets, collars raised, shoulders hunched, displaying that most famous of British traits—unwavering stubbornness.

As morning arrived, the rain began to taper off, eventually stopping altogether around 7:00 a.m., the sun trying to break through the low-lying clouds but not having much success. The temperature rose a few precious degrees, but whatever heat the enduring crowd gained was quickly lost in the escalating winds that whipped through the square. It was a terrible morning to be outside in the elements.

But it was a grand day for an execution.

Most of the run-of-the-mill hangings were done right inside Edinburgh Prison, with no fanfare or thought put into it other than carrying out the Lord Advocate's orders according to the law of the land. The execution of William Burke was far from run-of-the-mill though, and there was such a huge public outcry about the well-publicized Westport Murders that the Crown had no choice but to make the hanging public. To accommodate as many people as possible, some who would even rumored to be travelling from other cities to attend, the authorities chose a site known as Libberton Wynd.

Libberton Wynd Lawn Market was a continuation of Edinburgh's High Street, lying between the head of the West Bow Municipal Buildings and the impressive crown-shaped spire of St. Giles Cathedral. The market square was basically a large grassy park within the city. But seeing as it was normally filled with row upon row of street merchants' and food vendors' tents, selling their wares to the public, there were no trees or bushes to get in the way. The massive wooden gallows had been constructed at the east end of the square, near the front entrance of the cathedral. Workers from all over the city had donated their time and labor to help build the structure, more than happy to be a part of this highly anticipated killing.

By 8:30 a.m. the market square was teeming with people: young and old, rich and poor, ranging in ages from toddlers riding on their father's shoulders all the way up to elderly men and women limping along High Street with crutches to support their frail legs. Everyone and anyone in the city wanted to be here to bear witness to the execution, either to see justice carried out on a heinous criminal, or simply to say that they were there to see the poor bugger die—it mattered not—as long as they were there. With the rain having stopped, and the icy wind settling down somewhat, the mood in the crowd was boisterous and loud. Despite the hour and the supposedly serious occasion, there were people singing and dancing and drinking, having themselves a tremendous time.

The only thing this party was missing was the star of the show.

* * *

Billy Burke could hear the raucous crowd of what he considered ghoulish people outside in the square, but he was in no hurry to meet any of them. He'd been brought from the prison the day before, and had spent most of yesterday afternoon and evening listening to the construction workers endlessly banging their nails into the scaffolding and platform he'd soon be walking out onto. It hadn't made for a relaxing or peaceful last night on earth but there was nothing he could do about it. Billy had long since made peace with God and with his imminent death but with the situation as it was he wasn't exactly in the best of moods as they came to collect him.

"You ready for this?" the burly guard named McDaniel asked.

"Go on and fuck yourself, mate," Billy said, not even opening his eyes.

"Aye, and I might do just that once I'm done dealing with the likes of you. On your feet, scum. It's time to meet your maker."

When Billy opened his eyes, he saw that there were four men standing at the door of his makeshift cell, each looking as tall and wide as a Clydesdale horse. The sight of the huge men nervously guarding the room's only exit, as if he might try and make a break for it, made Billy sit up from his cot and laugh.

"Bloody Hell...you sure you don't need to get a few more blokes to walk me out? I'm a dangerous man, you know. Haven't you been reading the papers?"

"Think we'll manage," McDaniel said, with no hint of a smile. "Let's go!"

Billy sighed, but reluctantly did as he was told. Once in the hallway, he was joined by a thin-faced Catholic priest dressed in a brown cassock, who walked along beside him in case Billy wanted to speak. He didn't. He'd met with this same priest last night and had said everything he'd wanted to say to the man (and to the man's boss upstairs) already. This morning he just wanted a little peace and quiet. The sooner they got this over and done with, the better.

Billy exited out into the market square through a side door in the municipal office and was greeted with a rapturous chorus of cheers, jeers, screams, and whistles as he was led slowly across High Street and walked toward the gallows. He'd known there was going to be a big crowd waiting outside, but wasn't quite prepared for what he was seeing. The gathered throng of people was enormous, as if every man, woman, and child in Edinburgh had shown up to see him hang. It wasn't far off the truth, either.

Fear took a hard and sudden bite out of Billy's bravado and his legs involuntarily stopped moving. He'd thought he'd prepared himself for what was about to happen but obviously he'd been wrong.

One second the idea of dying and moving on to the next life had been a peaceful, almost comforting thought, but faced with the cold, stark reality of the moment was too much for Billy and he refused to walk another step. Unfortunately, the quartet of beefy guards escorting him was ready for just such a development. He was quickly grabbed and forcibly dragged the rest of the way.

"Now, now, Billy," McDaniel said in his ear as they walked, shouting above the din of the bloodthirsty horde. "Keep a stiff upper lip, hear? Rumor has it even Sir Walter Scott is here to see you off. Wouldn't want to disappoint him now, would you?"

"Bugger Sir Walter…and bugger everyone else!" he screamed, his heart racing the closer he was dragged to the steps of the scaffold.

Billy didn't give a damn about Sir Walter Scott, or anyone else for that matter—famous or not. Even if King George and the entire Royal Family had camped out in the front row he'd still tell them all to go straight to Hell. He maybe owed the families of his victims his life, and the devil his soul, but as far as he was concerned he owed the vermin gathered here to watch him die absolutely *nothing*!

Don't let them see your fear, he thought. *Don't give the bastards the satisfaction!*

Easier said than done, of course, but Billy tried his best to rein in the terror gripping his body; trying his best to at least exit this world with his self-respect intact. Up the scaffold steps they went, Billy being dragged up two steps for every one he managed on his own. At the top, Billy finally got a good look at the rope and noose awaiting him, and for some reason it made him feel a tiny bit better. He was frightened, sure, but he was also exhausted from the trials and the written confession and the days and nights freezing his arse off in the damp, moldy prison. Part of him—no matter how scared he felt inside—was ready to get this over with. Taking a deep breath to steady his nerves, Billy walked the final ten feet to the noose all on his own.

The trap door beneath his feet creaked loudly with his weight, but held. He was just wondering what would have happened if he'd have fallen through the board and broken his legs in the fall—*would they have to go down to the ground and carry him back up here?*—when McDaniel was beside him slipping the noose over his head and yanking the knot tight.

"Say hi to Satan for me, mate!" the burly guard said, a smile on his face as he walked away without waiting for a response. That was good; Billy had none for him.

A fancily dressed officer from the Magistrate's Office climbed the stairs and walked over to introduce himself to Billy and the clergyman, who was still standing by in case he was needed. Billy couldn't make out the man's name over the roar of the crowd, not that he cared. The tall, feminine-looking man turned and shouted for the noisy audience to calm down. It took a moment but soon he had everyone's undivided attention.

"Good morning, ladies and gentlemen. I can understand your anger and vindictive attitude for the condemned man in front of you but I must insist you act with the decorum such a solemn event deserves. After all...a man's life is about to be forfeit for his crimes. The least you can do is show the man, if not respect...then at least a shred of decency."

The crowd started to boo and shout even louder, such was their bloodlust and bitter contempt for the Westport Killer. In a different time and place, Billy would have found the situation hilarious and made fun of the silly toff himself, but as it was he just stood there trying not to shake, and waited for the man to proceed.

"Have it your way, then," the officer continued, removing a paper scroll from his jacket pocket. "William Burke, it is by order of the Lord Advocate of Edinburgh, operating under direct authority of King George IV, that you have been found guilty in the murders of Mary Patterson, James Wilson, and Mary Docherty. Today, in the presence of God and in front of these witnesses, you are to be hung by the neck until declared dead. Do you have anything to say for yourself before the sentence is carried out?"

Billy had been waiting for this moment, preparing all those long, lonely nights in prison to come out here and tell the world how he had his share in all the terrible things that had happened, but that he certainly wasn't the only one who should be blamed. He intended to tell them—whether they'd listen or not—about his mate William, Ambrosious Black, and Magenta Da Vine. Surely they'd all played their part in this, and for the life of him Billy couldn't understand how the Crown could possibly lay all the blame at his feet. As much as he truly didn't harbor any ill will against William for saving his own skin when he'd been offered the chance (he'd have done the same), that still didn't mean he had to be happy about it.

Billy opened his mouth to speak...

...and then he spotted something huge flying over his head, slowly circling the market square. It was the owl—Black's beast—silently watching everything on the ground below. Just the sight of its razor-sharp beak and talons stole Billy's breath for a moment, making him lose his train of thought. He watched the bird of prey circle once more then land on an exposed wooden beam beneath an open window on High Street. Inside the room, a tall man with white hair and a white beard stood looking over at him.

Mr. Black! Billy thought, a sliver of fear entering his heart, even under the circumstances. *Why would he be here?*

The mysterious sculptor stared back at Billy, and then raised a single finger to his lips, motioning him to be quiet.

Screw you, mate, Billy thought. *I'll do nothing of the sort.*

Billy opened his mouth to speak...but nothing happened. His voice was suddenly and inexplicably gone. He tried again, but nothing more than a tiny squeak escaped his lips. *What's happening? Why can't I talk?*

"Suit yourself," the officer from the Magistrate's Office said. "Perhaps in this case, silence is for the best. And for what it's worth...may God have mercy on your soul. Gentlemen, you may proceed."

No! Billy thought, trying his best to shout, to scream, to holler out any words at all at this point, but no matter how hard he tried, he could produce no sounds from his throat. *I've been hexed, I have! Bloody well cursed!*

Billy's eyes returned to the open window across the street where the sculptor was still watching him intently. It was difficult to tell, what with the man's beard in the way, but Black appeared to be smiling. The last thing Billy saw before someone behind him pulled a black bag over his head was the massive owl spreading its wings and launching high into the dreary morning sky. Moments later, without warning, Billy was flying too; although *his* journey would last but a few short seconds and the only place he was headed was straight down.

Chapter 16

Although Billy Burke admitted to taking part in many murders—even he hadn't been sure of the exact number—he had only died on the gallows officially charged with killing three. His hanging at the Libberton Wynd Lawn Market had drawn the biggest crowd ever to witness a single execution in Scottish history. And in what many agreed was a perfectly ironic twist of fate, as the law of the land dictated, his deceased body was immediately turned over to the local surgeons for anatomical study and dissection.

For better or worse, Billy's suffering was over.

William Hare wasn't about to get off quite so easily.

Not that he'd likely have gone even if he'd been allowed; William wasn't in attendance to witness his friend's death. He was still locked in his cell at the prison; technically a free man after completing his duties as King's informant, but unfortunately for him, his life still in grave danger. While it was true the crown had legally forgiven him with a full pardon, the vengeful citizens of Edinburgh were a different story altogether and had no intention of letting the murdering Irishman off the hook for what he'd done.

Vigilante mobs lined the street day and night outside the prison, waiting for their chance to get their hands on Hare, so for his safety he was kept incarcerated for an extra week until some of the heat began to die down. William was finally released at one o'clock in the morning through a seldom used side entranceway. He was still worried about the mobs spotting him, but his fear of a crowd of angry men was nothing compared to what he felt when he saw the four-wheeled Hackney cab waiting for him at the first crossroad.

And the familiar, long-legged beauty standing beside it.

"Move your arse," Magenta Da Vine said. "Get in before you're spotted."

William did as he was told, nodding to Big Josh, the huge smiling man who was steering the horses, and soon the cab dashed off into the quiet night, its wheels making far more racket on the cobblestones than he would have liked. In truth, he would have preferred to just walk, and had secretly hoped he might have had time to sneak home, pack a bag, and disappear out of the city before anyone knew he'd been released. He should have known he'd never be that lucky. He had a debt owing, and come Hell or high water the actress intended on making him pay.

"Evening, Mr. Hare," Da Vine said. "I trust you're pleased to see me and looking forward to completing our little arrangement, yes?"

"Certainly, ma'am. Be glad to have a' this over and done with, if you don't mind me saying so."

"Couldn't agree more. Where we headed?"

Despite the chill of the February night, William was starting to sweat. He'd played this moment over and over in his head this past week, and no matter how he thought things through he couldn't come up with a scenario that would guarantee his long-term survival. They were alone for now, sure, but once the actress had her hands on the Carpenter's Cup, what would stop her from having her baldheaded goon driving the cab get rid of the only living witness?

The answer was: *Nothing!*

"Umm…don't take this the wrong way, but I'd prefer if you dropped me off at the lodging house and I'll bring the Grail round to the Ripley within an hour. I gotta get out of this city. I just wanna pack a bag and once I deliver your cup I can be on my way."

Magenta began to laugh.

"I don't think so, William. What's the problem?"

"Well...to be honest, I'm worried your boy up there will slit my throat if I take you straight to the Grail."

"And how does that change if you bring the cup to me?"

"It doesn't, but I figure I can pick my time to drop it off and at least get a head start. I don't want no trouble, ma'am...I just want to live."

"And you think you could run away from me if I wanted you dead?"

"I'm just asking for a chance. I'm pretty fast when I wanna be."

"Not fast enough," Da Vine said, her toothy grin even more predatory and unnerving than usual. "Luckily I have no intention of killing you. We made a deal, William, the cup for your life, remember? I intend to honor that."

"What guarantee do I have of that?"

"Absolutely none. Now where's the Goddamned Grail?"

For just a moment, the actress' eyes appeared to flare bright red in the darkness of the cab but surely it must have been a trick of the light outside, her eyes reflecting the open flame of a gaslight as they raced on by. At least that's what William told himself to refrain from screaming. He swallowed down a mouthful of acidy fear and said, "Okay...okay. Just take me home. I'll get it for you."

"The cup is at the lodging house? I thought you said it was hidden somewhere I'd never find it."

"You wouldn't. It's hidden in the loo."

"Pardon me?"

"It's at the bottom of the privy."

"You took the Holy Grail, the most priceless, sought after artifact in all of Christianity, and *dropped* it in the toilet?"

"It was the only place I was sure no one would find it. Don't worry, it's safe. It's sealed inside a bag and tied to a rope. All I have to do is reach in and pull it up, quick as you please."

"You're a bigger idiot than I thought. You better hope it's still there."

"It will be. No worries."

Magenta passed the information on to her lackey and then they rode in silence the rest of the way home; William still trying to come up with his escape plan, Da Vine simply too disgusted with Hare to speak. When Big Josh pulled into Tanner's Close, he rapped on the roof of the cab to let them know they'd reached their destination.

"Let's go," Magenta said.

"No way. The privy's at the back of the house right next to the room Mr. Black's staying in. Trust me, we don't want to wake him up. Just stay here. I'll be back in two minutes. Promise."

Against her better judgement, Da Vine sighed and said, "Okay, but hurry up."

Hare was out of the cab and inside the house as quickly and quietly as a burglar. He hadn't been kidding about not wanting to wake the sculptor up. All Hell might break loose if Black and Da Vine were to face off over who was taking the cup and the last thing William wanted was to be stuck in the middle of that fray. If only he knew how prophetic his fear actually was, he might have knocked on the sculptor's door and let the inevitable confrontation begin, but he was still relatively clueless as to what he was really a part of so he tip-toed down the back hallway as silently as possible. His new plan was to give the actress her golden prize, grab a few supplies and his secret stash of cash, and disappear before Maggie or Ambrosious Black were any the wiser. He'd make his way back to Ireland, or perhaps head for England where hopefully no one would know who he was. He'd change his name and start a new life far away from all this insanity.

William made it to the privy and had to blindly grope around in the filthy hole until he chanced upon the rope he'd hidden within. He could actually hear Mr. Black snoring loudly through the paper-thin walls, the perfect reminder that he needed to be as quiet as a mouse. Twenty seconds later he had his hands on the leather, waterproof sack and tried his best not to think about what was squishing between his fingers as he untied the knot at the top.

Once he had the cup, he dropped the soiled sack and rope back in the smelly hole and snuck to the front of the house. Da Vine's cab was still parked out front, the actress anxiously awaiting his return.

"That was quick," she said, her eyes never leaving the smooth chalice cradled in Hare's hands.

"Told you I would be. Like I said, don't want any problems. I just want you and Black gone."

"Give it here, then."

William wiped the golden cup on his shirt, trying to clean it as best he could but also stalling for time. He still wasn't sure he was doing the right thing here, but then again, what choice did he have? More afraid than he'd ever been in his life, William walked over and handed the actress the Grail.

"There. We're even," William said, backing away from the cab. "Now go away and leave me the hell alone."

Da Vine smiled wickedly and sat back in her seat, out of William's line of sight. "Whatever you say, boss." The actress started to laugh and just as the horses began to walk away, the entire inside of the hackney cab began to glow a brilliant blood red that was blindingly bright. William shaded his eyes from the unearthly light and fell to his knees in the street. The last thing he heard (if in fact he heard anything at all) was the mysterious actress whispering directly into his confused mind, saying, "Pleasure doing business with you, Mr. Hare."

* * *

At the rear of Log's Lodging House, the great Snowy Owl Nazza screeched, and Ambrosious Black bolted upright out of a sound sleep. Instantly he felt the same alarming shift in the balance of nature that the bird of prey obviously had. He hadn't felt panic like this in a very long time and his heart was starting to race hoping things weren't as bad as they seemed.

Outside, the sculptor could hear the sounds of a team of horses racing away into the night. Ambrosious started to climb to his feet to see what was going on, but out of nowhere a great wave of pure hatred and ice-cold menace struck Black like a physical blow, pummeling him back onto his bed. Black gasped for breath, suddenly knowing what must have just happened.

And he also knew who was to blame.

"Oh my God!" he said. "What has that fool done?"

Chapter 17

William Hare was scared to open his eyes but he was even more afraid to keep them closed. He didn't want to look, but he desperately needed to know if Da Vine was truly gone. Part of him was sure the sound of the receding horses was merely a trick and she would be standing two feet away, eyes like burning flames, ready to pounce at his throat the moment he looked up. He compromised and only opened one eye, squinting through the fingers of the hand he was shielding his face with, attempting to peek without being obvious about it.

Tanner's Close was empty.

She's gone, William thought, relief flooding over his still trembling body. He'd never experienced anything quite like what had just happened. He'd given the actress the golden chalice and like something straight out of a nightmare the inside of Da Vine's cab had lit up with that unnatural red glow, and a feeling of intense fear instantly slammed into him, driving William to the cobbled street. It was as if a giant invisible hand had reached out of the Hackney carriage and squeezed the breath from him. The only word that came to his uneducated mind to describe the darkness that had swept over and through him, was *evil*. That's what it had been. *Pure evil*.

"What have I done?" William whispered, unaware that at the rear of the lodging house Ambrosious Black was being startled awake and wondering the same thing.

William had no answer to his question, but he was sure of one thing: He had to get away from here as soon as possible. Edinburgh had become a more dangerous prison to him than the actual jail he'd just been released from. At least in his moldy damp cell he'd been relatively safe. Out here on the streets he had mobs of angry men and woman looking to string him from the nearest gaslight, a mysterious woman who was quite possibly a witch, and an old man who was – hell, William had *no idea* what Black was, or what he'd gotten himself and poor Billy into the middle of. Nor did he want to know. All William wanted to do was skip town and start fresh somewhere far, far away.

He didn't even want to bother waiting to pack a bag of supplies or any of his personal belongings. He'd rather leave now with only the clothes on his back than risk hanging around the extra ten or twenty minutes it might take. He wasn't leaving without his stash of money, though. Couldn't even if he'd wanted to. How could he disappear and start a whole new life if he was penniless? Clothes and food and a place to sleep didn't come cheap. Neither did the booze and the women William promised himself once he'd made his getaway and put a little sanity back into his life.

But first, the money...

William entered the lodging house as silent as a ghost, hoping to be in-and-out as quickly and discreetly as he had twenty minutes earlier. Everything was still dark and quiet, the way he'd left it, and he took a deep breath to steady his nerves. A shot of fine scotch would have done a better job of it, but that would have to wait. William headed for the common room where there were no embers glowing in the fireplace. There were kindling and several logs in the hearth but no one had bothered to ignite the wood. Maggie likely just had the fire all set, ready for the morning.

Thinking about his wife made William a little sad. Not that he loved her. Not really, anyway. It was just that a woman like her, who would let him stay out all night drinking and fighting and whoring and still keep his belly full and a roof over his head, was all right in his selfish opinion. It might take him months to replace her in London, or wherever he ended up. Oh well, that was a problem for another day. He could leave Maggie behind in a heartbeat if it meant abandoning all his other current problems. A clean slate was definitely the way to go.

William made his way over to the left of the fireplace and bent down in the corner of the room beside the exposed brickwork of the chimney. He thought he heard a faint scratching noise from somewhere close, but when he turned around there was no one there. It was probably nothing; maybe a mouse, so William returned to his work. Down near the floor, the second row of bricks up, one of the blocks could be wiggled loose from the others, and in behind it there was a small hollow where Hare kept all his earthly treasures. Hidden in the hole was just over one hundred pounds in carefully rolled up bank notes and a sterling silver pocket watch he'd recently nicked from a drunk down at the pub. William crammed the watch in his pocket and just as he was doing the same with a handful of money, something above his head moved, catching his eye. It was too dark in the room to make out details but when William looked up he could swear there was *something* on the wooden mantel that hadn't been there before. Something large. And then William stood up and noticed the yellow eyes looking at him.

The Owl!

Black's monstrous beast perched on top of the fireplace mantel watching Hare's every move. William had been through enough frights for one night and this pushed him over the edge. He stepped back and was about to let loose a scream, when suddenly a giant hand clamped over his mouth from behind and stifled him into silence. A cold icy voice whispered in his ear.

"Not a sound, William…or I'll have my friend pluck your tongue out. Maybe your eyes too. Understand?"

Hare slowly nodded his head and was released. He knew exactly who had spoken to him but he spun around quickly to see Black anyway, panic causing his heart to race and making him breathe hard as if he'd been running. He glanced at the front door, thinking running was exactly what he should be doing right now, but decided against it.

"Mr. Black? What in blazes are you—?"

"Be *QUIET!*" Black said, his voice so cold and angry William immediately did as he was told. "I've no more time for your nonsense, so take a seat and listen. I don't want to tell you what I'm about to, but you've left me no choice."

William slumped into a nearby chair like a scolded boy, his frightened eyes trying to dart between the bird of prey on the mantel and the enraged sculptor but he was having trouble seeing either in the dark room.

"Can I draw back the curtain or maybe light the fire?" Hare asked. "I can't see a bloody thing in here."

"Scared of the dark, are we?" Black rubbed his hands together and a reddish-blue flame appeared out of nowhere to rest in the palm of his right hand. "Only reason the fire's not lit is that Maggie's afraid the mobs will burn down the lodge if they think you're inside. She hasn't so much as lit a candle after dark for two weeks now, but if you want a roaring fire…you'll have one!"

Black hurled the mysterious flame toward the hearth and the stacked up logs immediately burst into fully engulfed flames, the light in the room going from midnight to noon within seconds. The owl on the mantel squawked and flew away. William sat back in his chair in bewildered awe.

"How did you do that? I mean, Christ, am I going daft or is everyone I know around here in league with the devil?"

"No, not everyone, William…just the woman you gave the Holy Grail to."

"How did you—?"

"Keep your bloody questions to yourself. Doesn't matter how I know; I just do. Let me guess, okay? Young, beautiful, dark hair, long legs, lots of cleavage…am I getting close?"

"That's her all right. Miss Da Vine. She seemed to know you too."

"Da Vine? Is that what she's calling herself this time?"

"Aye. Magenta Da Vine."

Black nearly laughed at that. "Magenta? And you actually believed her?"

"Well, she did tell Billy and me it was one of those...what do you call it...stage names. She's an actress down at the Ripley theatre."

"She's a monster, William, and you're a fool! The only thing keeping her young and beautiful is her evil. She's no more an actress than I'm a sculptor-for-hire."

William wasn't sure what to make of that and was about to ask but Black carried on, starting to pace the small room as he spoke.

"I should have known she was here. Blast it! I tried to see you and Billy but they wouldn't let me in. I never dreamed things were as bad as they were. What were you thinking, man? I told you to bring the Carpenter's Cup to me."

"You didn't tell me *anything*! You just kept telling Billy and me that we'd know it when we saw it. What were we supposed to do? You were paying us...she was paying us, but she also had two goons who were gonna slit our throats if we crossed her."

"Billy would have been better off with his throat slit. I hear they've sent him to the surgeons for dissection and plan on displaying his bones in a glass case at the university. You did a fine job helping your mate out, William. A fine job indeed."

William hung his head low, honestly ashamed for what had happened to his only friend. "I didn't want any of that to happen but it was him or me. Miss Da Vine told me one of us had to go to the gallows for what we'd done and—"

"She got you the deal with the crown? It was *her* that saved your useless neck?"

"Aye...in exchange for what we found in the grave. I didn't really have a choice, did I? I also didn't think it was real. Neither did Billy. We thought it was just an expensive gold cup. I mean honestly...the Holy bloody Grail? That's just a legend, right? A silly story told around campfires and pubs."

Ambrosious Black exhaled a long slow breath, nodding his head, no happier than he was a minute ago, but at least now understanding what had happened. "William, William, William...unfortunately your stupidity knows no limits. The Holy

Grail is much more than a legend, young man, and it's anything but silly. I take it you're well aware of the Knights Templar, yes?"

"Of course. It was a Templar's grave we found the cup in."

"Was it?" Black said, only a little surprised. "Makes sense, I suppose."

"Big man; and it looked like he'd just died a fortnight ago. More magic I'm guessing?"

"Certainly. Protect the Grail and it will protect you. For a while at least. That brave man willingly sacrificed himself to hide the chalice from evil."

"What? You mean he wasn't already dead when they put him in the box? How can you possibly know that?"

"Because it's the way it has to be. The power in the Carpenter's Cup would sustain him...keep him alive. That knight, whoever it was, probably lived for years below the ground, ready to protect the Grail if anyone found out where it was buried and tried to dig it up. No food, no water, no light. Only prayer. Even after his drawn out death, the Grail would slow his decomposition down to almost nothing, which is why he looked the way he did when you saw him."

"Even if I buy all that, why in blazes would any bloke allow himself to be sealed inside a casket and buried alive? It's madness!"

"It's *faith*, William. He believed in the Grail, and in protecting it from falling into the hands of evil."

"Oh bollocks. Nobody would throw their life away like that."

"Not many people today, I'll grant you that. It was a different time and a different place. Magic was everywhere and the power of the Holy Grail wasn't questioned. Not by the Knights Templar anyway...or by me."

"You? You speak like you were there."

"I was. Not when the Grail was reburied...before that. There's an old story that perhaps you need to hear."

Black ended his pacing and took a seat over by the roaring fire. As he spoke he gazed into the flames, hardly looking in William's direction, his thoughts lost in a time long, long ago. He began by telling a grand tale of the Templars and their return from the Holy

Land with the Carpenter's Cup. It was a dark tale, not at all like Mallory's glorious pageant of chivalry and romance. It was a story of suffering, and rivers of blood.

"Joseph, the Arimathean merchant, had used the carpenter's cup to collect the blood of Christ, that was well known, but what was not so well known was the fact the Arimathean also collected the blood of Escariot after his suicide, using the same golden cup to capture precious drops of the traitor's life juices. This tainted the Grail, spoiling its glorious goodness with evil incarnate. Good and evil together as one.

"This cup was eventually passed into the hands of Jacques de Morlay, preceptor of the Knights Templar, who was sworn to guard it. Since that day, the battle has raged between good and evil, each side knowing if they possessed the Grail they could harness the divine power within. In the hands of the church, or a pure soul like that of a Templar, the righteous power of the Lord shines through, putting an end to disease and suffering and making miracles possible. In the hands of someone whose heart is cold and black and filled with the Devil, the tainted side of the Grail can bring destruction and chaos and maybe even open up the gates of Hell itself."

"That's why it had to remain hidden," William said, his face visibly drained of color even in the flickering light of the fire.

"Exactly. It's why a brave knight decided it was worth sacrificing his life for, why I've spent my entire life trying to track it down to make sure it would always be safe, and why a foolish grave robber, who should by all rights be dead with his idiot friend, shouldn't have given up the most powerful artifact in history to an evil sorceress."

"Sorceress?" William said. "But I had no idea Da Vine was anything other—"

"Stop calling her that. It's just more of her trickery and lies. She's the Witch of Lyonesse. She's been known by a dozen names but her real name is Morgana Le Fay."

"Hold on. You're back to talking rubbish again. The witch you speak of wasn't real. Morgana's just legend, same as King Arthur, and Excalibur, and the Knights of the Round Table...and...and..."

"And what?" Black asked, his voice cold and low again."

"And the Grail, I was gonna say." William gulped down a few mouthfuls of air and thought about everything he'd just learned. "It can't be true...can it? Christ, that would make you...*no!*"

"My name's not Ambrosious Black. The Welsh and the Irish remember me as Myrdinn, the bard and prophet, but to the English and the Scotts I'm known as—"

"Merlin the magician!" William finished his sentence for him and then settled into a brooding silence. Black just let him be, knowing the simple man would need time to let it all soak in. Eventually, William raised his eyes and spoke again. "You're serious, right? I mean, this is all real? Everything you've told me?"

"Every word, yes."

"And you're the good guy."

"I'm no saint...but yes. I serve only two people: The Forever King, and our blessed Lord on high. I'm charged with protecting the Grail and stopping the witch. She'll destroy the world if we don't get that Grail back."

"We? What do you mean...*we?*"

"I need your help, William. I wouldn't have told you any of this if I could find her and do this myself."

"But I can't help you. I'm a bad man...I've done terrible things."

"Aye, you have...but it looks like God's about to give you a chance to make up for everything evil you've done. One last chance to do what's honest and right."

William wasn't convinced there was anything he could ever do to right the wrongs in his life, but something stirred to life in his dark heart and he knew he couldn't refuse the old man. "Okay. I guess I'm your man."

"Excellent," Merlin said. "Here's what we're going to do..."

Chapter 18

Calton Cemetery was still shrouded in fog, but a glimmer of sun was rising in the east and would hopefully start to burn it away, layer by wispy layer, for another day. A huge bank of dark clouds hung in the sky threatening a storm, but it was too early yet to tell. Merlin stood in the cold, early morning mist with his eyes closed but his mind wide open. He was deep in prayer and meditation, and if anyone had taken the opportunity to check they'd have found out his respirations were down to five breaths a minute and his heart rate had been cut in half from the times it normally beat. It was his way of preparing his body and mind for battle; his calm before the chaos; his moment of serenity before the coming storm.

Behind the magician stood the newly erected stone effigy of Robert the Bruce, towering over the white-haired old man like a frozen giant. The city council had hired him to build a statue to commemorate the Battle of Bannockburn, but Merlin's thoughts drifted further into the past than that, back to an age of blood and clashing steel that history had somehow forgotten and pushed into myth and legend. A time when the Forever King still proudly walked the land, surrounded by brave men in shining armor who were honorable and just. Together, with Merlin's help, they had purged Britain of the ruthless heathens and the immoral nobility who foolishly believed they were above the laws of God. Together they'd searched for the elusive Holy Grail, determined to find it and keep it safe forever but it wasn't to be.

The witch Morgana was searching for the Grail, too. Even then, when Merlin had thought she was just a silly woman who had lost her way in the world. She had doubts about the Lord and her faith had been shaken by the cruel death of her father, but Merlin had never believed she would give her soul to the devil the way she so eagerly had. She'd always had the gift of magic in her (as many people did back in those days), but her powers had grown a thousand-fold after her soul had willingly been corrupted. She'd raised a small army of devil worshippers, cutthroats, and mercenaries and launched a hastily planned attack against the king's disciplined and far better-trained knights.

The confrontation was more of a slaughter than an honorable battle, the deep green grass of the field painted red with the blood of Morgana's woefully prepared troops. In the end she accomplished what she'd set out to do that day though, albeit purely by accident, and it was the darkest day in Merlin's long life. The king had ridden out on his warhorse at the end of the fray and while dismounting to join his men, the horse's front hooves slipped on the blood slick grass, its normally sturdy legs sliding out from beneath it. The huge animal tried to correct itself, but in the process toppled over and landed on its left side, accidentally crushing the king beneath its massive bulk.

By the time Merlin made it to the king's side, the horse had regained its feet but the damage was already done. The greatest warrior the land had ever known was dying on the battlefield, his pelvis bones crushed and nearly every rib shattered from the horse's tremendous weight. What Merlin remembered most – and the image that still haunted his nightmares all these years later – was of his beloved king staring up at him in helpless agony, blood draining out of both of his eyes....

Merlin snapped back to reality, a light rain starting to fall from the unsettled sky. The fog in the cemetery disorienting him for a moment, but when he turned to see the intricate sculpture he'd recently done for the city he remembered where – and more importantly – *when* he was. Perched on the Scottish King's shoulder was the Snowy Owl, carefully watching its master and patiently awaiting orders. It didn't have to wait long. Merlin took two more deep breaths, willing his breathing and heart rate to return to normal and then addressed his feathered companion by name.

"Nazza, my friend. If today doesn't go our way I want you to get as far away from here as you can. Understand?"

The bird of prey swiveled its head to look down at the old wizard, then turned away again, ignoring him. Merlin grinned despite the gravity of their situation, unable to help himself. "You're as stubborn as Lancelot, you are...but not nearly as pretty. At least go fetch me my staff from where we left it outside of the city. I have a feeling I'm going to need it soon. Go!"

The white owl immediately took to the air, heading off into the fog and the rain without making a sound. "And hurry up about it, too," Merlin called after it but it was already lost in the gloom.

"I'm hurrying as fast as I can, gov," William's voice answered back, his footsteps announcing his arrival before his body materialized out of the fog. "It's a long way to run, you know?"

"I wasn't talking to you," Merlin said, but couldn't be bothered to explain the situation. "Well...did you deliver the message?"

"Aye, but it wasn't easy. Half the town wants to see me hang, remember? I had to peek in the windows of three different pubs but I eventually found Big Josh, one of Da Vine's...I mean Morgana's fat goons, and waited for him to head for home."

"And did you remember what to tell him?"

"I told him to tell his boss we had a major problem. Said that you'd found another golden cup here in Calton and you're claiming that you've found the *real* Grail. I told Big Josh to tell her she might have a fake on her hands. Said she'd better come to the cemetery this morning to straighten this mess out."

"Perfect. She'll come too...I know she will. Even if she knows I'm lying, she'll come to try and kill me, once and for all. Come on; let's get back to the gravesite so we're ready for her."

* * *

Dawn had arrived but the sun was hidden behind the thick layer of storm clouds already, leaving the sky an ominous charcoal grey. Thunder rumbled somewhere off to the west of the city but for now the rain had stopped again. It had taken William a little over half an hour to re-dig the grave Billy and he had found the Carpenter's Cup inside. He'd been drenched with sweat by the time his shovel scraped the top of the wooden box clean and he'd pried open the lid to reveal the giant man lying within. It had only been a matter of weeks but the knight's skin was turning a sickly shade of yellow-grey and the smell of the dead Templar was noticeably worse than the last time they'd opened the makeshift casket. Not a horrible stench yet, but the corpse was obviously suffering the effects of being separated from the Holy Grail; its protective magic no longer preventing the flesh from starting to rot.

"He's in worse shape than I remember," William said.

"Aye, he would be. That's okay...he'll do. Put this in with him same as the real one was sitting." Merlin handed William a smooth-sided golden chalice that looked remarkably similar to the one he'd recently handed over to Morgana.

"Wow, you made this just from my description? It looks real."

"It's only an illusion. See for yourself."

William looked back down and was surprised to see an old tarnished metal wine glass in his hand. Seconds later it changed back into the golden chalice. "That's incredible."

"It's child's play, but it will have to do. Put it back wherever you found it."

William laid the false Grail down on the large knight's chest and maneuvered the Templar's hands until they were shielding the cup in the same way they had for hundreds of years. "There...that's about as good as we're going to get."

William climbed out of the grave and sat down on the damp grass to catch his breath. Another rumble of thunder drummed above his head, the storm getting closer. Merlin walked to the side of the hole, looked down at the dead man, and said a silent prayer. When he was through, the wizard held his hands out over the cadaver's body and began to speak in an ancient language only a few people on earth might still be able to translate. Merlin knew the words though…and so did the fallen knight.

"*Sarannha de nedro ank. Terannha de nedro ank. Monutaris de tartarum arturus feh…hades de nedro ank!*"

The wizard spoke in this strange forgotten language for another minute but he ended his conversation with the dead man in English.

"Thank you brave knight…for your sacrifice and for your faith. You've earned your rest in paradise but the world still has need of your services this one last time."

William had no idea what all that gibberish had been about, and to be honest he didn't really want to know. He just wanted this craziness over and done with so he could get out of the approaching storm and make good his escape.

"What now?" he said.

"We wait."

"What's going to happen, though?"

Merlin turned his milky-white eyes to the dark rumbling clouds above but shook his head. "You'll have to ask the sky, William. Only the thunder knows…"

* * *

The fog had completely vanished by the time Morgana made her appearance, walking between her henchmen Angus and Big Josh. It was just like a woman to show up fashionably late. And fashionable she was, twirling a small parasol above her head to protect her coiffured hair and dressed in a tight black dress with a plunging neckline which left nothing to the imagination. The witch looked more like she was stepping onto the lawn of some fancy garden party than walking onto a field of battle, but seeing as she believed today would settle her claim on the true Grail as well as finally getting rid of her archnemesis once and for all, maybe this *was* a celebration of sorts. Stunningly beautiful or not, she was rotten to the core inside and needed to be stopped.

"Good of you to show up, my lady," Merlin spoke, tongue-in-cheek. "I was beginning to think you'd lost your nerve."

"Don't flatter yourself, old man," Morgana said, moving closer.

"That's far enough," Merlin said, once Morgana and her men approached within fifteen feet.

"I hardly think you're in any position to be making up the rules," the witch said, but stood her ground anyway. "I'll do as I damn well please. Good of Mr. Hare to dig your grave for you, though. Thank you, William."

William had no idea what to say and no interest in getting involved in this if he could help it, so he remained quiet.

"The grave's not mine. Not yours either, unfortunately. It's already occupied you see...by the true Grail Keeper. Have a look for yourself."

"Rubbish, wizard. We both know I've already got the proper one. The *only* one!" As if to add weight to her point, the large mountain of a man to her right held up the golden chalice.

Merlin tried his best not to stare too hard at the object he'd been searching for most of his long life.

"Do you now. Are you sure? You'd *better* be!"

"Step away from the hole, Merlin. You try my patience for the last time."

William began to edge away to his left but Merlin stood his ground. One of Morgana's henchmen, a tall broad-shouldered muscular man, stepped forward brandishing a long thin-bladed knife.

"You heard the lady," Angus Brooks said. His baldheaded ally Josh moved forward as well, a blade appearing in his massive hand too. "Aye...step off!"

Merlin smiled at the intimidating men, then glanced wryly at Morgana as if to say, *you're kidding me, right?* "By all means, good sirs. Anything you say."

The magician walked over beside where William had slunk away to, allowing Morgana and her friends access to the Templar's grave. Morgana peered into the freshly dug hole, somewhat taken aback when she saw the red cross on the giant dead man's tunic. A shadow of doubt crept across her pretty features and her eyes flashed to the golden cup she'd brought with her today.

"Give me my Grail, Josh, and get in there and check the grave."

"Right away, ma'am."

Accomplishing Morgana's request was easier said than done for the big man. With his bulk, it was proving quite difficult to maneuver his fat body down into the grave and he twice nearly pitched face first down onto the corpse. In the end, Big Josh had to sit down in the wet grass and slide into the hole.

"Get on with it, man!" Angus said. "Search along the side of the body. It could be down behind his head too."

"Shut yer gob...I know what I'm doing!"

"Find the blasted thing, then. You'll be swimming soon if those clouds let loose."

"Okay...okay."

Big Josh knelt down with his knees on the exposed side rails of the wooden box and began searching around the dead Templar's legs and sides. He easily found the old sword lying alongside his leg but ignored it for the moment. He was already sweating and breathing hard, the air wheezing in and out of his lungs sounding like a broken steam engine. Eventually he saw the way the dead man's hands were cupped upon his chest and noticed something golden glinting between the Templar's grey fingers.

"Hey, I think I've found something," Josh said, his face beet red from his exertions. "Just a second...looks like gold!"

As soon as the fat man touched the knight's hands Merlin shouted, "Now!" and the normal fabric of the world began to come undone. Inside the grave, the dead man's eyes snapped open and the corpse of the knight reached up and shoved Big Josh backwards with the palm of one massive hand. Josh started to scream, trying to climb to his feet and out of the hole as fast as his overweight body could move but he wasn't nearly fast enough. The Templar sat up in his box and drew out his long-unused sword in the blink of an eye, savagely swiping the razor-sharp blade across the exposed neck of the fat man. Death obviously hadn't stolen much of the warrior's strength as he effortlessly lopped off the goon's head, a geyser of blood shooting straight up into the air and falling like hot crimson rain. Big Josh's headless body continued to try and climb out of the hole, and very nearly succeeded before tumbling backwards onto his back and wedging himself against the dirt wall and the outside rim of the casket. His bald head spun end over end, finally coming to rest at the feet of his mate, Angus Brooks.

Angus was shocked into silence for a moment, not sure what the hell had just happened, but when he saw the huge Templar rise to his feet and start to climb free of his grave he snapped out of his reverie and started to scream. "You bastard!" he shouted, running toward the ancient soldier clutching his knife, revenge on his confused mind.

"No, stop!" Morgana said, trying to warn him but it was too late. Angus had a full head of steam, blindly moving forward, and there was no turning back now. They met just as the knight made his way to solid ground, Angus taking the first wild swing at the dead man's heart with his thin blade.

The Templar had been trained well, and dropped to one knee in a defensive position, the goon's knife sailing high and wide. Before Angus could strike again the knight came up to his full height, bringing his sword up with him through his assailant's right forearm, severing his knife-wielding limb just shy of the man's elbow. Although not a killing blow, the Templar's attack left his opponent defenseless. Angus's thin-bladed weapon dropped harmlessly to the grass still clutched tightly in his spasming fingers.

Where mercy might have been given in a fair and honest fight, today there would be no such compassion offered. The emotionless knight grabbed Angus around his throat and lifted him high off the ground, blood soaking into the front of the Templar's white tunic as the goon tried to grab the dead man with his missing limb, only now noticing it was gone. Seconds later, the knight ran his sword up and through Angus's chest, sliding the blade in under the helpless man's ribs, directly piercing the heart, and pushing out through his right shoulder. Impaled on the sword, Angus was already dead; dying without so much as a whimper, never mind a scream. The knight released his grip on his opponent's neck and allowed Angus's large body to drop heavily to the bloody grass. All total, the one-sided battle was over within thirty seconds.

* * *

"What's going on?" William said, turning to look at Merlin, bewildered and more than a little shaken by what he'd just witnessed. He'd killed men and women with Billy, but he'd never witnessed violence and bloodshed such as this. Merlin seemed unfazed, a slight smile on his weathered face.

"If you don't know by now, you never will."

"But even with the Grail's magic, I could smell his flesh rotting. That knight had been dead for hundreds of years!"

"He still is, fool. I'm not really a necromancer...I can't reanimate the dead. If I can get to them before they die, I can sometimes heal them, but not once they've crossed beyond the veil like our brave Templar here."

"Well he's moving around awfully well for a dead man."

"Aye...just pray he doesn't decide to move in our direction."

"You mean you're no' controlling him? He's running wild."

"Course not. I just cast a spell that called his soul back into his flesh. He's a weapon of the Lord now."

A few weeks ago William and Billy would have burst out laughing at such a ridiculous statement, but now Burke was dead, Hare's life had been turned upside down, and the seven-foot-tall walking dead man with a blood-smeared sword was ample proof that powerful magic was still at work in the world.

"Will he kill the witch?" William asked.

Merlin seriously thought his response over for a moment, and then regretfully said, "I highly doubt it...no."

* * *

The knight took a moment to wipe the gore off of his sword and then nudged Angus's fallen body with his leather boot to make sure he was really dead. He obviously was, so the Templar turned his glazed, jaundiced eyes toward the witch. Morgana actually seemed more annoyed by what had transpired than afraid. When the warrior charged toward her she simply uttered a few secret words and conjured a bright red ball of energy into her open hand. The witch hurled the glowing sphere into the chest of the dead man and it hit and drove him backwards almost thirty feet, the Templar tossed like a rag doll through the air and landing on his back.

Unable to be injured since he was already dead, the warrior climbed to his feet and once again began his attack. His sword held on high the Templar moved in for the kill, only to be met with another energy ball that hit him with the strength of a charging warhorse at full gallop, sending him sprawling onto his back again. Twice more the knight regained his feet and twice more the witch knocked him back down, neither side giving an inch but neither finding any advantage either.

"Enough of these games!" Morgana screamed, her frustration reaching the boiling point. Using her thumbnail she gouged a thin cut in the palm of her left hand and let some of her corrupted blood dribble into the Holy Grail. Like Merlin had done earlier to cast his spell on the Templar, the witch began to speak in a long-forgotten tongue, waving her free hand in circles above the golden chalice.

"*Mehatta suchem terra terra...kono de basilisk metta saron...*"

Within a heartbeat there was a deep rumbling noise that at first could have been mistaken for more thunder in the stormy sky but instead was coming from the ground beneath Morgana's feet. She continued to chant and became more animated with her hand gestures and gyrations, backing up a little as something monstrous began to push itself up and out of this desecrated burial ground's soil. Whatever it was, it was huge.

And incredibly angry...

* * *

The first sign of the emerging creature Merlin saw from his vantage point was a huge blast of fire that erupted out of the upheaving ground. Following the flames came the elongated snout of a massive reptilian beast, its green scaly mouth opening to reveal row upon row of razor-sharp teeth. The animal's impossibly long front claws burst out of the dirt to furiously scratch and claw its way out of its earthly prison.

Just the sight of the creature made Merlin's blood run cold. The power it must have taken for Morgana to conjure a beast such as this was truly mind-boggling. Her magic had always been impressive but the witch had never been *this* powerful before. Obviously she'd tapped into the power of the dark side of the golden chalice, her evil abilities growing stronger the longer she possessed the Grail.

"Mother of God!" William screamed. "Look at the size of that monster! It's some kind of crocodile *thing*. Got to be forty or fifty feet, nose to tail."

"That's not the worst of it...*look!*" Merlin said, watching in awe as the great beast finally gained its feet and unfurled thick twenty-foot-long leathery membranes along each side of its body.

"Bloody Hell! It's not a croc, it's a...a..."

"A dragon," Merlin said, finishing the sentence for the grave robber.

"But that's impossible. They're no' real."

"You said the same thing about the Grail, if I remember correctly. Stop doubting everything. The sooner you learn to let go of reality and just *believe*, the better your chances are of getting out of here alive."

Together they watched as the sword-wielding Templar attempted to battle the dragon, silently charging the beast. The dragon let the warrior get quite close and then let loose an eruption of smoke and fire from its throat, engulfing the valiant knight in a devastating cloud of flames. He was dead so he didn't scream, but when his tunic and hair ignited he dropped his sword and tried to protect himself; perhaps a memory of self-preservation from before his premature burial. When the flames died away, the knight's skin was charred black, his clothes, hair, eyes, fingers, toes, and genitals all gone – burned to ashes. Even with all that damage the brave Templar tried to stand and fight some more, still swinging his scorched fists into the beast's mouth as the dragon swiftly flowed across the grass and swallowed the dead man whole.

Its appetite barely wetted, the winged creature picked up the scent of Angus and Big Josh, the other recently killed men, and went in search of more human meat.

"How can we fight something like that?" William asked, equal parts fear and awe in his voice. "It's like something straight out of a nightmare."

"We can't fight the dragon," Merlin said. "But I know someone who can! Quick, come with me. We've no time to waste."

The white-haired magician took off at a run, not bothering to check and see if William was going to follow or not. The last thing Hare wanted to do was race after the wizard but there was no way he was staying here to take on the dragon on his own. No matter where the wizard was headed, as long as it was away from the fire-breathing dragon, it was a step in the right direction, as far as he was concerned. With no other options to choose, William swallowed his fear and gave chase.

* * *

While the dragon was busy feasting on the remains of Morgana's henchmen, Merlin ran back to the twelve-foot-tall statue he'd sculpted for the city council, William Hare hot on his heels. From out of nowhere, a massive shape flew over William's head and he dove to the grass, sure that the dragon was about to attack but it was only Merlin's Snowy Owl, returning to its master's side. In its hooked claws, the bird carried an eight-foot-long scepter made of a dark gnarled wood. There were strange symbols and pictures carved into the staff and at the top end, a large orb was attached, made from some type of smoky-green glass. William watched as the owl dropped the wooden staff into Merlin's hands and then immediately banked away from the cemetery and flew out of sight.

"Thank you, my friend," Merlin called after the bird, but immediately turned his attention back to the statue before him, his mind back on the task at hand. The wizard walked completely around the stone giant twice, thinking as he walked, trying to convince himself his plan might just work.

"What are you doing? I doubt that stick will save us from the dragon. We should run, take a lesson from that damn bird of yours and try to get clear of the city and—"

"No, we don't run. We can't. Morgana's beast will hunt us down."

"What do we do, then?" William said, panic in his voice.

"King Robert made his final stand at the Battle of Bannockburn and many of the brave men buried right here in this cemetery stood with him. We're going to make our final stand here too."

"Oh, bollocks to all your talk about bravery and heroes. I don't give a damn about Robert the Bruce…I just want to survive and get as far away from here as I can. That monster is going to burn us alive!"

"Precisely why we can't fight the dragon ourselves. Luckily we have someone with us who can't burn."

William looked up at the towering Scottish King and had to ask, "So you're going to bring the soul of Robert the Bruce into this statue, like you did with the Templar?"

"Aye, something like that, only this isn't a statue of the Bruce. A few minutes ago I told you to stop doubting everything you see…well you also need to stop believing everything you hear! I lied to the city council."

"Who is it, then?"

Merlin rubbed his hand against the leg of his beautiful sculpture. "Many lifetimes ago a great king fell beneath his mount when the horse's legs slipped out from under it. It was a freak accident but the king was mortally wounded…crushed and dying in front of my eyes. Before he passed on, I was able to cast a spell that let me keep a tiny bit of his essence, to allow most of his soul to travel on to its reward in Avalon, but to let me keep some of him alive within me. I took a vial of his blood that day too."

"When we finished constructing the statue that day, I used his blood along with some of my own and added it to the wash bucket with a dozen other herbs and potions. I soaked the entire statue in the potion, smoothing and polishing the stones with old magic to what you see before you now: The once and Forever King, Arthur Pendragon, Ruler of Camelot! If anyone can slay the dragon, it will be him."

"King Arthur!" William said, shocked but no longer doubting anything the old wizard told him that might get him through this day alive. He could still remember the stinky smell of whatever it was Merlin had coated the statue in that day. "But the statue is made of stone, not flesh like the knight. How can a soul be put into rock?"

"Have you ever heard of a golem? A doppelganger? A soul can be reanimated into any likeness of the original host. It will be King Arthur in every aspect other than his flesh. He'll be even more powerful this way…and practically indestructible!"

"Well, whatever you're going to do, best do it quick…look!"

Off to the south, Morgana's winged beast had taken to the air and was wildly circling the cemetery blasting mouthfuls of flaming death thirty feet long. Its feast of its master's goons apparently over, the dragon was still hungry and on the hunt for more. It wouldn't take long before it zeroed in on Merlin and William and moved in for the kill.

Merlin set his staff aside, turned to the statue and started muttering in that same strange language he'd used before, a sweat breaking out on his wrinkled brow as he used his own energy to draw the Forever King's soul away from Avalon. It taxed the wizard incredibly, twice causing the old man to fall to his knees but both times Merlin regained his feet and carried on. A low rumble shook the nearby headstones and an emerald glow started leaking from the ends of the Merlin's trembling fingertips, seeping into the dark stone until the entire statue was bathed in a magical green light.

And then King Arthur opened his eyes.

William watched helplessly as Merlin collapsed to the ground, exhausted from his efforts, and raced over to help the old man back to his feet.

"Are you okay?"

"Don't worry. I'll be fine," Merlin said, his strained voice indicating anything but. "Look...he rises!"

True enough, impossible as it seemed when William looked back up at the twelve-foot-tall statue, it was stretching its neck and flexing its left arm. With a thunderously loud CRACK, the golem broke free from its pedestal base and stepped down onto the damp grass.

"But how...?" William started to say. "How can stone bend and move like—"

Merlin dropped back down on one knee and pulled William down beside him. "On your knees, man! And lower your eyes. Have you no respect? You're in the presence of the King, for God's sake."

William felt a bit foolish kneeling in front of a stone statue but did as he was told. He very nearly wet his pants when the towering warrior began to speak.

"Merlin? Is that really you my friend?"

"Aye, my King...it is I, your humble servant."

"And who are you, young man?"

When William remained silent, Merlin nudged him hard, whispering, "Answer the King when he speaks to you!"

"William Hare umm...sire. I'm nobody really."

"Your soul is tainted, boy. Your heart and mind impure. You will have much to answer for when your days are done."

William had no idea what to say to that so simply said, "Yes sir."

"Where am I, Merlin? Why have you summoned me from my place of peace? And what type of armor is this? I feel...*strange*."

"My apologies, but I could only work with what I have. You're in Edinburgh...in Calton Cemetery. The important thing is I've finally found the carpenter's cup, my liege, but it has fallen into Morgana's evil hands. We need your help to get it back."

"Morgana!" Arthur shouted, his gravelly voice suddenly loud and angry. "The witch is *here*?"

"Yes, and she's conjured a hideous fire beast from the pit of Hell to destroy all that we fought for, sire. I didn't want to disturb you but I couldn't think of anything else. I need you, Arthur. Your people need you!"

"Then they shall have me. You've done well, Merlin. I feel bigger...stronger than ever before. Where are Morgana and this beast of hers?"

William risked raising his head and meekly pointed a finger up into the air. King Arthur and Merlin both followed his finger skyward just in time to see Morgana's dragon swoop by fifty feet over their heads, bank to its right and ignite a wooden tool shed on the ground with one giant ball of its fiery breath. Morgana was headed toward them as well – umbrella twirling in her right hand, the Holy Grail held casually in her left – walking like she was out for a pleasant morning stroll. The cold, hungry look of anticipation on her face told a different story though.

There was no more time to waste.

"Stand aside, Merlin," the stone king said, striding off into battle. "I'm going after the beast. You keep an eye on the witch!"

Merlin retrieved his long staff from the grass and the semi-transparent sphere at the top end immediately lit up to a bright emerald green, pulsating with an internal power in the magician's hands. Merlin smiled and moved toward Morgana. "With pleasure, sire!"

William Hare just stayed where he was and kept his mouth shut, perfectly content to be left out of whatever madness was about to happen...

* * *

King Arthur moved quickly into position, getting a better feel for his newer, larger stone body with each powerful stride. He felt impossibly strong but he also felt angry, the witch ultimately responsible for his death. There was no way he could allow her or her minions from Hell to use the power of the Grail to wreak havoc on an unsuspecting world. She needed to be stopped and she needed to be stopped *now*. Once and for all.

Above him, Morgana's dragon caught sight of him running toward it and circled lower to the ground, sweeping past the reanimated king close enough to see what it was up against. The beast raced by less than six feet over Arthur's head, its reptilian eyes open wide, its huge nostrils flaring, probably not smelling any of the normal smells associated with these human creatures. The beast flew higher into the stormy sky, looking confused but not in the least bit bothered.

Not what you were expecting, huh, big guy? Arthur thought, smiling.

On its second pass the massive dragon came in low, scaly belly scraping the grass as it rocketed straight at Arthur, its mouth opening wide and preparing to unleash its unholy inner fire. The king stood his ground, unflinching, as the beast roared and spat out a thirty-foot-long inferno, the flames hitting him in the chest and engulfing his entire body for at least five seconds. When the dragon closed its fearsome jaws and banked skyward again it surely expected to see its opponent on fire, burnt black like the last knight it had faced. Arthur wasn't going away quite so easily.

The King of Camelot opened his eyes to find himself undamaged, the flying monster's fire having no effect on his stony body whatsoever. Well pleased, Arthur drew his stone sword and prepared for the dragon's next attack.

"My turn, beast!" he shouted. "Come and get some of this!"

* * *

When Merlin approached the witch, she was laughing. Morgana set her parasol and the Grail both down on the grass at her feet, quite enjoying herself.

"Isn't that cute?" she said. "You've brought to life a cute little stone soldier with a cute little stone sword. He's simply adorable! Hope all that rock doesn't give my dragon a sore stomach."

Merlin wasn't sure how a twelve-foot-tall warrior could ever be described as "little" but he let her snide remark slide. "Actually he's not a soldier at all...and that cute little sword happens to have a name you just might remember. It's called *Excalibur!* Ring any bells in that pretty little head, witch?"

The smile faded from Morgana's lips. She looked back over at the stone man, perhaps seeing him in a whole new light. "Excalibur? But that would mean..."

"All hail the Forever King!" Merlin said, not being able to keep the satisfied grin from showing on his face. Hopefully his long white beard would cover it. "We're taking the Grail back, sorceress. The Carpenter's Cup was meant to represent all that's good in this world, not to be twisted and used in your sick little plans. I can't let you keep it."

"You can try and take it back, old man. You and Arthur both, but I'm the only one walking off of this battlefield alive today. Your dead King can give you a personal tour of Avalon shortly."

"A much better place than you'll spend eternity, witch. I can assure you of that!"

Morgana screamed in anger, hurling a blood-red energy sphere at the magician's chest. Merlin was nearly caught off guard but managed to get his staff raised just in time, the powerful spell deflecting off the enchanted wood and fragmenting into harmless fireworks above his head.

"That the best you've got?" Merlin asked his opponent.

"No," Morgana said, her tone ice cold. "Not even close."

The witch bared her teeth and prepared for her next attack...

* * *

King Arthur made the mistake of looking over at Merlin when the wizard had deflected Morgana's first strike. He watched the energy sphere explode into a million twinkling lights and by the time he looked back to where the dragon had just been flying his adversary was gone. Seconds later, the beast attacked at lightning speed from behind, grabbing Arthur around the waist and dragging him along the ground for a hundred feet before driving his body into the dirt and biting down hard.

The dragon's bite would have easily sheared through flesh and bone and crushed most types of armor, finishing this fight in a spray of blood, but the stone that made up Arthur's new body was made from a special type of mineral classified as corundum, a high quartz material as hard as granite and only topped by diamond as one of the hardest rocks on Earth. The beast's bite produced nothing but a series of tiny scratches across the King's waist, chest, and back. The dragon screamed in pain as four of its giant hand-sized teeth broke off on the stone and it was forced into releasing its squirming prey to swallow a mouthful of its own syrupy blood.

King Arthur rolled free of the dragon's bleeding mouth and thrust his stone sword deep into the beast's right eye. Excalibur punctured the thick protective lens and Arthur was showered in a soup of viscous jelly as the eyeball completely ruptured, emptying onto the ground. The dragon howled in agony and rage, launching into the air and savagely clawing at some imagined opponent it could take out its frustration on. Blinded in one eye but more dangerous than ever, the fire-breathing beast banked left and circled the stone warrior on the ground, stalking him, always keeping the man in view of his good eye. Even from the ground Arthur could tell what the monster was thinking, its primitive brain searching for his weaknesses, waiting patiently to strike again…

* * *

Merlin deflected yet another energy sphere, his strength starting to wane. The proximity to the Grail was giving Morgana an endless source of power, and her strikes were hitting the old wizard hard and fast, like he was standing directly in front of the business end of a long range cannon. The sculptor knew he couldn't keep the sorceress' blows at bay for much longer – not like this. He'd managed to launch a few volleys of his own from his emerald scepter but for the most part Morgana's evil power had kept him constantly on the defensive.

I've got to get her farther away from the Grail, he thought, knowing she wouldn't be nearly as strong if he could lure her onto neutral ground.

With no great plan in mind, Merlin turned and started to run. He play-acted a slight limp as he ran, leaning heavily on his wooden staff, hoping a false sign of weakness would make the witch overconfident and sloppy. Obviously Morgana wasn't the only one here who could act, because his ruse worked. When Merlin glanced over his shoulder he saw Morgana laughing at his painful gait, and saw her start to jog after him. Forgotten for the time being, back on the grass, she had left behind her umbrella and the Grail.

"Where do you think *you're* going?" Morgana shouted after him, easily closing the distance between them. "There's no rest for the wicked, old man! Not today!"

The witch threw her hands skyward and drew power from the black storm clouds above. The smell of burning oil filled the magically charged air and when Morgana pointed her long finger from the cloud to Merlin's back, a lightning bolt flashed across the darkened sky shooting straight toward the retreating wizard. Merlin dove for the ground just in time, the electric bolt missing his head by less than a foot, singeing the hair on his bushy white eyebrows and very nearly igniting the hair on the back of his head. The lightning bolt tore into the cemetery grass twenty feet in front of where he landed, instantly creating a deep crater in the earth, dirt exploding everywhere.

When Merlin regained his feet, he saw a second large hole in the ground and realized he was back at the Templar's grave, empty now other than for half of a human leg lying in a pool of sticky blood – all that remained of Big Josh's oversized body from the dragon's feast. The wizard moved off to his left to avoid falling in either of the holes and turned back to the witch just in time to see another lightning bolt headed his way. Acting purely on instinct, Merlin held up his scepter like a shield, the enchanted wood taking a direct hit and snapping into splinters in the magician's scorched hands. The power of the blast hurled Merlin's burning body fifteen feet through the air, knocking the wind from his lungs as he landed flat on his back in the cool wet grass.

The injured magician still had his wits about him, rolling on the damp grass to put out his smoldering clothes. The flames finally out, Merlin was about to try and stand up, but Morgana was suddenly standing right above him. He scurried backwards in the grass, in pain and more or less defenseless against the powerful witch without his staff.

"There's nowhere left to run, wizard," Morgana said coldly, some of her true hideous features starting to show through the cracks in her beautiful veneer. "It's time to die, old man. Time to *suffer!*"

Merlin could do nothing but watch the sorceress come closer...

* * *

The dragon looked like it was becoming impatient, not used to feeling pain or being unable to kill its enemies. Blood ran freely from its vacant eye cavity, and the monster kept snapping its jaws at thin air, desperate for revenge and the desire to inflict pain on someone else. King Arthur knew it would make its move soon, its bloodlust too great to wait much longer. It knew nothing other than killing and eating, and although the beast might know it wouldn't be filling its belly with him today, it would still want to somehow crush or break him to pieces, anything that would steal the life from him.

Maybe its rage is its weakness, Arthur thought.

"Come on, you big ugly brute," the stone King screamed, taunting the beast. "Lost your nerve, have you?"

Arthur had no idea if the dragon heard him, or even if it did, whether or not it comprehended his words, but when he shouted the monster tilted its scaly head to listen and roared in anger. Diving to pick up speed, the dragon leveled off and came charging straight at the King, spitting fire and screaming holy hell as it barreled closer at top speed. Arthur stood as tall as he could manage, even going so far as to balance up on his toes to make the dragon misjudge its attack height. The beast kept its mouth closed, looking like it intended to ram Arthur rather than bite him, but at the last possible second the King dropped to his knees and held Excalibur above his bent over body. The stone blade caught the beast under the chin, piercing through its scales and thick reptilian skin, the dragon's momentum carrying it forward, helplessly gutting itself on the stationary magic sword from throat to belly. A literal river of gore flooded out of the massive wound, the dragon's internal organs splashing to the ground a second before the beast itself, the monster dead before it could even slide to a shuddering stop.

Arthur stood and barely glanced in the dragon's direction, the blood and horrendous stench alone more than enough for him to know the battle was over. The stone King's thoughts – and eyes – turned toward Merlin and the witch, wondering how his most trusted ally was faring with his fight. Not very well, unfortunately, by the looks of things. When Arthur looked to the far side of the cemetery, he saw Merlin lying injured on the grass and Morgana standing above him, ready to deliver the killing blow. Even though he knew he'd never make it in time to help his friend, King Arthur took off running, moving as fast as his powerful stone legs could carry him…

* * *

Morgana was having trouble controlling her outward appearance, her lust for power and the imminent murder of her archenemy an intoxicating mix rushing through her old veins. Her beautiful raven-black hair was greying and drying out at the roots. Her smooth youthful skin was cracking and showing dark lumpy welts that bled freely down her exposed arms and neck. And where normally her smile would reveal perfectly straight white teeth, when the witch opened her mouth to speak all Merlin could see was a set of rotted black stumps.

"I've been looking forward to this for centuries," Morgana said. "I could make this quick and easy on you…but I don't want to!"

Merlin kept sliding his body backwards along the wet grass, worm-crawling away from the witch but there was nowhere for him to go. The lightning bolt had injured him more than he'd originally thought, burning his clothes and skin, but more importantly messing with his head. His mind was cloudy and he had a splitting headache, finding it nearly impossible to concentrate hard enough to cast spells of any significance. He conjured a small energy sphere of his own and hurled it at Morgana's chest but she batted his weakened attempt away with a flick of her hand, laughing at his declining strength.

"No, I think I'll take a more *personal* approach to this," the witch said, her hands starting to glow, her fingers starting to extend and curl into long razor-sharp claws. "I'm going to rip your heart out with my own hands, old man!"

Merlin slid back another foot and his right hand hit something hard and made of metal. Without looking down, he felt around in the grass, hope igniting a small fire within him. It was a sword – the Templar Knight's sword, dropped and forgotten when he'd been attacked by Morgana's dragon. Merlin concealed the long metal blade with his leg and waited for a chance to strike. Perhaps there was still time to turn the tides of this fight after all. It would all come down to the timing.

"You ready to finally see your precious Avalon, wizard?"

"Ready as I'll ever be," Merlin said, and he was surprised to realize he was telling the truth. He'd lived a long, hard life, and if today was to be his last he was okay with that, more than ready to move on to his just reward. Still, the stubborn magician within him held onto the flame of hope, not ready to give in to the witch's evil. If he fell to Morgana today, the world would be a much darker place in the days and years to come. For that reason alone, he had to win this battle. "Get it over with witch...before you fall apart at the seams. Wouldn't want anyone to see the ugly hag you *really* are under that pretty little façade."

Morgana screamed and lost her mind with rage, running the last few steps toward Merlin with her monstrous hands clawing at the air, aiming for the wizard's eyes. Merlin rolled to his left, bringing the knight's sword up in a heartbeat and sat up to meet the witch's charge. With both hands, Merlin thrust his weapon into Morgana's belly, shoving it in deep until he heard the blade scrape against her spine. The witch gasped, not yet feeling the pain, shocked that her enemy wasn't bleeding beneath her fingers by now.

"How...?" she said, but that was as far as she made it.

Merlin twisted the sword's handle ninety degrees and viciously pulled left, ripping the blade out through the witch's side, nearly cutting her in half. Blood sprayed into the air first, followed by Morgana's perforated stomach sack, a chunk of her severed liver, and a mile of ropey, stinking intestines. The witch fell to her knees, trying to hold her insides from falling out but the damage was already done. In the end she looked over at Merlin with wide, fearful eyes.

"But you can't defeat me. I can't die...*can* I?"

Merlin climbed to his feet, seeing the desiccated old witch for what she really was now, her evil unable to mask her hideous appearance any longer. Her flesh was grey and wrinkled, covered in dozens of weeping sores. Her hair was turning white, falling out in huge clumps and the smell of her putrid organs spilling out onto the grass was so nauseating that Merlin couldn't stand to look at her another second.

"Rot in Hell!" Merlin said, swinging the Templar's sword in an arc parallel with the ground, severing the evil hag's head from her shoulders with one smooth stroke. Morgana's body swayed back and forth for a few seconds but then slumped forward onto the grass and lay still.

The Witch of Lyonesse was finally dead...

* * *

Morgana's head had landed face up in the grass and King Arthur stopped to take a look at the woman who had ultimately caused his death all those centuries ago. She hadn't made the horse lose its footing in the bloody grass that day but she had been the reason his army had been there in the first place. With a scowl of disgust, Arthur kicked the head away, sending it flying through the air to bounce and roll into the nearby open grave. "Good riddance, witch!" the stone King said. "Your death was *long* overdue."

The rain started to fall hard as Arthur walked over to where Merlin sat recovering in the grass near the rest of Morgana's bloody corpse. The wizard's eyes were glazed and he was breathing hard. His clothing was ripped and burned and his long white hair and beard were singed a dirty grey-black in spots.

"You going to be okay, old friend?" Arthur asked, placing one of his huge stone hands on the magician's shoulder.

"I'll survive," Merlin said. "Unfortunately."

The wizard's words made the King smile, knowing what the old man was feeling. "Don't worry, Merlin. Your reward will be waiting for you in paradise. It's just not your time to claim it yet."

"I know. But how much longer must I wait. This old bag of bones gets wearier by the year. Some days I'm fine, but to be honest, many of them I pray for rest."

"And you shall have it, my friend. Just not yet. The world still needs your magic and your wisdom."

"For what?"

"Well, for one thing, it needs you to make sure the Grail is safe."

"Yes," the magician agreed. "I'll keep it with me from here on out, never letting it out of my sight again."

"No Merlin," Arthur said. "That would be a mistake. We hunted the Carpenter's Cup for years, thinking it could only be safe with us but the Grail is too powerful for anyone to possess. Even for you, my friend. Its vast power cannot be controlled. Today has proven that to me."

"What would you have me do, then?"

"It has to be re-hidden. Lost again…and hopefully never found."

Merlin nodded, knowing Arthur was right. If anyone possessed the Grail – even someone pure of heart like him – he'd eventually be tempted to use its power. The dark side of the cup wouldn't rest until he did. No, it was far better to bury it again and let the world think the Grail was nothing but fiction and fanciful legend, blissfully unaware of the truth.

"You're right, of course," Merlin said. "Man was never meant to possess the power of God. I'll take care of it, my King."

Arthur helped Merlin to his feet and together they walked in the rain back toward the fallen dragon. With the witch dead and gone, her magic was disappearing from the world too, the massive beast starting to bubble and dissolve in front of their eyes, melting back into the same ground it had come from. By the time the authorities checked the cemetery the dragon would be gone, Arthur would be back in Avalon, the Robert the Bruce statue would be back standing in its original pose, and Merlin would have William fill in the Templar's grave with Big Josh's and Morgana's remains hidden within. If they were lucky, the rain would wash away the blood on the grass and no one would be any the wiser that an epic battle had taken place here today.

"Where's your friend?" Arthur said, looking around the cemetery but not seeing him by the base of the statue where they'd left him. "Has the coward run off?"

"He's no friend of mine," Merlin said, but he couldn't locate William either. A bad feeling crept into his heart then, and he began to run as fast as his tired, injured body would allow. "Follow me," he yelled at the King. "And hurry!"

Merlin ran to where he'd started his fight with the witch, frantically searching for what he knew should be there. And then he spotted something lying in the grass. With his heart thudding in his chest from the exertion, he raced over and skidded to a stop, not believing what his eyes were seeing.

"Oh my God!" he screamed, his eyes following a set of male-sized boot prints in the mud leading in the direction of the city street.

Morgana's small umbrella lay in the grass beside Merlin's feet.
The Holy Grail was gone.

Chapter 19

Where could someone like William Hare hope to run that he wouldn't be found? Where could he hide? He was one of history's most notorious criminals: the lazy husband who'd become the grave robber, who'd become a ruthless killer, who'd sold his partner's soul to the devil to buy his own freedom. How could he possibly have taken the Grail knowing the struggle between good and evil that it represented? It was almost inconceivable that after the magical battle he'd bore witness to, he still hadn't learned his lesson that crime didn't pay. Was he flat out crazy or just plain stupid and filled with greed, knowing the carpenter's cup was worth a fortune to the right bidder? Even so, there was a huge difference between something worth a mountain of money— enough to live his life in the lap of luxury—and something that was truly *priceless*. No dollar amount could ever be placed on the golden chalice, and no amount of wishful thinking and misguided hope could ever prevent William from eventually being caught.

Knowing Merlin would be coming after him, and having already decided he had to flee Edinburgh before a lynch mob got their hands on him, William made his way to the biggest city he knew—London, England—hoping to become lost in the vast throngs of people there. Only in a new city, in a new country where no one would know who he was or what he'd done, could he hope to become invisible. That was what he was counting on anyway, when he rented a small flat above a brothel in the seedy area of town known as Whitechapel. The poor working-class slum reminded him of Westport back in Edinburgh and he felt right at home amid the hookers and the drunks and the con artists who lived and plied their trades there.

In short, William fit right in...

* * *

For two full weeks Hare actually thought he'd made a clean getaway, holed up in his pigsty of a room, not daring to go outside for a pint at the pub or call a floozy up to join him for the night in fear someone would recognize him or worse yet, try to steal the Grail. His first clue that he'd been found was when he heard a flutter of powerful wings on the edge of sleep, and woke to find the great Snowy Owl perched on his window sill, silently watching his every move. The bird flew away before he could leap from his covers but it didn't matter—William knew the gig was up.

Dammit all to Hell! William thought, his heart suddenly trip hammering with fear inside his ribcage, urging him to run, but he was too afraid to move. "I've got to get away," he said out loud, hoping hearing the sound of his own voice would stir him into taking action. He had to at least try, right? But where could he go? Panic induced thoughts of Ireland or even America filled his head; *anywhere* in the world a better hiding place for him than here in—

The door to his hovel suddenly burst open, Merlin storming into the room looking far bigger and nastier than William could remember. The Magician was dressed head to toe in mud-splattered black clothing, his hair and beard a tangled mess from being on the road for so long. The wizard's mouth was pulled tight with rage, his eyes literally burning with hellfire in the darkened room. Knowing full well he was in a dire situation, William immediately dropped to his knees and began to beg for his life, a large part of him knowing he was probably wasting his breath.

"I'm sorry, Merlin, please...forgive me. I didn't know what I was doing. You have to believe me. I just couldn't help myself."

"Where is it?" the wizard said, pointing an accusing finger toward William's chest. "No more games. Lie to me now at your peril!"

William had no intention of lying.

"I have it, and it's safe as can be. I never even thought about—"

"Where is it, thief?" Merlin screamed, his voice thunderously loud in the small enclosed space.

William scurried off his knees over to the wooden drawer beside his bed. "It's here, sir! Right here…safe as houses just like I said." William dug the Grail out of the drawer where he'd been storing it since arriving here in London, and handed it over to the angry wizard with a hopeful smile plastered on his filthy unshaven face.

Merlin examined the Grail for a moment, making sure it was undamaged, and then turned his burning eyes back onto William. He said one word to the thief and it was the last word he'd hear before his eyes rolled back into his head and he dropped to the floor unconscious. The Magician waved his hand and said, "Sleep!"

And so William did.

* * *

When next William woke, he found himself squeezed into a tight place that smelled of oil, earth, and wood. He was surprised to find that he was outside somewhere and that it was unusually dark and quiet for the middle of a large city. His surprise turned to fear when he realized he was lying inside a wooden box, a makeshift casket of some sort. He tried to move his arms and sit up only to find that he couldn't move a single muscle on his entire body. He tried to scream out for help, but even his voice had been stolen from him for the time being. All he could do was lie there in this claustrophobic place, staring straight up into the smog and star-filled night sky.

And then Merlin stepped into his view.

"Ah...there you are. Nice of you to rejoin the land of the living. Thought I'd lost you there for a minute. You've been asleep several hours already."

The Magician was speaking quietly and seemed to be in a much better mood than when he'd kicked down William's door earlier tonight. There was even a hint of a smile touching the corners of the wizard's mouth but for some reason his newfound mirth made William even more afraid of the magician than when he'd been screaming.

William tried to speak, tried to ask where he was and what Merlin was going to do to him, but no more than a tiny incoherent mumble exited his frozen lips. He had no way of knowing it, but his mate Billy had known exactly how he felt at this moment, back when he'd been standing on the gallows with a rope around his neck.

"Don't waste your breath, William. You're under a spell. There's nothing you can say to save yourself, anyway. The die's already been cast. You're a liar and a thief and a murderer and a fool...and for your multiple crimes against man and your meddling with the Grail I condemn you to this one final act of goodness that may someday wipe away all your sins and allow your soul peace. Then again...maybe it won't."

William fought against the wizard's spell, trying to break free from the magical bonds holding him still and leaving him mute. Nothing he tried worked and he was left with the horrifying fact that he was helplessly stuck in this shallow grave and at the magician's mercy. The only things he could control were his eyes.

"If you're curious, we're still in Whitechapel, just off one of the main crossroads. It's a small park but I'm not sure if it even has a name. Not that it matters. Not where you're going."

Merlin reached down and grabbed something down by William's feet. When he brought it into view, it was clearly a thick rope running through some sort of wooden pulley but from where

Hare was lying he couldn't tell what the other end was tied to – until Merlin started to let out some of the slack and the box William was stuck inside began to lower deeper into the ground.

No! William screamed in his mind, his eyes opening wide with fear.

"You see, King Arthur made me promise I'd hide the Grail from the world again. Morgana's evil plans and to a lesser extent, even your brainless treachery convinced him – and me – that the Carpenter's Cup was too powerful to be left in the hands of mankind. It needs to disappear again, to be buried deep where it will hopefully never be found."

The wizard let the coffin drop another six inches but then cinched the rope off, halting its descent. From out of his baggy jacket, Merlin produced the golden chalice and took a moment to shine its smooth sides before bending down and placing the Grail on William's heaving chest. Without any effort or thought of his own, William's hands both crossed over his breast and cradled the carpenter's cup to his body. Merlin also placed a silver-colored sword into the box, laying the blade along the side of William's right leg.

"The Grail needs to be hidden but it also needs to be guarded...*protected* the same as it was last time. Unfortunately I don't have any Templar Knight who's willing to sacrifice himself for the cause, but that's where you come in, of course. Willingly or not, your suffering will not be forgotten. Like I said...it may even one day wash your sins clean but that's in the Lord's blessed hands, not mine. If it were up to me, you'd stare at the top of this box forever!"

Merlin smiled coldly and slid the lid of the coffin into place, banging a dozen nails into the wood, sealing William inside. The darkness closed in on William and he would have screamed his throat raw if he'd been able to. The coffin began to descend again, Merlin lowering the box deep into the cold earth, so deep it would hopefully never be disturbed again.

"Goodbye William," Merlin said, his voice muffled by the lid and the tunnel of dirt. "Always remember you brought this fate upon yourself. May God have mercy on your wretched soul."

And then other than the sound of dirt raining down on the lid of the coffin to fill in the hole, William heard nothing at all. In time, perhaps he'd learn to pray for an end to his damnation but for now he could do nothing except lay there in the dark, staring up at the memory of a starry sky he'd never see again, and weep.

His hands involuntarily tightened around the Holy Grail.

Epilogue

William Hare died a slow and horrible death inside the deeply buried coffin, clutching the Carpenter's Cup to his chest, his fingers still protectively wrapped around his golden treasure in the dark. And like the body of the Templar Knight who'd lain buried in Calton Cemetery in Edinburgh, his flesh would decay, though slowly, preserved by the Grail's magic. Years later, the dark power of the chalice would merge with his corrupt soul and although his body was trapped within the grave, some essence of his evil rage would escape the cold earth and linger in the dingy streets of Whitechapel, searching for a new vessel to taint. The darkness would enter the malleable flesh of a newborn babe, only a few streets from where Hare was buried alive.

After the pain and the midwife's happy sobs, seeing her healthy boy was almost too much for the young mother. She held him close, whispering his name, the name that best suited him. After all, a baby boy needed a good strong name. "Jack."

And Jack would grow up to be quite famous in his own right...

Author's Note

For those who don't already know, the core story of William Burke and William Hare is sadly all too true. They really were two lazy Irish friends who lived in Edinburgh, Scotland in the late 1820s. An old man's death in the Log's Lodging House set them on the path to infamy, leading them to the vile acts of grave robbing, bodysnatching, and ultimately becoming the first documented serial killers in British history. When they were eventually captured, neither man could honestly remember the number of people they'd killed, but the generally agreed upon body count was sixteen or seventeen.

I've obviously taken a great many liberties with my version of their story so I wanted to take a moment to address some of them. First and foremost, the real murders and grave robbing took place over a much longer period of time – at least a full year and a half. I condensed that down to several short months so it would fit in with the time it took for Ambrosious Black to carve his statue for the city council. I couldn't squeeze in all the murders and facts in that shortened timeframe, but I also didn't feel I needed to. I think you got the gist.

Another point some might take issue with is that I've set things up having William Hare as the smarter, savvier leader of the two killers. That could easily be argued, especially since the Edinburgh Crown Attorney judged Burke to be the mastermind behind the murders, which is why he allowed Hare to go free if he cooperated and presented King's evidence against his friend. My research indicated there was a chance the Crown had been duped though, with Hare only pretending to be a simpleton following Burke's brutal commands. We'll never know for sure, but the story worked best for me having Hare as the leader, so I went with it. In the end, both men were equally guilty, and in a perfect world both should have faced the gallows together.

Along with Burke and Hare, both of their wives were questioned in connection with the crimes. I really only introduced Hare's wife Maggie. I made her more of a sympathetic character, totally innocent of her husband's evil deeds, but in reality there is a lot of evidence that ties the wives into the murders as well. Perhaps not in the dirty deeds themselves, but there was a lot of money coming into the two households and the women surely must have known far more than they claimed at the eventual trial. Both wives were questioned but ultimately released, and both lived out their lives in hiding, forced to flee the city and move in with sympathetic relatives.

Dr. Robert Knox, the man who was buying the cadavers for his dissection school, obviously knew what was going on as well. He claimed total innocence, of course, and was released a free man – but the evidence shows that the only reason he wasn't implicated in the murders was because of his affluent place in society and some well-placed "donations" he may or may not have made to certain city officials at the time. Regardless, just being associated with Burke and Hare destroyed his reputation and he was forced to close his surgical school and move to England to escape the shame and the wrath of the Scottish people.

William Burke died as I mentioned in the story, swinging from the gallows on January 28, 1829, paying the price for everyone involved. There is some conflicting data as to whether he was officially convicted of three murders, or if after the judge declared him guilty of killing Mary Docherty, the other charges against him were deemed unimportant and dropped. He'd hang the same for one murder and they could only kill him once, so why bother proceeding to the other charges? After Burke had been declared dead, his body was immediately donated to the surgeons for dissection and his skeleton was cleaned and hung in a glass case at the University of Edinburgh. You can still go there today and see his bones for yourself. There's even a medical book on display there, bound in Burke's skin.

Of William Hare's fate, no one really knows. When he was released from the Jail a full week after Burke's execution, he needed to be snuck out a side entrance to avoid the angry crowds that were waiting to get their hands on him. History tells us that somehow Hare made it out of the city and then disappeared into the sands of time. No one knows if he lived a long happy life or if he was perhaps captured by the mob and secretly killed. There are several stories of him making his way back to Ireland, or even as far as London, England, where I decided he should go. Although we will never really know, I like to think that wherever he went he was haunted by a great Snowy Owl in his dreams. And if by chance William Hare did somehow fool the lawyers and the judges during his murder trial, perhaps my ending is some small measure of fictional karmic payback. Hey, you never know.

Anyway, thank you for taking the time to read my story. It was a lot of fun for me to write and I hope you enjoyed it. I urge any of you who might be interested to go online and do a little research on good ol' Burke and Hare. Their escalating series of crimes is a fascinating story that is well worth reading.

Gord Rollo
February 9th, 2013
Great White North

GORD ROLLO was born in St. Andrews, Scotland, but now lives in Fonthill, Ontario, Canada, with his wife and three children. His short stories and novella-length works have appeared in many professional publications throughout the genre and he is currently at the end of a four-book novel contract with Dorchester Publishing in New York City. His novels include: *The Jigsaw Man*, *Crimson*, *Strange Magic*, and *Valley Of The Scarecrow*, all of which are being rereleased in brand new e-book and trade paperback versions through Enemy One Press. Besides novels, Gord edited the acclaimed evolutionary horror anthology, *Unnatural Selection: A Collection of Darwinian Nightmares*. He also co-edited *Dreaming of Angels*, a horror/fantasy anthology created to increase awareness of Down's Syndrome. He recently completed his newest book, a horror/dark fantasy novel entitled *The Translators* and can be reached through his website at www.gordrollo.com or www.enemyone.com or through his agent Lauren Abramo at labramo@dystel.com.

East End Girls

Rena Mason

JournalStone's DoubleDown Series, Book I

LIMITED EDITION HARDCOVER
__6__ OF 100 COPIES

JOURNALSTONE PUBLISHING

East End Girls

By
Rena Mason

JournalStone
San Francisco

JOURNALSTONE
YOUR LINK TO ARTISTIC TALENT

Copyright © 2013 by Rena Mason

All rights reserved. No part of this book may be used or reproduced by any means, graphic, electronic, or mechanical, including photocopying, recording, taping or by any information storage retrieval system without the written permission of the publisher except in the case of brief quotations embodied in critical articles and reviews.

This is a work of fiction. All of the characters, names, incidents, organizations, and dialogue in this novel are either the products of the author's imagination or are used fictitiously.

JournalStone books may be ordered through booksellers or by contacting:

JournalStone
www.journalstone.com
www.journal-store.com

The views expressed in this work are solely those of the authors and do not necessarily reflect the views of the publisher, and the publisher hereby disclaims any responsibility for them.

ISBN: 978-1-936564-82-8   (sc)
ISBN: 978-1-940161-16-7   (hc – limited edition)
ISBN: 978-1-936564-79-8   (ebook)

Library of Congress Control Number: 2013935628

Printed in the United States of America
JournalStone rev. date: June 7, 2013

Cover Design: Denis Daniel
Cover Art: Alan M. Clark

Edited By: Norman Rubenstein

Dedication

for Rob, Gehret, and Parker
—the West End Boys

Endorsements

"Historical fiction is difficult to write, because the writer must carefully attend to period language, culture, events, and avoid anachronisms—all this while telling a compelling story. In *East End Girls*, author Rena Mason accomplishes all this with ease. In addition, her story is woven into the time and events of the most intriguing of serial killers—Jack the Ripper. Believe me: This is an exciting read by a young star on the rise. *East End Girls* has my strongest recommendation."—**Gene O'Neill**, *Dance Of The Blue Lady And Other Stories* (coming June of 2013, Bad Moon Books)

"*East End Girls* takes the story of Jack the Ripper and turns it upside down and inside out with the precision of a surgeon. It is a marvelous read from beginning to end, with delightfully bloody twists and turns that are as dark and dangerous as an East End alley. With this book, Rena Mason proves she is a rising new voice in horror."—**JG Faherty**, author of *The Burning Time, Cemetery Club, Carnival of Fear,* and the Bram Stoker Award® nominated *Ghosts of Coronado Bay*.

"I hadn't read any work by Rena Mason before but I'll certainly be following her now. *East End Girls* shows she's a very talented newcomer with a very inventive story about Jack the Ripper. I loved everything about this book and was just sorry to see it end. It's very evocative and entertaining, and I can't wait to see Mason's next book."
– **John R. Little**

Acknowledgements

A big thanks to Gene O'Neill and Gord Rollo, the "Burke and Hare" of horror writers, Alan M. Clark, Norman Rubenstein, Christopher C. Payne, JG Faherty, R.J. Cavender, and Chris Marrs.

"It is the same woman, I know, for she is always creeping, and most women do not creep by daylight." —Charlotte Perkins Gilman

Chapter 1

Steam rose from Eliza's gloves as hot blood continued to gush out of the wailing prostitute. "For the love of God, hold her still," Eliza said to the prostitute's friend, who nodded and strengthened her grip. "It'll be the end of us if a copper hears." *The end of me anyway, my life, and good family name.*

She had been christened Catherine Elizabeth Covington on June 3, 1870. Her parents, Lord and Lady Covington of Northumberland call her Eliza, but the East End prostitutes knew her simply as 'Jane.' Where or how she got the nickname, Eliza never learned or cared to find out.

It was times such as this that made her wonder why she was wearing a hooded cape like a villain, kneeling in a back alley of the loathsome Whitechapel District with her hands between the legs of someone so far beneath her both metaphorically and literally. Then she would remind herself it was in pursuit of finishing up at the London School of Medicine for Women to become a physician like her father, and this thought alone was enough to keep her going. Eliza dreamt of being the first female doctor to care for a member of the Royal Family. Why not? Times were changing fast, and she was ready to do whatever it required to see her dream realized—even despicable things such as what she was doing now. The vile creatures of the East End had been a way to advance her knowledge, and they got something out of Eliza's charity and studies, too.

The uterine curette had slipped from Eliza's grasp and she'd inched her fingers further up inside the harlot in search of the bulbous metal handle. The other end was shaped into an open oval. Sharp around all its edges, the instrument was perfect for scraping the inside of a uterus. The woman squealed and clamped her legs together, making the task more difficult.

"Keep her calm," Eliza said, looking up and around for anyone who might be passing by.

The woman repositioned her hands on her friend's legs, held them firm, and then spread them farther apart. "You sure you know what you're doin' Miss Jane? Seems a lot of blood for such a little thing."

The prostitute patient began squirming again.

"It's perfectly normal," Eliza said. "But there would be less of it if she were to just keep still!"

The friend turned her head toward the patient and whispered. "Be calm now. She'll be done soon enough."

Up to her elbow in filth, Eliza thought of the mess that would be left on the sleeve of her frock coat. Granted, it was one she wore specifically for university and these ventures in the East End to blend with the residents of the area, but still, she would have to wash most of it herself before handing it off to the servants. She knew choosing a black one would be smart, because she *was* smart and of superior intelligence regardless of what Professor Huxley had to say. He could go hang himself.

"I got it." Eliza said. With a firm grip on the handle, she roughly circled the instrument inside the prostitute one last time, then she pulled it out. A warm gush of bubbling crimson and gore followed.

"Ugh," the friend leaned away and gagged. "It's done then?"

"Yes. She should rest for the night." Eliza said.

"I'll make sure of it Miss Jane. And er...I ain't got nothing to pay for your services, less you want a little piece of me." The woman smiled, exposing her yellow teeth and furrowing the dried dirt caked over her brow and on her cheeks.

"That won't be necessary, but see to it this doesn't happen again." Eliza pulled strips of fabric from her medical bag and stuffed them into the patient's vagina using the curette she had removed a moment earlier. She'd been stealing the servants' undergarments and shredding them for just this purpose over the last few months, and if any of them had noticed, they'd never mention a thing about it to her. Eliza knew it was a very clever idea—*superior intelligence.*

"I swear this dollymop won't be seeing the likes of 'ya again, Miss Jane."

"That goes for you, too."

"You know I got experience compared to her. Not like me to get knocked up."

"Fine then." Eliza stood, looked around to be sure she had all her things.

"And what about that mess on the ground between her legs?"

"Clean it up or leave it. I'll have no part."

"And the pieces? What am I to do with those?"

"Scoop them up and get rid of them. Here's some cloth." Eliza unlatched her medical bag once more and handed the prostitute a larger swatch of fabric. "Burn it all if you can."

Eliza stepped into the fog and made haste.

London haze in general was abysmal, but the murk that permeated the East End was rife with smoke and a wretched stench of the poor. A few blind turns past derelicts and common people coming and going from whatever business occupied them and soon the more familiar look of Wentworth Street would come into view. The busier thoroughfare would make it possible for her to catch a hansom cab back to London Hospital. During the ride, she would remove her cape and frock coat, change her shoes and tidy up. When Eliza was really a mess, she'd go into the hospital and wash before taking another cab from the hospital back home to Queen Anne Street, near Regent's Park. Until then, she was fortunate the despicable fog hid her from the police and criminals alike.

Some nights she would walk along the wet, rugged cobblestones and ponder her future, which appeared dimmer than the East End lamplights that were useless in the fog, their glow seemingly miles away. Her wedding, set to take place in several months to Sir Osborne's son, Henry, however, felt close enough to smother her. As dismal as the walks in the area were, the people of the East End had an unexplainable energy about them that was missing from her own life, and she envied it. So many East Enders had a bad criminal nature and without a care. It seemed hardly fair sneaking around to further her education.

If I became a vile, loathsome creature, the East End would welcome me into its bosom.

Chapter 2

Because of the hour, Eliza used the servants' entrance when she arrived home. It also gave her the opportunity to rinse the sleeves of her frock coat and cape before exchanging them with Margaret for a plate of cold supper. Margaret was married to Mr. Daniel Sutton, the Covington's butler. Together the couple took charge of the other servants and gardeners.

After dining, Eliza visited her father in his study and poured him a glass of his favorite brandy. It had been a nightly tradition since she could remember. As a young girl, Eliza wanted so much to understand his work, be a part of it. She was fascinated by his knowledge of medicine and his dedication to the Royal Family. If any of them fell ill or were injured, he was called for at all hours, even if he was exhausted after seeing other patients all day. A phaeton carriage would arrive and be waiting outside to speed him away. There were quite a few physicians that cared for royalty, but it was well-known that Lord Covington was one of Queen Victoria's favorites.

However, it wasn't until Eliza showed medical interests in her later studies that Lord Covington finally took notice of her pursuits and approved. Since then, they would spend hours at night discussing new procedures, illnesses, and medicine in general. Nothing made her happier.

This evening was different, though. The air was heavy and grave as Eliza approached her father's study. She could hear other men in the room, so she gently leaned against the door to listen. Their voices boomed and vibrated through the solid mahogany, but she couldn't discern any of the conversation. No longer able to stand it, she rapped on the door with her fist.

"Who is it?" Lord Covington asked.

"It's me, Father. Can I come in?" Eliza could hear some protest from the men in the room. "Is that Henry in there with you?"

"Come in, Eliza," her father said.

She turned the knob so quickly she almost fell into the room.

"Close the door behind you. We wouldn't want your mother to hear. Gentlemen, this is my daughter, Eliza."

Two men quickly stood from chairs by the fireplace.

"Eliza, this is a colleague and old friend from my university days you've never met, Doctor Rees Llewellyn." His name was said with great reverence. "And this is Detective Sergeant George Godley." His introduction was made with little to no sentiment. "Please gentlemen, continue. Don't let her looks fool you. More than likely, she's brighter than the three of us together."

"But sir," the detective said.

"That's Lord Covington to you, Godley."

"Gentlemen, please," Eliza said. Seemed she came at the right time. Eliza walked over to the brandy tray, poured some into a snifter then brought it to her father who was seated at his desk. He acknowledged her with a nod and they stared into each other's sky blue eyes for a moment, his expressing seriousness and hers curiosity.

Eliza turned her head toward Detective Godley and Doctor Llewellyn. "Would either one of you care for some brandy?"

"No thank you, Miss. We're here on business," Detective Godley said.

"Quite the beauty she is," Doctor Llewellyn said. "I hear congratulations are in order, Miss Eliza.

She looked up at him with no idea of what he meant. For a moment she thought perhaps her father had told him about her progress toward becoming a physician.

"For your upcoming nuptials to Henry Osborne," he said.

"Oh yes, thank you doctor." She sat down and made herself comfortable in a high-backed chair next to her father's desk. For several moments, the rustling of her starched skirts, the occasional crackle from the fire, and Godley's labored breathing were all that could be heard.

"Come now gentlemen, let's get on with it. We haven't all night," Lord Covington said. "We're discussing murder, Eliza."

Detective Godley gasped. The shortness of breath suited him. He was a stout man stuffed into an old jacket that was far too small. The plaid, tan vest underneath was pulled so tight, it protruded his rotund belly. The man's face was flushed, and his hair, black as night, was matted to his head with some kind of cheap tonic that reeked of wet animal.

Doctor Llewellyn, who was tall and lean in comparison, turned to face her. "A few women have been found with their throats slit this summer at the East End. But this last one...this last one had her abdomen cut as well." When he spoke, his face appeared worn, as though he'd had a rough life. But otherwise, he was clean-shaven, and his dark blue suit was kempt. He looked much older than her father did, even though he had said they'd been university colleagues.

"They think perhaps this fiend is evolving, Eliza," Lord Covington said. "It happened near the London Hospital." He gave her a stern look, but mentioned nothing to the men of the volunteer work she sometimes did there. Fortunately, her father knew nil of the loathsome deeds she endured in order to learn the female anatomy, for he would never approve.

"Are you certain it is the same murderer?" she asked.

Detective Godley gasped again and plopped himself down into a chair. The color in his face had gone, and he was quite pale.

Doctor Llewellyn walked over to the brandy tray and poured some into a glass. He stepped over to the detective and handed it to him. "Drink this, Godley. For heaven's sake man, pull yourself together. This woman is practically a physician already from what I hear, and surely she's cut a few bodies open herself. We speak of nothing she hasn't done or seen."

Eliza glanced at her father and they both smirked. The detective took the glass with a shaky hand, downed the brandy in two hardy swallows, then handed the snifter back to Doctor Llewellyn.

"The cuts are always the same," Doctor Llewellyn said. "From left to right."

"So either your villain is left-handed, or he gets at them from behind," Eliza said.

"See, Rees, I told you she was sharp," said Lord Covington.

Doctor Llewellyn raised the empty glass in his hand and nodded at his colleague. "That is correct, Miss Covington."

"Was there anything else, besides the abdominal cut?" she asked.

"She had been drinking and was probably strangled first. There was little blood loss at the scene. Her innards were protruding from the open wound, and there were numerous slashes crisscrossing her abdomen," Doctor Llewellyn continued.

Detective Godley began coughing. Then he stood upright. "Please, sirs, and lady," he said. "You'll have to excuse me. I've been feeling a bit under the weather."

Doctor Llewellyn took the detective's empty glass and set it down next to the brandy tray. "Yes, it is getting late. I suppose we've overstayed our welcome."

Lord Covington rose from his desk. "It was good to see you again Rees after all these years. Don't be a stranger. I'll be sure to have Lady Covington add you to the wedding party, and please consider joining us for Michaelmas."

"Thank you, Thomas. Please give my regards to Lady Covington. And if you can think of anything else that might help with the case…or even you for that matter, Miss Eliza," he turned toward her and bowed slightly. "Do send us a message. But I'm hoping this is the end of it. I look forward to seeing you again in September under more celebratory circumstances."

"Until then, Rees," said Lord Covington. He came out from behind his desk and shook hands with Doctor Llewellyn.

"It was a pleasure to meet you both," Eliza said.

"The pleasure was all ours young lady." Doctor Llewellyn raised her hand to his lips and kissed it gently.

Detective Godley stood by the door, looking a bit green in the face. He held up his hat. "Good evening Lord Covington. Miss Eliza."

Godley opened the door and Mr. Sutton, the butler, who'd been waiting just outside the study, motioned for the two men to follow him out.

Eliza walked over and shut the door after they went. "Father, why haven't I met Dr. Llewellyn until now? Does Mother know him? You've never mentioned him before."

"He was a good friend at University, but he had some problems his last year. Got addicted to laudanum from what I heard. It was a sad business, too. Rees was one of the brightest students who ever walked those halls. Seems he pulled through after the rest of us had finished up and moved on. Was never able to recover his reputation, though."

"Why was he here with the detective?"

"He's a police surgeon now."

"What a shame," Eliza said.

"Indeed." Lord Covington looked over to his wall of books and appeared to study them for a moment. "I don't want you anywhere near London Hospital in the evenings. It's too dangerous."

"But Father, I'm only there twice a week, and I have my wits about me."

"I know that, but it's of little help when there's a maniac on the loose."

"It sounds like he's after drunken East End girls anyway, not medical volunteers who help the sick and the poor."

"I won't speak any further on this subject, Eliza. You are not permitted to go to the East End. I will have a meeting with Professor Huxley and that Miss Anderson first thing tomorrow."

She lowered her head, turned around, and started for the door.

"Is there anything else you'd like to say to me young lady?"

"Good night, Father."

"Good night," he said. His tone softened. "You'll see that it's in your best interest to stay away. Besides, your mother has been blaming me for keeping you from your wedding plans. Henry's a good man, Eliza. He'll make a good husband."

"Yes, Father." A single tear rolled onto her cheek as she opened the door and stepped out of the room. Months ago, he was in full support of her attending university and all the work that went with it. She couldn't understand why a few murders now would make him change his mind. People died in the East End all the time. It wasn't unusual to have a body floating in the Thames there at least every other day. No, it couldn't be that her father was so worried about it. This change of heart must be because of her mother. Eliza's familial and social commitments would be the death of her. There had to be a way of escaping them, and she was desperate to find it.

Chapter 3

At breakfast, Lady Covington was alone when Eliza came into the room. "Where's Father?" she said.

"He told me he had to leave early and speak to Professor Huxley this morning."

"Oh." Eliza sat down. Mrs. Sutton appeared with a plate of toast with jam, and a cup of tea with a bit of milk. "Thank you," Eliza said.

"You're welcome, Miss Eliza. Did you sleep well? You look a bit pale this morning."

"I slept fine."

"She's right," Lady Covington said. "You don't look so well. Maybe you should stay home today."

"I could have Mr. Sutton send a note to Professor Huxley," Mrs. Sutton said.

"You can rest and I'll show you what I've chosen for the silks, the flowers, and the—"

"I'll be leaving as soon as I finish my tea, Mother. I assure you, I am quite well."

"You speak to me the way your father does."

Mrs. Sutton quickly exited the room.

"Well, I am his daughter."

"I won't have it, Eliza. I've been burdened with the details of your wedding these past few months and a bit of help now and then would go a long way. A young girl your age should be happy to be marrying a man from a good family and with future prospects."

"Yes, but—"

"Not running around all over London attending university, laboring as if you were a man, and God only knows what else. It's not proper, don't you understand? You're fortunate Henry tolerates it and loves you enough to allow you this whim, but be sure that when the wedding is over you will be doing your duty as his wife, not doctoring anyone but him."

Eliza clenched her fist and slammed the butter knife onto the table.

"It's all such a waste of time," her mother continued. "Why can't you see it? You are so much like your father it's hardly tolerable."

"Well Mother, you won't have to take too much more. I'll soon be married, away, and out of your hair for good."

"Don't be that way Eliza."

Eliza knew there was no point in arguing with her mother. After years of watching her father lose battles it was obvious neither of them would ever win one. "I'm sorry Mother, it's just that exams are coming up and there's so much to study for. Regardless of whether or not Henry lets me practice doctoring, I'm determined to finish my studies."

"Yes dear. I understand. It's just that…"

"What is it Mother?"

"It's Ann Williams, dear. She's been out of sorts lately and I really wish you would see her more often. You two used to get along so well. I worry for her health."

"I've been a little busy, and I'm sure she understands."

"Please, promise me you'll call on her soon. The last time I saw her out, she seemed dire."

"I'll visit her in the next few days, I promise." Eliza swallowed the last bit of her tea and placed the delicate china cup on the table.

Mrs. Sutton came back into the room. "Shall I have Mr. Sutton ready the carriage?"

"I'd much rather take a hansom."

"Now you're being ridiculous," said Lady Covington. "These new ideas of yours are preposterous. You can't tell me every girl there doesn't already know who you are."

"It makes no difference. I'd still prefer a cab."

"Be home early today. Henry's joining us for dinner. It'll do you good to see him and maybe he can talk some sense into you."

Lady Covington was ringing the bell for Mrs. Sutton again when Eliza rose from the table and left the room. She put on a hat before stepping out of the house, and made sure everything she needed was in her medical bag. Outside, Eliza looked up the street and saw the Williams's home at the crest of the hill. It had been a while since she'd spoken to Ann. Eliza truly hoped she was all right, but it would have to wait. The most important days of her life were coming, and nothing would distract her from her studies. Too much depended on it.

* * *

"Miss Covington, would you please point out the deceased's fallopian tubes," Professor Huxley said with a sharp tone. His voice echoed and bounced off the cold, stone walls until the words seemed to come from the cadaver itself. She could feel his dark, beady eyes glaring at her through his wire-rimmed spectacles. He was awkwardly tall and thin with a tendency to lean over and watch her work, intimidating her whenever the opportunity arose, as now.

Eliza looked down and saw a swirling puzzle of bluish-purple innards. "Here, sir." Thinking herself clever knowing there are two ovaries, she pointed to one thing and then to another on the opposite side which looked similar.

"If we were to have it your way Miss Covington, women would not be able to reproduce. Those are arteries of the kidneys. Your knowledge, or rather, lack thereof, astounds me. I suggest you study up on the subject," he whispered over her.

"Yes, Professor Huxley," she said. The heat of embarrassment flushed her face. Before she could retort, he'd moved on to the next student, taking away her opportunity. Eliza hated her lack of a quick wit.

The classmate, Jessica Blake, was always ready with her correct answers. They were all just jealous, but being made a fool of wasn't something she was familiar with or would ever get used to. Between her parents, Professor Huxley, and even Henry, it would be a feat if she ever accomplished anything other than marrying a good man. But, like she'd told herself so many times before—one had to stay determined in order to succeed.

After class, she approached the professor when all the other girls had left. "Professor Huxley, may I have a moment?"

"Yes. What is it Miss Covington?"

"My father, did he—"

"Yes, Lord Covington paid me a visit this morning."

"And you told him…"

"I told him you were excelling in all the facets of doctoring Miss Covington. I may be a simple professor of medicine at a university for *females*, but I am no ignoramus as to my position and rank in society."

"Did he mention London Hospital?"

"Yes, it seems you are no longer permitted to go there in the evenings. I didn't have the courage to tell him that you were never assigned to volunteer there at those hours. I do admire your determination Miss Covington, but you should take care in your extracurricular means of study. I can promise you that you will graduate from this university and then be married to Henry Osborne, after which you can finally give up the notion of being a medical doctor. It will give me great peace, and I will be able to sleep at night knowing you are not out there practicing any kind of medicine, on any living person. Good day, Miss Covington." Professor Huxley turned around and walked away from Eliza.

She stood in the center of the room unable to move for some time after hearing Huxley's harsh words. Eliza leaned against the wooden table where the cadaver was earlier. It was the only thing keeping her upright for the moment. The sun crossed a high window, moving a slow shadow across her face, and she finally snapped out of the trance. It was time to get home and dress for dinner. Henry would be there and if nothing else, perhaps he could cheer her up. Give her a bit of good news after Professor Huxley's extreme display of discontent. Eliza knew she wasn't the smartest girl at the school, but she didn't think she was the most ignorant either. It was imperative she get more practice in at the East End. She would have to be very clever to keep it from her parents and extremely sharp to stay away from a possible madman on the loose. It was a challenge she felt up for.

Chapter 4

Eliza couldn't sit still and kept rearranging the silverware around her plate. During the meal, she continuously sneaked glances at Henry, who looked dashing in a fashionable new navy pinstripe jacket. She'd already told him several times since he'd arrived how handsome he was, and her mother couldn't have agreed more. Her father, however, told him he looked quite ridiculous—but he'd always been more on the conservative side of fashion.

The jacket wasn't the reason she was so excited. It was Henry announcing why he'd worn the jacket. Right before dinner, he said he wore it to tell them about some especially good news after the meal. Henry was a handsome young man with brown hair he kept neatly slicked back and a thin moustache. Eliza didn't like his eyes, though. They were brown and narrow, making him look as though he were always keeping something secret. Regardless, she could hardly wait to hear what he had to say.

"Please Henry, what news?" she whispered into his ear. Before moving away, she gently breathed down his neck.

His smile grew wicked. "Clever girl, are you trying to seduce me?"

"Is it working?"

"Father's always told me I'm good at keeping secrets, and I'm not about to give this one up."

"Not even for me?"

"You'll be my wife soon, and then there will be nothing kept hidden between us." He raised his glass and took a sip of wine while staring into her eyes.

Eliza knew that what he'd said wasn't true. Henry was a man's man, all about business. His father, Sir Osborne, was a banking magnate in London. It was well-known that the patriarch of the Osborne fortune had numerous affairs with other women all throughout England and even Paris. Henry was every bit like his father, and he'd most likely behave in the same manner. A husband's infidelity was almost expected. But why, she'd never understand.

The world was changing. Women wanted rights and were getting them. The poor wanted rights now, too. Parliament was in an upheaval over it. The conditions at East End were inhumane, and in these times of rapid modifications, it shouldn't be fair that men could still cheat. But some things Eliza knew would never change and this made her angry.

She thought of her good friend in the house on the hill, Ann Williams. The last time Eliza spoke with her, Ann was still upset over her inability to have children. She had also hinted that she thought her husband might be having an affair. Maybe this was why Lady Covington wanted Eliza to visit with her so badly. Although she seemed quiet and demure, and in her own way really did care, her mother had an insatiable penchant for gossip.

Finally, dinner had ended and everyone gathered in the parlor afterwards to hear Henry's announcement. Even Mr. and Mrs. Sutton found an excuse to come in and stay longer, rearranging dessert plates around on the sideboard table. Henry sat next to Eliza and then stood when Lord Covington entered the room. Beads of sweat formed on Henry's upper lip and he couldn't stop rubbing his hands together. Eliza couldn't remember if she'd ever seen him like that before, not even when he asked her father for her hand in marriage. The suspense was astounding—and giving her a headache. She hoped he would say whatever it was soon so that she could excuse herself and get some rest.

"Please, Henry, sit," Lord Covington said.

"I'd rather stand if you don't mind, sir. This is big news."

"Well, get on with it then lad, before you explode. Eliza looks as if she might faint."

Eliza looked up at Henry and rolled her eyes then smiled to give him some encouragement.

"As you all know I'll be taking over the business when my father retires, but…"

Eliza took hold of his hand. He squeezed her fingers and continued. "He is sending me to New York City, in America, to establish one of our banks—and there it is."

The room went quiet. Eliza pulled her hand from his grip and let it drop onto the chaise. Her father was right; she might faint after all. Lady Covington let out a high-pitched whimpering sound like a wounded cat. Mrs. Sutton gasped and knocked over a crystal goblet of water. Mr. Sutton hurried over to help her clean up the mess.

"Well," Lord Covington broke the silence, walked over to Henry and shook his hand. "Congratulations, son. No doubt you'll be off right after the wedding."

Lady Covington mewled again.

Eliza stared straight ahead, and Henry, trying to catch her eye responded, "Yes, of course. I wouldn't think of leaving London without my wife, Eliza. I've waited long enough to have her hand in marriage. Our engagement has been extended more than most."

The word *wife* suddenly triggered hatred within her. She wouldn't be a good one. He deserved someone better. She had to speak up. "But my education, Henry, it would all have been for nothing there."

Lady Covington stopped squealing and glared across the room at Eliza. It was as if little pins shot out of her eyes and pricked Eliza all over.

Henry sat down and took Eliza's hands into his. "Oh my dear, there will be so much for you to see and experience in America, you may forget about wanting to be a doctor." She tried to pull her hands from his, but he held tight. This was an aggressive side of Henry she hadn't noticed before. "But there are universities there for women, as well. If you really have your heart set, I'm sure there are places where you can practice medicine."

Eliza knew he was lying, but there was nothing she could say.

It was what her mother wanted to hear, and Henry knew it.

"See Eliza, there's still hope after all," her father said. There was a deceitful tone in his voice, and for the first time in her 21 years, she saw the *man's man* side of her father. Eliza couldn't believe what she was hearing and wanted to run out of the room screaming.

"Yes," she said, her lie coming as quickly as his. "That would be wonderful Henry." Then she leaned up and gave him a peck on the cheek.

Mr. and Mrs. Sutton left the room with the wet linens. Her father stood.

"Come on now, Henry, let's leave these women to their chatter." The men left for Lord Covington's study to drink brandy and smoke cigars. Despite how angry she was at the both of them, Eliza wished she were there—anywhere but alone in a room with her mother.

"You truly will be leaving me soon." Lady Covington began to whimper. "What am I to do with my only child gone? And so far away."

"If you don't mind, Mother, I have a bit of a headache. I think I'll go upstairs and retire early this evening."

"You do look pale, dear. I don't blame you for feeling ill with such news. I think I should be happy, but I'm feeling quite sad. Will you let Mrs. Sutton know I'll be retiring early as well?"

Eliza rose from the chaise, walked over and kissed her mother on the forehead. Lady Covington grabbed Eliza's hand and kissed it. "Oh, my little girl," she cried.

For the third time this evening, Eliza pulled her hand away from someone and walked out of the room. A part of her was numb—another felt dark and enraged.

Chapter 5

Nearly a month later, Eliza still felt dull and out of sorts about the idea of moving to America after the wedding. The uncertainty drove her hard into her studies, and she was more determined than ever before. There were more late nights spent at the Royal Free Hospital, plus daytime volunteer work, all in addition to her curriculum. She took whatever work she could to improve her medical knowledge, but it still wasn't enough. Eliza knew she needed the East End. It needed her, and she wanted it. All she had to do was walk the streets with her medical bag in hand, and she would be approached by the sick or injured and sometimes by prostitutes hoping she could take care of their business in the back alleys they were so accustomed to. If she was going to be forced to live a life she didn't want, she would first do what she could and learn as much as possible in the East End.

It was late when Eliza snuck out. She had to be certain everyone was asleep. With her bag under her arm, she walked as far as she could from the house before taking a hansom to Whitechapel. The fog was so thick she could hardly see the cab driver. By the time she got there, it had started to rain. Eliza pulled the hood of her cloak over her head and kept her bag slightly open in case she needed to reach in for a weapon. Wet and cold, she stood by a building prostitutes frequented, and waited. Raindrops pitter-pattered against the tin roofs around her. Chimney smoke from the workhouses and homes of the poor blackened the fog, making it look green in the dim lamplights. Every breath inhaled was poison, so she folded the bottom part of her hood over her mouth.

After a few minutes, she heard muted footsteps. The water and haze distorted sounds, and Eliza couldn't tell from which way they came. She reached into her bag and carefully felt around for the handle of her surgeon's knife. Nimble fingers searched out the smooth mahogany, sized for a man's hand. The blade end was the same length, made of durable, sharp stainless steel. Against an attacker, the surgeon's knife would be a menacing weapon. She was happy to have it in her bag; a gift from her father. It wasn't long before she was approached.

Two women, drunk as she'd ever seen anyone, stumbled up and nearly knocked her over. "Sorry miss," one said while brushing off Eliza's cape with filthy hands. She had dark hair and a plump face compared to the other woman, who was rail thin; both were obviously working women.

"See you got a medical bag there, Miss. You wouldn't happen to be called Jane, would 'ya?" the one with the long scrawny face asked.

"I am."

"Good. Ah…Emma here's got a little problem she needs you to take care of." The prostitute patted Emma's belly and giggled.

"Do you have a doss for the night?" Eliza said. "A room is best to do the work."

"No miss, we spent it on drink. Besides, looks like the rain's lettin' up."

"Is there any place else?"

"Right around the corner will do. Emma here's not picky. Not a lot of folks out this time of night."

"Fine then, let's get to it." Eliza walked about 20 yards until a street pump for water caught her attention. This would be good for cleaning up afterward, so she turned left and walked down a long corridor behind a three-story building that was partially lit up from a lamplight in the rear yard. She figured it was as good a place as any, and she would have plenty of room to work. Two small outbuildings weren't too far off in the backyard and she hoped one was a lavatory where things could be discarded. "Lie down here,"

Eliza told the prostitute, Emma. "Use the bottom doorstep to rest your head. Help her—what's your name?" she asked the other prostitute.

"Catherine, miss," she slurred, then belched.

"Not your real name!" Emma scolded.

Catherine shrugged her shoulders and both women giggled.

"Keep your voices down, or I'll leave this minute!" Eliza said. Catherine looked properly chastised. Eliza often wondered why these stupid, disgusting animals worried so much about using their real names. She didn't care one way or the other who they were because it was unlikely she'd ever see them again. "We must keep quiet unless you want trouble from the tenants."

Once they had Emma positioned correctly, Eliza lifted the prostitute's skirts and readied her instruments. First, she took out a piece of wood wrapped in cloth that was a little longer than a finger and just as thick. "Here," she told Emma. "Bite down on this to keep quiet when the pain comes." Emma nodded and put the stick in her mouth.

Eliza pulled down the woman's filthy drawers. She left her gloves on and inserted two fingers deep into Emma's vagina while pressing the woman's abdomen with her other hand. She was sure she felt a lump that wouldn't normally be there. The patient grunted and her musculature stiffened. "Try and calm her," Eliza told Catherine. "It will make things go easier."

While Catherine patted her friend's head and whispered everything would be all right, Eliza pulled the long curette from her bag and slowly inserted it into Emma. The woman wriggled and bucked like a wild animal and her friend was worthless at holding her still. Emma bit down hard and grunted, swinging her head back and forth. Tears streamed across her temples. "I can't do this," Catherine said. She got up and ran off with her hands over her mouth. Eliza heard the prostitute's footfalls tap loud and quick at first, then they grew faint, until they faded to nothing.

"Don't worry," Eliza told Emma. "We don't need her, but you've got to hold still."

Emma nodded and Eliza continued circling the curette. She

grabbed another instrument with a sharp hook at the end, inserted it, and pulled when she felt it had caught on something. Emma's eyes bulged and she screamed with the bit still in her mouth. "Almost done," Eliza said. She yanked hard and a glob of tissue came out with a rush of bubbled blood that reeked of feces. "Dammit," Eliza said, knowing she'd hit bowel.

Emma began to scream louder and louder. Eliza was in a panic, didn't know what to do. She thought first of what Professor Huxley would say. He would tell everyone he knew she was a horrible surgeon. Her father would be so disappointed. Her mother would be ashamed, and Henry would never take her as his wife. Eliza leaned forward and tried to shush Emma, pinning her arms to her sides to keep her from flailing about. They struggled, and when that didn't work, she grabbed hold of the sides of the bit in her mouth and pushed down. Emma freed herself and reached into her pockets for something. Eliza grabbed her hands, tore the fabric of Emma's dress, and loose junk from the pocket flew up into the air then landed scattered about. Emma tried to fight. Eliza twisted up the scarf Emma had around her neck and began choking her, used her thumbs to push hard against her trachea until Emma passed out. Crazed, Eliza searched in her bag for the surgeon's knife. She held it up and stared at the glinting blade just as Emma started coming to.

Eliza leaned over her body then used the scarf to turn her head to the right. With little life left in her, Emma didn't put up much of a fight when Eliza took the surgeon's knife and cut across her throat from left to right. Eliza let go of the handkerchief and quickly began her work down below. There couldn't be any evidence left behind and she would have to move fast.

It was fortunate she'd been there to hear the details Dr. Llewellyn gave when he and Detective Godley came to visit her father—almost as though it was meant to be. And her own father gave her the best bit of advice. If the killer was evolving, then this would be his next step. Taking a thing—a prize.

Eliza opened Emma up and heaped her innards on top of her chest to get to the uterus. It had to go. Everything that could lead back to this failed abortion had to be taken and discarded. The extraction took less than a quarter of an hour. Then she wrapped the uterus and other parts of incriminating evidence, into a large swatch of fabric from her bag and tied it off with a piece of string. Quietly, but very alert, she went up to the front of the building, set the organs down next to the water pump and rinsed her hands off best she could. It started to rain again. Eliza put the bundle into her bag and hurriedly walked down the street. Every footstep was a loud splash against stone. She caught a hansom cab that delivered her close to Regent's Park, where she got out and walked the rest of the way. Eliza clutched her medical bag hard against her chest as though it might open and spill out her horrible secret.

When she got home, Eliza used the servants' entrance, went down into the kitchen, took the bundle from her bag and placed it onto the fire along with her gloves. The flames grew to life with her offering, but she added two more logs to be sure. Her hands wouldn't stop shaking. *What if the police don't believe my cover-up? That won't, and can't happen.* Before anyone in the house woke up, Eliza rinsed her cape and frock coat best she could then went upstairs to change for breakfast.

Despite all the feelings roiling inside, hunger rose above all else.

Chapter 6

"You look flushed this morning, Eliza. Are you feeling all right?" Lady Covington said.

"The other day I was too pale, and now I'm flushed. Are you sure it isn't your eyes?" Eliza sat down at the table and thanked Mrs. Sutton for a cup of tea.

"That's no way to speak to your mother," Lord Covington said.

"See how she treats me, Thomas?"

Eliza rolled her eyes. "Oh Mother, you know I don't mean it."

"Then don't vex me like that," Lady Covington said. "After church will you go over the flower arrangements with me?"

"I can't today. I'm playing tennis with Henry, Henrietta, and her husband, Arthur."

"How is his sister getting along since her marriage?"

"I've not heard much about it."

"That's because you've got your nose in books all day. It would be to your advantage after your own wedding to listen to what's happening in society."

"But I don't really care what happens with society."

"You will when it pertains to your husband, dear."

"Ladies, please, might a man have a piece of toast without the bickering?"

Mrs. Sutton entered the room, placed fresh jams on the table and set a folded paper down next to Lord Covington. "I thought you might like this right away, sir." He nodded. Then she stepped over to Eliza and poured more tea. The maid leaned over and whispered in her ear. "Nanette says your frock coat and cape are soaking wet. What would you have her do?"

"Wash them," Eliza said. "I decided to walk home yesterday and got caught in the pouring rain."

"Yes, Miss."

"Did you say you walked in the rain yesterday?"

"Yes, Mother." Eliza watched and waited for her father to open the paper.

"Are you trying to catch a death of a cold?"

"No, Mother. What news, Father?"

He looked up from the paper. "Walking is a healthy thing," he said. "It's good exercise."

"Yes, but in the rain, Thomas?"

"Well, maybe when it's pouring out take a cab next time, Eliza." He went back to reading the paper. "Hmm…seems there's been another murder in Whitechapel."

"That's horrible," Eliza's mother said. "Must we discuss this while we eat?"

"Thank you, Father," Eliza said. "May I be excused to dress for church?"

"Yes, you may."

Eliza took the stairs down toward the basement washroom and found Nanette, one of her best servant girls, standing over a large wash basin. Eliza picked up a can of soap on the shelf next to her and threw it against the wall in front of the maid. White powder exploded everywhere and the young girl screamed and turned around.

"Was there a problem with my coats, Nanette?" Eliza said with clenched fists.

"No, Miss, they were just so wet and heavy like they'd been left outside in the rain. They smelled funny, too. I thought that perhaps you'd want to throw them out." The maid trembled and rattled off her words.

"You know those are the clothes I wear to school and to work in."

"Yes, Miss."

"Well, they'll have to do until I'm finished then, won't they?"

"I'm sorry, Miss."

"Don't be sorry, Nanette. I'm a bit out of sorts this morning, that's all. Please, just wash the clothes when I bring them to you, with no comments to Mrs. Sutton or anyone else. Do you understand?"

"Yes, Miss."

"Then hurry up and clean this mess before someone sees, and don't tell a soul what happened here, either." Eliza walked upstairs and dressed for church. No doubt the news of the murder had spread throughout all of London. She meticulously scanned over images in her mind regarding the night's event. Eliza could think of nothing she might have forgotten or left at the scene in her rush to clean up and leave.

During the entire sermon, she kept her eyes down and thought of the other prostitute, Catherine. What if she told someone? Eliza doubted a woman of her nature would go to the police. Still, she would have to find her somehow and figure out a way to strike a bargain to her keep quiet.

A match or two of tennis would help her think things through. Her mind was always more clear when she was active. Sitting stagnant in church with her thoughts running in circles did nothing to help. It was suffocating, which made her think of the grip she'd had on Emma's scarf when she was strangling the girl. Her hold had been firm; so much so, she could hardly believe her own strength. Eliza moved her hand over her bicep muscle and marveled at the definition in her arm. All the tennis matches and archery competitions had made her stronger than she realized. She looked up from the pew and smiled.

* * *

Henry took Eliza home in his phaeton carriage and she wondered where her heart was. Would she ever fall in love with him? Her mother told her it would come with time, but shouldn't she feel the least bit for him now? *Love and marriage are useless things. Life and death, those are real.*

Eliza knew that once she became a fully-pledged physician she'd have some control over what was real. But losing control, like she did last night, had also been liberating. This kind of freedom without conscience could get her into a great deal of trouble. She had to be careful. Perhaps someone at the Royal Free Hospital would know of a prostitute named Catherine.

"What occupies your thoughts so, Eliza? Say it's me."

"Of course it is." Eliza was pleased with her increasing ability to lie so easily. "You, our wedding, our future lives in America."

"I hope you'll be happy, dear."

"I'm sure I will."

"Good. Good."

Henry's driver brought the carriage to a halt in front of the Covington residence then helped Eliza step out. "I'll see you soon," Henry said from the door.

"Goodbye, Henry."

Eliza sensed unease when she walked through the front door. She removed her hat and gloves. Mrs. Sutton came into the foyer and took them from her. "Lady Covington would like to speak with you."

"Is there someone else here?"

The maid looked from one side to the next then whispered. "More detectives and the police surgeon have come again. Something to do with the Whitechapel Murderer, I presume."

Eliza started for her father's study.

"Miss Covington, your mother is waiting for you in the parlor."

"Yes, of course, but—"

"Trust me when I say you wouldn't want to be in the same room with that severe bunch. Even your father looks more stark than usual. Best you be on your way to see what Lady Covington requires."

"Thank you Mrs. Sutton." Eliza headed for the parlor, slowing her pace when she passed her father's study. Men's voices boomed through the closed doors, making Eliza's heart race. Perhaps they'd caught on, which hastened her steps. If anyone knew what was happening in the house, it would be her mother.

"There you are, Eliza. Where have you been?"

"I told you earlier Mother, with Henry playing tennis."

"Oh, yes, now I remember. These events have me so distraught I hardly know what to think. It's horrible of these men to keep your father from his dinner. A man needs his nourishment, and he's not getting any younger or healthier."

"Mother, it's important. They need his help."

"His help? Why on earth do they need his help?"

"Well, he's esteemed, Mother. They trust him."

"I suppose, but it is very inconvenient."

"Who is here speaking with him? Are they the same men from before?"

"How would I know?"

"Mother, you must have some idea."

"I can't believe you're more concerned about what is going on in that room full of men than the reason I called you here."

"All right, why did you send for me?"

"The dressmaker is coming tomorrow afternoon."

"Oh, mother, how can you think of such things when father is in his study talking to detectives about murder?"

Lady Covington raised her voice. "If I don't, it will be your wedding day, and you'll be walking up the aisle in your nightclothes. What is murder to humiliation? I won't have it. You need to be home early tomorrow for the dressmaker, and I'll have no more talk of death or detectives."

"Yes, mother." Eliza had never seen her so upset. No sense in vexing her any further. At least she could be at ease knowing none of them suspected she was guilty of murdering a prostitute. If they had, she was certain her mother would hysterically inform her.

* * *

Dinner was served late that evening, and Lady Covington made sure to tell everyone she suffered from a cruel headache, so most of the conversation centered on her health. After pudding,

Lord Covington returned to his study and Eliza followed. She could no longer contain her curiosity. The door was barely closed when she spoke. "Father, please tell me, what news of the Whitechapel Murders?"

Lord Covington furrowed his brow. "You shouldn't concern yourself with these matters; although I can tell you that I knew this kind of thing would only get worse. They've got Inspector Abberline on it now. Expect to have it wrapped up soon."

"He's that good?"

"I've never heard anything other than exceptional remarks about him."

"Hmm…"

"What is it? You seem a bit out of sorts. Your mother again?"

"I have to be home early tomorrow to meet the dressmaker."

"Is it all that bad? You are getting married soon."

"No, that's not it."

"Second thoughts are normal. You'll get over it eventually, and you know I'd love nothing more than to have you practicing next to me. But as it is, I'm up half the night listening to your mother worry about your future."

"I'll be fine."

"Truly?"

"Yes, Father. Good night." Eliza went around the desk, leaned in and kissed his cheek. He looked more tired tonight than usual. She was sure his mind was occupied with thoughts on how to catch a madman, and so she did not want to keep him from his bit of solitary peace and quiet.

In her room, Eliza noticed her cape and frock coat hanging over the cabinet door of the armoire. Nanette had done a good job getting them clean. Eliza sighed. She'd be unable to walk the East End tomorrow in search of the prostitute, Catherine, but at least there'd be time to ask around the Royal Free Hospital. Degenerates from many London districts came there at one point or another for care. Someone was bound to know of one or two women named Catherine.

She hoped.

Chapter 7

Professor Huxley stood in the center of the room with a scalpel in one hand and the decapitated head of a man in the other. He made a circular incision around one of the cadaver's eye sockets then set the blade down on the table. "Move in closer, ladies. Mr. Smith here won't bite. He just wants to get a better look at you is all."

Everyone stepped in while Professor Huxley dug his fingers into the dead man's orbit. There were wet slushy sounds as he moved his digits about. When he pulled the eyeball out, it made a small pop. He proceeded to walk around with the head and the eyeball, showing everyone the ocular nerve and muscles.

All this time and the professor still continued to try and elicit some form of dramatic reaction from the women in class—perhaps with the hope some of them might change their minds. None of them would. They were all determined, just maybe not as much as Eliza, but who knew. Maybe she didn't give them enough credit. The university accepted students from near and far and from every walk of life. *Anyone* could apply, which was why her mother had been so against it. But the world needed more female physicians who understood and cared about the human condition as well as physiology and pharmacology. Doctoring encompassed so many facets of life, and Eliza knew she had what it took to be one of the best. Nothing would stop her from obtaining that goal. The title would earn her respect among her peers. Maybe other high-society women would take notice and try to further their education. It wasn't enough to be a lady from a good family who was destined to marry well. Not anymore. Times were changing.

After class, Eliza gathered her things and left the schoolhouse on Handel Street in search of a hansom cab to ride home. As she walked past the side of the old red brick building, she felt as though someone down the alleyway, between buildings, was watching her. Moving quickly and often looking behind her, Eliza had the sense of being followed and stalked. When she finally hailed a cab, it had never been such a relief to get in one. Eliza knocked on the underside of the roof with her fist to get the driver moving. As soon as they rounded the corner, she felt safe again. The sensation of being watched—gone. She sat back and sighed in relief, and wondered if it was her imagination. Who would wish to seek her out? Then she thought of her father and the detectives. Perhaps they were having her followed for safety reasons. She wouldn't put it past her father. It couldn't possibly be because they suspected her.

* * *

Upon arriving home, then entering her mother's parlor, Eliza had stepped back in time. Long panels of glorious white and ivory silks and laces were strewn across every piece of furniture. Strands of pearls and sparkling beads hung from the backs of chairs. Having gowns custom-made and sewn by hand was a regal indulgence. In an era when too many clothing factories were popping up and putting out ready-to-wear attire, and most ladies of society were traveling to Paris for their gowns and wedding clothes, superior London seamstresses such as Mrs. Plympton, were becoming more rare with each passing year. The Covingtons would never use anyone else, and her father insisted on spending their money in England. They preferred traditional methods and Eliza supported their ideas wholeheartedly.

"Good afternoon, Miss. It's good to see you again." Mrs. Plympton stepped up and shook hands with Eliza.

"What took you so long? We've been waiting nearly an hour," Lady Covington said from across the room.

Eliza rolled her eyes and Mrs. Plympton smiled. "Shall we get started then?" the seamstress said. "Oh my, what a lovely broach." She reached her hand up and gently touched it.

"It's my great-grandmother's."

"Will you be wearing it on your wedding day? I can design a special place for it on the neckline with some small ruffles encircling the piece, perhaps."

"That sounds lovely, Mrs. Plympton."

The broach was a bouquet of flowers made of fancy-cut diamonds and pearls. Eliza received it from her mother for her sixteenth birthday. The party was a glorious affair. *Hard to believe that was only two years ago.*

With the help of Mrs. Sutton, who was already there eyeing the fabrics, Eliza removed all her clothing except for her corset and drawers. Lady Covington sat in her favorite chaise, sipping tea, and nibbling on biscuits in between ordering everyone around.

"Your daughter has a very muscular build, Lady Covington," Mrs. Plympton said, sounding slightly shocked. She measured the length of Eliza's arms and legs, her waist, and every other part of her body with a measuring tape she uncoiled from an ivory case.

Lady Covington rose from the chaise to have a look. She put her hand around the bicep muscle of Eliza's right arm. "It appears you're right, Mrs. Plympton. What have you been doing girl, rowing boats down the river?"

"Tennis, Mother. And the archery events, when I can attend."

"Eliza is quite the archer, Mrs. Plympton. She has several winning pins. Tennis offers no such trophies," Lady Covington said the latter with less enthusiasm. She'd never been a fan of Eliza playing lawn tennis, always said it was much too physical a sport for a lady.

"Indeed, more active women tend to have bigger muscles."

"This won't affect the sleeves of her gown will it?"

"Not at all, Lady Covington, unless she carries a bouquet of iron flowers down the aisle."

"That is not the least bit amusing, Mrs. Plympton. You don't know how I've toiled over this wedding. I've done nothing but plan, organize, and worry for months. My daughter here shows no interest, and it wouldn't surprise me the slightest if she were to carry iron flowers."

"Is that so? Why do you put the task all on your mother?" Mrs. Plympton asked Eliza.

Lady Covington pulled a lace-edged handkerchief from up her sleeve and used it to dab her forehead as though she were overworked and perspiring. Eliza couldn't think of a time when she ever saw her mother do a bit of work, so the act was ridiculous and typically overdramatic. "Ouch," Eliza said. One of Mrs. Plympton's pins had stuck into her side a bit.

"Sorry," Mrs. Plympton said.

Lady Covington walked back over to the chaise and sat down.

"You've known my mother for years now, Mrs. Plympton," Eliza said in a soft voice.

"Why yes, nearly two decades."

"Then you of all people should know my mother has been planning this wedding for all that time."

Mrs. Plympton giggled and quickly put her hand over her mouth. When she was done, she went back to draping and pinning. "How right you are, Miss."

"I am simply my mother's daughter."

"Well said. And what's this I hear about you going off to America after the wedding?"

"It's true. Henry's father wants him to start up one of their banking establishments."

"I'm sure you'll be fine."

"It's not England, though. I will miss...everything." Eliza sighed.

"I'm sure you will."

With the mood turned melancholy, Mrs. Plympton began chatting with Lady Covington about some of the other ladies in town. Eliza stared off into space, her mind empty of thought.

Chapter 8

Dinner was early at the Covington house. Eliza joined her father in the study afterward and they had hardly begun to discuss the day when Mr. Sutton knocked on the door to announce the arrival of Inspector Frederick Abberline and a Doctor George Phillips.

Two men entered the room and immediately removed their hats at the sight of Eliza. "Good evening, gentlemen," Lord Covington said. "I was sure to dine early this evening in case you came again. This is my daughter, Eliza."

The inspector gently shook hands with her as did the doctor. Then they stared at one another, then at Lord Covington, and then at Eliza.

"My daughter's studying to be a physician at the London School of Medicine for Women," Lord Covington said, when the silence grew awkward.

"Interesting," said Inspector Abberline. He was a portly man, like Detective Godley. What little hair he had was a mix of red and gray. His moustache, beard, and sideburns were overly bushy as if to make up for the lack of it on top of his head. "Does she know of the murders in East End?" He said in a soft-spoken voice. The inspector's demeanor reminded Eliza of Henry's father, the banking magnate.

"Why don't you ask her?" Lord Covington said. He looked at her and winked.

"Well, Miss, have you thoughts on the Whitechapel killings?"

"Yes, inspector."

"And do you think it's possible a woman could have had a hand in it?"

"Inspector!" Lord Covington said. "What are you suggesting?"

"Doctor Phillips and I think there's a slight possibility a midwife would have what it takes to dissect these women the way we've been finding them."

"The knowledge, yes," said Lord Covington, "but the strength? Just look at Eliza. She has the skills to perform surgeries, but under a different set of circumstances entirely. Her patients are anesthetized, sedated. Even a drunkard puts up a fight, and she hasn't the build."

"Unless the victim has blacked out," said Doctor Phillips.

"Let her speak," said the inspector. "Answer the question please, miss."

"If they're already unconscious by strangulation," Eliza said. "Why bother stopping the job to slit their throats? It seems to me the perpetrator prefers to see the blood spilling out of his victims. More male in nature, I would think."

"Yes, I see your point. Thank you, Miss," the inspector said. He turned toward her father. "It was simply a theory, but after taking into consideration the barbaric nature of the crimes and the appearance of your daughter here, Lord Covington, I'm beginning to think it isn't possible. Her figure is so slight a strong wind might knock her over."

"Not all women are frail and weak, sir, no matter their physical appearance," Eliza said.

"Now this I know firsthand, Miss; my wife is neither one of those, but nor does she appear to be." All of the men roared with laughter. "However more masculine her figure may be compared to yours, Miss, she is also incapable of the heinous brutality exhibited by this madman."

"So, you are convinced the killer is a man now?" said Lord Covington.

"Yes, indeed I am."

"Good. Then the timing for your visit here was just right and my daughter's presence was to your benefit."

"It wouldn't be anything but, Lord Covington. Such a lovely girl."

"Eliza, pour us some brandy if you please, and then leave us to the rest of the evening. I will catch up with you on your progress tomorrow."

"Yes, Father."

Eliza did as she was asked, and the men became more involved with conversations about the murderer. When Inspector Abberline mentioned that the most recent victim's name was Annie Chapman,

Eliza was a bit surprised, yet her hand remained steady as she poured. She listened closely while they surmised that perhaps it might be a butcher, maybe even a doctor. But then Lord Covington mentioned the Hippocratic Oath.

"That doesn't rule out a failed doctor," Abberline said, and the others agreed with nods and 'ayes' that it was a possibility to consider.

Eliza left the room, relieved the inspector no longer had his sights on the possibility of a woman being the murderer. The next step was to find Catherine, the friend of Annie Chapman.

* * *

It was early afternoon when Eliza left the Royal Free Hospital. All week she sensed someone watching her, following her through the streets as she searched out a hansom. Eliza even started making the cab drivers take different routes and circle the park. Most of the time, it was only when she was on foot that she felt stalked. Still assuming it was someone her father had convinced to protect her, she did her best to ignore it.

Having time, Eliza took a cab to the London Hospital in East End to make some inquiries. After she paid the driver, Eliza pulled the hood of her cloak over and joined a crowd of factory workers heading back to work after their break. She walked past an open doorway and suddenly stopped when something inside caught her attention. The workers passed her by, and jostled her a bit as she stood there and stared at a blazing hearth fire. The image of a burning, sizzling uterus filled her vision, until someone inside closed the door. She blinked several times to clear the sight from her head then walked on.

Distracted by the grisly image, along with the feeling of being followed, Eliza inadvertently walked toward Spitalfields, near where she had killed Annie Chapman. Unnerved by her choice of direction, she turned around on Thrawl Street and walked back toward London Hospital when a scruffy young boy ran up to her in a fit of hysterics. Eliza jumped back.

"Miss!" the boy said. "My mother needs help. It's a baby."

"Where?" The fear and panic in the boy's voice charged Eliza.

He started running back toward Spitalfields and Eliza followed, glad now she kept herself active with sports, despite her mother's protests.

They arrived at one of the small shanties that lined Brick Lane. The boy came to a wooden door that was nearly falling off its hinges, flung it wide open, and pulled Eliza in.

"Mum, please help."

There was a small cot in the corner of the room where a woman was lying, moaning, and rolling back and forth. Eliza hastily removed her cape and frock coat, threw them over a chair, and rolled up her sleeves. She went up to the bed and saw the woman's face frozen in what at first appeared to be a smile and then resolved into a grimace of pain as Eliza drew closer. The woman's hands clutched the bed sheets in a death grip. Beaded sweat covered her forehead and her nightgown appeared damp, clinging tight to her bulging pregnant belly.

"Boy! Run to the London Hospital as fast as you can and find a Doctor James Riley. Tell him..." *Tell him what? I can use my influence to help this woman, but father, I don't know...oh bloody hell!* "Tell him Miss Covington sent you to fetch him. He needs to bring a carriage. Go now!"

The boy ran and slammed the door shut on his way out. The top hinge broke, and the door fell to one side leaving an open corner above. Eliza turned back to the woman and pulled the bed sheet down. Below the waist, her gown was soaked with blood, sweat, and amniotic fluid.

"What is your name?" Eliza said. There was a basin on a small table nearby.

"Louise," the woman said between grunts.

"Is this water clean?"

The woman nodded.

"How long has it been since the pain started?"

"'Bout three hours."

Eliza put her medical bag at the end of the cot and opened it. She pushed Louise's legs up, and they fell open and apart. "This is going to hurt," she said. "You will feel a lot of pressure. Try very hard to be still."

Louise nodded.

Eliza brought her fingers together into a point as best she could, then inserted them into Louise's vaginal opening. The woman let out a bloodcurdling scream that made Eliza see stars for a moment.

"Shush," Eliza said. "We don't want anyone barging in here thinking I'm hurting you. Pull the sheet up and bite down on it."

It didn't take long for her to feel the baby was breech. "Take quick short breaths," Eliza said. "That's good. And do *not* push. The baby's turned around." Eliza felt movement inside. "It's alive!"

Louise attempted a smile that quickly became a grimace, which was followed by a series of pants and grunts.

"I've got to rotate it," Eliza said. With her right hand still up inside the woman, she toppled her doctor's bag with her left hand and fingered through the items until she found a small leather case. Eliza popped it open and pulled a scalpel from its sheathed location. She looked up over the woman's belly to see her face. "I need to make a cut first. Brace yourself."

Eliza brought the scalpel forward and made an incision from where her forearm was inside Louise, nearly all the way down to her anus. The skin pulled apart and blood quickly filled the exposed area of open flesh. The woman screamed through the sheets and Eliza felt her pain—the pain only women seem to know and can relate to one another through.

"You're going to feel more pressure now," Eliza said as she pushed her other hand into Louise. She felt resistance. "Stop it! Don't push!" It let up and she continued.

Slowly, Eliza turned the baby until she felt its head. Louise was a hardy woman and did rather well considering Eliza was nearly up to her elbows with both hands and forearms inside her. She continued to scream, then grunt, and take quick short breaths.

"We're close," Eliza assured her, knowing she needed to work fast. She repositioned her hands and moved out just a bit. A contraction was beginning. "Push now, Louise. Push!"

The woman pushed, the contraction did its job, and Eliza had to pull the baby's head very little as her arms and hands were expelled from Louise's vagina, the infant right behind them.

Eliza caught the baby, held it up, and slapped it. When the newborn made its first wail, Louise let out a sigh and collapsed her legs onto the bed. Instruments in the open leather case at the foot of the bed flickered in the candlelight. Eliza pulled the case closer and removed a clamp. She put the umbilical cord between its metal teeth and brought them together. Then she took out a pair of scissors and cut the cord. It seemed she worked well under pressure, but she'd always known this. Delivering a breech baby was part common sense. *What do you do if a baby's positioned backwards? Turn it around.* Still, she was thankful for the midwifery classes at the university.

Louise tried to look up and see what Eliza was doing. For a moment, it was Annie Chapman's face she saw. Her eyes opened wide as saucers and she looked down expecting to see a bundle of gore in her arms, but instead saw the newborn. Eliza cut a clean piece of bed linen, wrapped it around the baby, and then handed it to the woman. "It's a girl," she said. "I've got to sew you up now."

Eliza stood and brought several more pieces of the cut bed linen over to the basin. As she wet the rags, the broken front door swung open on the one hinge and the boy barreled through it with Dr. James Riley close behind. "Thank goodness you're here at last," Eliza said.

"Looks like you've done just fine on your own."

"Yes, but..." Eliza thought about what to say. "I've got to get home, James. My father...I'm not allowed to be at London Hospital, the East End, because of the murders."

"And we've missed you very much." There was a slight smile on his face. Eliza knew he meant it. James had always been in love with her, but her father didn't approve. "But why—"

"Please, James. The baby was breech but I turned it around. She seems fine now. I was just going to sew her up. I thought she might need to go to the hospital."

"Don't worry about it. Take the carriage home."

"But how will you get back?"

"I'll walk, or take a hansom. You go on ahead."

"Oh thank you, James. You're a true friend."

He took a step closer to her. "It was good to see you again."

"And you too, James." Eliza leaned in and quickly pecked him on the cheek.

He smiled.

Eliza gathered her things and left without saying goodbye.

Chapter 9

Eliza couldn't get over her elation having just delivered a breech baby. The odds of that even happening and the infant surviving in the East End were staggering, but she'd done it. A part of her wanted so much to have the carriage stop at Henrietta Street so she could tell Professor Huxley, but she decided against it. The last thing she needed was anyone questioning why she'd been at East End, and she hoped James would not become a herald.

When Eliza arrived home, Mrs. Sutton met her in the foyer. "How was your day, Miss?"

"It was wonderful."

"Good to hear it. Your mother is in the parlor again and would like to speak with you."

"Can't it wait? I have to wash up."

"There's a man with her. They've been waiting a while."

"Please let them know they'll have to wait a little longer." Eliza huffed and headed upstairs.

She rushed cleaning up and changing, but was back downstairs within the hour. Before entering the parlor, she stood at the doorway and peeked into the room. A mousy-looking bald man wearing thin-wired spectacles sat in the Queen Anne chair next to her mother's chaise. There was a large group of assorted floral arrangements on her mother's Chippendale table in front of them. Lady Covington looked up and saw Eliza.

"What are you doing over there creeping about? Come in here and meet Mr. Grey. He's going to be doing the flowers for Michaelmas dinner. And if we like them, he may very well do the arrangements for your wedding." The florist got up, an eager smile on his face, and Lady Covington rose from the chaise. Together they walked toward Eliza.

"Mr. William Grey," the man said, extending his hand. "Hello, Miss."

Eliza went to shake it, but Mr. Grey gasped and jerked his arm away.

"What is it?" Lady Covington said. She looked down at Eliza's fingers, which were still in midair. "Catherine Elizabeth!"

Dried blood had caked around the cuticles, underneath the fingernails, and in the wrinkles of her knuckles. "Oh forgive me." Eliza lowered her hand. "I was sure I got it all off." She ran out of the room, while Lady Covington yelled for Mrs. Sutton.

A while later, Eliza returned to the parlor and there was tea and a tray of biscuits in front of Mr. Grey. For the next hour, they spoke of nothing but flowers. Eliza had never met such a man before—squeamish of a little blood but so knowledgeable about everything botanical. If he hadn't reacted the way he did when he saw her hand, her mother would never have noticed. This made Eliza dislike him. Particularly while watching him nibble on the corners of the biscuits and sipping tea. *Exactly like a mouse.*

"Pardon me, Mother, may I be excused? I'd like to lie down a bit before dinner."

"Yes, of course."

"Goodbye Mr. Grey. It was nice meeting you."

He stood up when Eliza did. "It was my pleasure. Oh, and silly me, I nearly forgot to ask. Please, tell me, what are your favorite flowers?"

"Lilies," she said, "white ones." Mr. Grey stood there, his face pale with wide eyes.

Lady Covington huffed. "Silly girl," she said. "Don't mind her, Mr. Grey. She knows nothing of feminine things such as flowers."

"Those are for funerals," he muttered. Eliza turned to leave the room.

* * *

As much as Eliza wanted to speak with her father after dinner, she was exhausted, and took her meal upstairs. Mrs. Sutton was kind and sympathetic, adding a piece of her scrumptious pear tart to the tray.

After eating, she rested her head on a pillow and quickly fell asleep. Eliza dreamt she was walking in the East End and Annie Chapman was following her. The uterus Eliza had removed and burned was dragging just behind the prostitute, connected by an umbilical cord that came out from the bottom of her skirt hem. "You won't get away from me," Annie yelled. "You're a murderer!"

Eliza quickened her pace, but so did Annie. In her haste, Eliza tripped on a broken cobblestone and fell onto the wet filth that covered the street. Her hand landed in one of the cesspool puddles and splashed muck onto her face and into her mouth. A bitter-tasting grit stuck to her tongue, and she turned her head to the side and spat. The prostitute caught up to her and launched her body on top of Eliza's, pinning her down. Eliza struggled, and when she tried to call out for help, Annie grabbed the back of her head and pushed her face down into a puddle. Eliza fought harder, kicking and grabbing at the woman. Her skin stung from scraping against the abrasive pavement. Then Annie grabbed her by the shoulders and started shaking her violently, smashing Eliza's face against the foul, slimy wet ground.

"Wake up, Eliza! It's a bad dream." Her father's voice called out. She opened her eyes and saw his hands on her arms.

"Father," she cried. He pulled her close to him.

"Do you want to talk about it?"

"No." She sobbed into his shirt.

"I was just going to bed when I heard you screaming. Did you have a bad day?"

She shook her head. "I had a fabulous day. You would have

been proud."

"I'm always proud, dear." He moved her away from him, and she lay back down in bed.

"Thank you, Father."

"Good night. We can talk about this in the morning if you like."

Eliza nodded and closed her eyes.

This time, no nightmares of the dead invaded her sleep.

Chapter 10

Lord Covington wasn't at breakfast the next morning. "Where's father," Eliza asked.

"He was called out very early."

"The Royal Family? Is someone ill?"

"I don't know the details. You'll have to ask your father."

"You look a little tired."

"Well, it's no wonder with his coming to bed so late then having to leave at all hours."

"Maybe you should take a nap."

Lady Covington sighed. "I suppose I will. For once I've a break from wedding planning."

"Then make good use of it. I'll try and come home early."

"It would be nice to have you home. You'll be leaving me soon."

"Please, don't start." Eliza downed her tea, grabbed her toast, and rose from her seat. "I've got to go."

Her mother was still talking when she went out to the foyer to put on her coat and grab the doctor's bag. Eliza made sure she'd had her cloak as well, hoping to try the London Hospital again if she finished before schedule. There was also the issue of talking to James about keeping quiet regarding what happened. Then she had the other prostitute, Catherine, to locate and take care of.

Despite the promise she'd made to her mother, she knew it was going to be a long day.

* * *

"Miss Covington, I heard news of someone delivering a breech baby at East End yesterday. Would you happen to know who that was?"

"Um...no, sir."

"I heard there were some great heroics and quick thinking involved."

"Indeed?"

Professor Huxley smiled and continued dissecting a cadaver spleen. Who would have thought the artery attached to it was so large?

At the end of class, the professor announced that three girls would soon be graduating. "Miss Blake, Miss Johnson, and Miss Covington will be moving on the latter part of this November." The rest of the women knocked on their books and cheered.

Eliza was in high spirits when she left Henrietta Street and took a hansom to the London Hospital at East End. So much so, she never noticed someone following her until, like in her nightmare, she stumbled on a broken cobblestone and fell onto her hands. This triggered the memory of the dream and a feeling of unease. Eliza looked behind her and caught a glimpse of a woman ducking into an alleyway. A couple of men walking by stopped and asked if she was all right, then helped her get back on her feet.

"I thought I saw someone down there." She pointed to the alley.

One of the men went to investigate. He walked halfway to the end. "No one here, Miss."

Feeling silly, she brushed herself off and thanked them, then went straight to the hospital.

Eliza greeted a few midwives and nurses she knew. "Where is Doctor Riley?" she asked Helen, one of the newer nurses.

"He's in C Ward, Miss."

"Thank you." Eliza headed to the area where they kept patients with breathing disorders.

Doctor Riley was writing in a patient chart when he turned and saw her walking toward him. He smiled and put the chart down. "I wasn't expecting to see you again so soon," he said.

"You didn't tell Professor Huxley did you?"

"Don't be upset."

"James, you—"

"Doctor Morton was the only person I told, and I swore him to secrecy."

"He's good friends with Professor Huxley. You knew that. How could you?"

"I had to tell somebody, Eliza. You were simply amazing."

"It *was* rather exciting news to keep quiet." She made a small smile. James was too innocent in his intentions to get distressed over. "Just promise me you'll tell no one else."

"I promise, and I don't think Huxley will say anything either. He's more afraid of your father than anyone I know. I'll never figure that one out."

"Father yelled at him once about a mistake he made regarding something he told a patient. Humiliated him essentially, and it hurt...practically ruined his reputation."

"Ah, that makes sense. Always wondered why a man would go into teaching women."

"James, you're horrible."

Doctor Riley laughed. "You know I'm teasing."

"Thank you again for coming to my rescue yesterday. It really meant a lot to me."

"You know I would've, I *would* do anything to help."

"I understand." Eliza leaned closer to him and kissed his cheek again.

"You really have to stop doing that, you know."

"Why?"

"It wrecks me for the next day or two."

"That's silly. Come on, I'll help you make rounds."

The two doctors worked side by side for the rest of the afternoon. Eliza used it as an opportunity to quietly ask patients she thought might be the street-working type if they knew any women named Catherine, and she would give them a brief description. She didn't gain any leads, but she enjoyed her time spent with James. Eliza had forgotten how fond she was of him. When they'd finished seeing patients, James walked Eliza out and they said their goodbyes.

Outside, it had begun to rain. Eliza pulled her hood over and walked quickly down the street. She passed an alley and heard someone shout out. "Miss Jane!"

Eliza stepped back, looked up and down the street to see if she saw anyone she knew, then headed down the alley. Behind some wooden crates, a woman was huddled against the wall. "Can I help you?" Eliza said.

"I'm sure you can." The woman looked up at Eliza. At once, she knew that long rat face. It was Catherine. The prostitute was filthy, and smiling up at Eliza with a missing tooth and a blackened right eye.

"What do you want?"

"You've got to know. Lucky I didn't turn you in."

"Have you been following me?"

"You bet I have. Can't let my future slip away, if you know what I'm saying."

Eliza's heart began to race. This harlot knew where she came and went. "What exactly are you saying?"

"Don't play dumb with me, miss. I want your money."

"I don't have any."

"You must have some! I've seen you take hansom after hansom. I was never able to follow you past East End. You could be heading home to Buckingham Palace for all I know. The one time I saw you on Henrietta Street I was taking a friend up to the Royal Free Hospital. She's all uppity these days and prefers it, and that's when I saw you leaving and followed you 'til you caught a hansom. So I'm smart enough to know you've got a lot of cab money, Miss." Catherine stopped talking. Her eyes targeted something on Eliza and then widened a bit.

Eliza looked down and saw her great-grandmother's broach through the keyholes of her cloak and frock coat. Her heart sunk.

"That'll do," Catherine said with a wicked smile pointing to the broach.

Eliza gasped and tightened the cloak around her neck. "I can't. It's a family heirloom."

"I don't care whose family it belongs to. If you want me to keep quiet, you'll be giving that to me."

Unable to catch her breath, Eliza began to hyperventilate.

"Don't go faking sick on me. I'll scream out, I will."

"I'm not." Eliza gasped and tried to think quickly. She reached into her pocket and pulled out a small silk pouch with a drawstring. "Take this," she said. "It's all I've got."

"Why thank you, Miss." Catherine snatched the pouch out of her hand. "But I'll still be wanting that pretty pin."

"Please, not now, let me think about how I'll explain it going missing. It's my mother's. She only leant it to me. The excuse will have to be a good one because she'll have every copper in London looking for it when it's gone. You see, this broach is highly unusual and, well, if you're found trying to sell it—"

"Fine, then! You think of a good way to hand it over. And don't you try and give me the slip. I know where to find you."

"Come to me in three days. I should have a plan by then."

"Aye, you better."

"But don't meet me near the hospital. It's too risky that I'll run into someone I know. Perhaps we've been seen already." Eliza turned and looked up the alley. No one was in sight.

"Where then?" Catherine said.

Eliza turned back. "Someplace farther away, but still busy," she mumbled while thinking hard and fast for a plan. "Mitre Square, about the same time as now."

"Don't try and cross me."

As Eliza's idea was coming to a realization, she felt herself mentally getting stronger. Then she became angry. "I won't. And don't ever threaten me again." She pointed her finger down at the Catherine's face.

The woman rose slightly, opened her mouth and put it around Eliza's gloved finger, then sucked it. Eliza pulled her hand away, repulsed by the harlot's vile actions. Catherine cackled as Eliza ran.

She heard coins jingling in the pouch from the alleyway behind her.

Chapter 11

Eliza barged through the doors of London Hospital out of breath and asking for Doctor Riley. When James met her in the lobby, she pulled him to a corner away from prying eyes. "James, I was robbed."

"What? Here, just outside?" He began to move toward the door.

Eliza grabbed his arm and yanked him back. "You can't make a fuss, James. I'm not supposed to be here."

"It's not right. We should send for the police."

"Absolutely not!"

Several people on the other side of the lobby, including the receptionist and two nurses, looked over at them.

"You're being ridiculous," he said. "You could've been hurt."

"But I wasn't. Please understand, James. My father—"

"Yes, don't remind me. I know his temperament all too well."

"Then help."

"How?"

"Have your carriage bring me home."

James stood there for a moment and appeared to be deep in thought. "I'll agree, with one condition."

"What is it? Anything."

"Promise you'll come back and work with me like you did today." He pulled Eliza closer to him and looked into her eyes.

Eliza turned her head and saw the other women in the lobby had continued to stare. "James, I—"

"It was one of the best days I've had in quite some time. Please, I'm not asking for anything else but for us to work together a few times more."

"All right. I'll try."

"Thank you." He lifted her hand and kissed it. "I'll send for the carriage." James gently released her hand, then walked over to the receptionist and nurses standing across the room. A moment later, the receptionist got up from her desk and walked down a long hallway and the nurses dispersed.

* * *

While the carriage horses clopped through the East End, Eliza took off her gloves, then reached up and caressed her great-grandmother's broach. There wasn't any conceivable way she could give it to a wretch such as Catherine. The mere thought made her seethe and grind her teeth. A moment later, she felt pain and moved her hand away. Eliza had been clutching the broach so hard some of the sharper edges of the setting had left minute pinpricks of blood on her palm. She put her hand up and licked the wounds, then put the gloves back on.

The carriage arrived on Queen Anne Street and the driver helped Eliza step out. She thanked him and then headed into the house. Nanette was in the foyer ready to take her hat, coat, and gloves. "Where is Mrs. Sutton?" she said.

"Last I saw, she was bringing your father tea in his study."

"My father's home?"

"Yes, Miss."

"For how long?"

"Since a bit after noon."

"He never comes home early. Is something wrong? What happened?"

"I don't know, Miss."

"Suppose I'll have to go and find out myself. Thank you, Nanette."

The maid curtsied and quickly left the room before Eliza could ask her anymore questions. Eliza slowly walked toward her father's study. She looked into the parlor on the way, hoping her mother would be there to distract her for a while. The room was empty. Knots in her stomach, she stood in front of the study doors gathering her thoughts before knocking.

"Come in, Eliza," her father said.

She turned the crystal knob, which stung her injured palm, and entered the room. Lord Covington sat in a chair next to the fireplace with a book on his lap.

"Hello, Father."

"Come in and close the door. Take a seat next to me here by the fire. You must be chilled. I saw you arrive in an open carriage."

Eliza walked over and sat in the chair opposite his, on the other side of the fireplace. "It's been a long day," she said.

"Was that Doctor Riley's carriage?"

"Yes, it was. I was on my way home and he saw me in Regent's Park. We spoke for a bit and he offered me a ride."

"Why didn't he come with you? I saw no one else in the carriage."

"He was waiting for someone."

"I see. And how is he? Gotten over you by now, I'd think."

"Yes, Father, I'm sure. We are only friends."

"Good. Good."

"What are you reading?" she said, pointing to the book in his lap, changing the subject.

"I was looking through this old picture book your mother kept."

Eliza got up and sat on the floor next to her father's chair. Together they went over the photos and Lord Covington explained each one. What the event was, where it was taken, and all the details. She watched her father's facial expressions go from joy at the earlier pages to somber toward the end when he got to a photo of his grandmother. Eliza treasured these dear moments spent with him; they melted her heart. Until she noticed the diamond broach her great-grandmother wore pinned to her dress.

That moment turned her heart to stone.

* * *

At dinner, Eliza ate very little and her mother took notice.

"If you don't eat, you will get too thin and your dress will have to be altered."

"Let her be, dear. She's had a long day," her father said.

Her mother sighed.

For the remainder of the courses, Eliza moved food with her silverware back and forth across the china without ever taking a bite. Her thoughts were miles away, but not filled with marriage plans, her wedding night, moving to another country, or regrets about James like her parents might have believed. Eliza felt an intense gnawing in her belly from the inside out over what to do about Catherine.

After dinner, she joined her father in his study hoping to discuss medicine and take her mind off of the predicament she was in.

"You seem bothered, Eliza. Pour yourself a bit of brandy and come sit by the fire."

"I'm all right, Father. Professor Huxley announced the graduates today."

"Ah, and it's all coming down on you like a ton of bricks now is it?"

"I suppose."

Eliza changed her mind and poured herself a bit of brandy, brought her father a snifter full and then sat down with hers, taking small sips while her father talked about his day.

"Mother said you were called in early today. Is everything all right with the Royals?"

"Yes, fine. One of the visiting little grand princes got a bit of the sniffles is all."

"Oh."

"We haven't spoken much about you going off to America. I imagine this must be weighing heavy on your thoughts, but you shouldn't worry. Henry's a smart man. He won't leave you alone in a strange place."

"He'll be busy working late nights, I imagine."

"What will you do?"

"Bring my graduation papers, find work if I can. Volunteer at hospitals if I have to."

"Do you think Henry would allow it?"

"If he doesn't want me to go mad he will."

Lord Covington laughed, then took a swig of brandy and swallowed. He said nothing.

"You don't think he'll want me to practice?" she said.

"I don't know. We haven't spoken about it."

"If you do, can you mention it to him? Persuade him, perhaps?"

"I'll try," he said, then took another drink.

Eliza wasn't comforted by their conversations this evening like she usually was. The talk only made her more nervous and upset about the future.

When she went to bed that night, she thought further on how to remedy the situation with Catherine. Dreams of hate and murder kept her mind occupied.

Chapter 12

"Mrs. Sutton, would you please send a note to Ann Williams this morning? Ask her if it would be all right if I call on her this afternoon."

"Yes, Miss."

"Well," her mother said. "It's about time. I'd almost forgotten myself."

"Do you think she'll see me on such short notice?"

"She hardly ever leaves the house these days. I'm sure she'll be happy for your visit, but why the sudden interest?"

"It's been too long, and I may not get another chance. Exams are next month, then graduation, then the wedding, and then I leave."

"Don't make it all sound so rushed."

"But it is."

"Oh Eliza, you have such a talent for dramatics."

"I do not."

Eliza's father entered the room. "It's too early for bickering, ladies." He took a seat at the breakfast table. "If you continue, I'll leave without taking a single bite."

Eliza and her mother both leaned back in their chairs and finished eating their toast.

"I say, now that's more like it," he said.

* * *

During classes, Eliza debated whether to go and work with

James as she'd promised. Then it came to her that it would probably be best if she went when it was time to meet Catherine again. The vivid dreams and nightmares she'd had the past couple nights—in bits and pieces—had given her an idea. A plan she knew would work if done exactly right. She just needed time and a clear mind to devise it and see it through.

More than ever, she looked forward to visiting with Ann Williams later that afternoon. Eliza hoped she might improve her friend's melancholy situation and forget about her own tumultuous one. At least for Eliza's sake, she was sure Ann would leave her house to attend the wedding in December. Eliza hated to see any acquaintance of hers upset or sad.

On her way home, she stopped at White's Chocolate House on St. James Street and had a cup to drink, then picked up several pieces of eating chocolate for Ann. For the first time in days, she didn't feel the presence of anyone watching her. She was certain then that it was Catherine who had been following her the entire time. There was no detective, no one her father had hired. Eliza was fortunate the woman never approached her in public. It was also good she hadn't gotten hurt. Catherine could have attacked her and simply stolen the broach. These thoughts made Eliza's heart beat harder and faster. She clenched her hands into fists. A slow-building heat full of rage moved from her chest upward, coating the skin around her neck and head with fire. Eliza, who was certain her face must be brick red, took in deep breaths to try to calm herself before arriving home earlier than usual. She didn't need any unwanted attention from her mother.

There was no one in the foyer when she came through the front doors, so she ran upstairs and began to change into something more appropriate for her visit with Ann. After she was dressed, Nanette came in and helped her fix her hair.

"Did Mrs. Sutton say that Mrs. Williams would see me? We could be doing this all for nothing."

"She did, miss. The carriage is waiting for you out front."

"Thank you."

"You're welcome, and don't forget the little box of eating

chocolates I saw on the foyer table. If Lord Covington or your mother sees them they might very well disappear."

Eliza laughed. "Funny how they say they dislike it, but behind closed doors…"

Nanette smiled. "I'll meet you downstairs to help you with your coat and hat." Then she left the room.

Moments later, Eliza was out the door and in the carriage to go just up the street. Any other day she would have walked, but it was drizzling out, and she wanted to look her best for Ann, whom she hadn't seen in quite some time.

When she arrived at the Williams's home, she was greeted at the front door by one of the maids, then brought to Ann who had been waiting for her in the atrium with a tray of tea and cookies on a side table. The Williams's house was lovely and Eliza had always thought it suited them.

Doctor Jonathan Williams was recently knighted by the Queen and worked sometimes alongside Eliza's father on more difficult cases. Ann had married him when she was 22. He was ten years her senior and it was a bit of a scandal because of his rank in society at the time, but then it was all soon gotten over because of his excellent skill and reputation.

Since then, Ann had gone into a deep depression because her father's tin business went under and as hard as she and Jon tried, she was unable to get pregnant. All the solemn news was too much for Eliza to handle with everything she had going on in her own life. She tried her best to comfort Ann and divert her attention when she could, but all Ann's woes, along with being unable to get pregnant, kept Eliza away. But she had the excuse of medical school and her own wedding to plan. Ann of all people knew the amount of work and education involved with becoming a physician.

When Eliza entered the room Ann looked up and stood to greet her. "You look absolutely radiant," Ann said in a monotone voice. Her face was peaked and expressionless.

Eliza smiled. She had hoped her attire and attitude would bring some cheer to her friend, but it didn't seem to have worked. Despite her kind welcome, there was deep hurt and longing in

Ann's eyes. "Forgive me for not coming to see you sooner. How have you been?" Eliza said.

The two women hugged. "Please, sit down," Ann said, pointing to the spot on the settee next to where she had been seated a moment ago.

Feeling the weight of the day's classes, and work, along with the sad expression on her friend's face, Eliza sank into the cushion when she sat. The Williams's maid began pouring them cups of tea. "Just a bit of milk in mine, please," Eliza said.

After the servant left, Eliza reached for Ann's hands and turned to face her. "Please, my dear friend. Tell me how you truly are and don't hold back."

Ann's eyes immediately filled with tears. Before Eliza could pull a handkerchief from her sleeve, her friend was crying. Eliza handed it to Ann, and she dabbed her eyes. "I'm sorry, it's just that things have been...well, they've been horrible."

"Please, tell me. What is it?" Eliza said. "Is it Sir Jon?"

Ann nodded.

"Has he done something against you?"

She nodded again.

"This is horrible news indeed," Eliza said. "Another woman?"

Her friend nodded again.

So, the rumors are true. Doctor Williams practiced at the London Hospital in East End. He performed abortions on prostitutes as well, but overcharged for them, which was not honorable in Eliza's eyes. She'd also heard stories that he might've been having affairs with some of these women. It disgusted her. She could feel hatred rising from the pit of her stomach.

Ann slowed her crying to whimpering. Eliza offered her the cup of tea the maid had just poured. She raised the cup and saucer and took a small sip. "Thank you," she said.

"Don't think of it," Eliza said. "Thanking me, I mean."

"I can do nothing but, and not about thanking you, but about *her*."

"Do you have a name? Is it someone you know?"

Ann shook her head, and then after a whimper, she said,

"Mary Kelly."

"I've not heard the name before."

"She might be a prostitute." Ann started crying again and Eliza took the teacup from her shaking hand and set it down on the table. Then she held her friend while Ann cried for at least ten minutes more.

"I will never quite understand how you endure it," Eliza said.

"Maybe after you're married it will come to light."

"I hope not. I'd like to leave some of *the ways* of English marriage behind when we go."

"That's a shocking thing to say."

"And what you've told me isn't? It pains me to see you like this."

Ann wiped her face one last time with Eliza's handkerchief, then handed it back to her. There were very few signs on her face that showed she had just been crying. She looked almost the way she did when Eliza first walked into the room. It was simultaneously sad and amazing to see her friend so changeable. Eliza worried that Ann might be skirting the edge of mental illness, possibly mania, and she wanted to help her friend before it was too late. Time was running out, though. She would be leaving very early the next year. Eliza wondered what she could do.

It was all the fault of the East End harlots. Eliza's hate for them had been gradually worsening, and this last bit of news had brought it to its peak. The prostitutes used to be a means of learning the worst cases of venereal disease and the female anatomy, but now they'd become a nuisance. Eliza thought about how it could be that these women's lives could be so intertwined with women like herself and Ann Williams. It just didn't seem possible. Times were changing, and she could already feel its effect on her.

And she didn't like it.

* * *

It had been three long days since Catherine threatened Eliza with a scheme of blackmail. Three days during which Eliza's loathing for the whores of the East End continued to grow.

She worked alongside Doctor James Riley, but he couldn't have enjoyed it the same way he did before, since Eliza was now always so distant and deep in thought about meeting up with Catherine and her visit the other day with her friend, Ann Williams. James tried several times to be humorous, or strike up a conversation, and failed miserably at getting her attention. It wasn't until he asked how she and Henry were getting along that she woke from her daze.

"What?" Eliza whispered.

"Have you heard a word I've said? What has your mind so occupied these days?"

"I'm sorry, James. It's the exams, the wedding, moving. Tell me something, do you know Sir Jon Williams very well?"

"I wouldn't say I know him *very* well, but I see him on occasion here and we talk about medicine. Why?"

"Have you heard any rumors about him?"

"These halls are filled with talk about other people, but I don't bother paying attention to any of it and neither should you."

"Do you think it's true he sees prostitutes?"

"Well, of course he sees them. Sir Jon is here every Friday to perform abortions."

"That's not what I mean, and I think it's wrong of him to make them pay so much."

"He accepts what they can afford. It's better than having one done on the street."

"You don't understand what I'm trying to say."

"And what exactly is it? You think Sir Jon is having an affair with a prostitute? Don't be silly. You need to get that notion out of your head. Talk like that can ruin your career. And his. Let's take a break and have some tea. Then we can discuss what it really is you're trying to say."

"I'll be fine."

"I know I made you promise to work with me a few more times, but I understand you're busy, and if you'd rather not—"

"James, I'm all right. A promise is a promise. Let's just finish up the day and go home."

Doctor Riley lowered his head. "My intention was for us to enjoy the last few times we would see one another doing something we both love, not for you to be in a rush and leave."

"Forgive me. Truly, I'm in no hurry to go. I never was. Please believe me when I tell you that I want to spend these moments with you. The memories I'll take with me and cherish always."

Eliza saw James's eyes well up. He turned away and spoke. "Don't apologize. It was my own selfishness that wanted this and if it hurts me, then only I'm to blame."

She took him by the arm. "I think I'd like some tea now," she said, and then she led him down the hall with a broken heart and a mind seething with rage.

* * *

Eliza left the London Hospital in the rain and told the driver to circle around before heading to Mitre Square. He did, and it gave her a little more time to ready herself. She put on her black cloak and pulled the hood over. There was a small pouch of money underneath where she kept the leather case of instruments. Eliza pulled it out and pushed it down into the pocket of her coat.

The driver stopped and pounded on the roof of the cab. Eliza stepped out, paid the man, and started walking in the rain. It wasn't long before she felt someone following her. *I know this game, and I can play, too.* She ducked down an alley, picked up her pace, and made a few quick turns, then stopped. Twenty feet in front of her, stood Catherine, looking side to side down backstreets in a frantic search.

"Lose something?" Eliza said.

Catherine swung around and gasped. "There you are, Miss. Thought you might be trying to give me the slip." She went over to where Eliza was standing.

"I would never do something like that."

"I knew you were a smart girl. Now, tell me your plan."

"Remember I told you if the broach went missing, the police

would go looking for it?"

"I do."

"Well, I've found a jeweler who will disassemble it for me so that I can give you the loose diamonds to sell individually. They'll be unable to trace it that way."

"Shame to break up such a pretty piece."

"Do you want the deal or not? It's the best I can do."

"How long will it take?"

"By Michaelmas."

"That long?"

"It's only two weeks, and besides, it's a delicate matter."

"I suppose it'll make for a great holiday surprise. For me anyhow." She cackled and then started coughing. Cleared her throat, then spat to the right. "What am I supposed to do in the meantime? I need a little drink now and then. Helps me keep my mouth shut if you know what I mean."

Eliza shoved her hand down into the cloak pocket and pulled out the pouch. "Here's five shillings. Should keep you quiet for a while."

"Indeed, miss. It will." Catherine smiled, exposing her missing tooth and grungy mouth.

"Meet me back here Michaelmas night."

"Good idea. Lots of people will be out celebrating, me right along with them."

"I don't want to see you until then, and if I feel you following me, the deal's off."

"No need to make threats. I'll leave 'ya be."

Catherine walked away shaking the coin pouch, humming a song Eliza didn't recognize, which didn't surprise her. She wanted nothing in common with this vile and loathsome woman.

Chapter 13

September 29th, the Covington house was filled with happy familiar faces ready for Michaelmas cheer. For Eliza, though, the holiday no longer seemed a joyous occasion as she often found herself checking the time. Doctor Llewellyn had come for dinner and Eliza's father was very happy to see his old friend again, but it meant she would have less time to spend with him. The men would finish their meals, then be drinking and smoking cigars until it was time to retire. Lady Covington would excuse herself and go to bed early blaming an exhaustion headache for all the work she did to make the dinner party a success.

"Eliza, there you are, darling. I've missed you." Henry stepped up, leaned in and gave her a simple kiss on the cheek. There was no passion in it. She felt domestic already and wondered whom he was truly saving his desires for.

"It's good to see you again," she said.

"I'm looking forward to when I see you every day."

She smiled. *I'm sure of it.* "I think it's time to sit down for dinner. We should go before my mother sends someone to look for us."

"I hope she placed us close to one another. Sometimes I'm certain your parents are determined to keep us apart until the wedding." He put his arm around her and pulled her close. Eliza moved out of his embrace. "What's wrong?"

"Nothing. Now come on." She took his hand and led him away.

The dining room was elegant. There were twenty chairs lining either side of the long rectangular king's table. Candlelight flickered off the silverware and set aglow the white and yellow rose bouquets. It appeared as though Mr. Grey and all his botanical knowledge had come through. No doubt, he'd be doing the flower arrangements for the wedding.

"There you are. Henry, you're over here next to me," Lady Covington said. He turned to Eliza and winked before walking to his seat. "Eliza, you're next to Doctor Llewellyn." Her mother pointed to the other end of the table.

Eliza grinned and hurried over. The doctor rose and pulled out her chair. "I'm delighted you were able to join us," she said.

"It was generous of your family to have invited me."

"Is your wife here? I'd very much like to meet her." Eliza looked up and down the table.

"She passed away two years ago."

"Oh, I'm so sorry." *I might've known that if Father had kept up your friendship.*

"Please, don't be. She's in a better place."

"Yes," was all Eliza could say. Doctor Llewellyn took a drink of wine and she did the same.

In perfect time, Mr. Sutton brought out a platter with a cooked goose on top. He set it down in front of them. Eliza eyed its spread legs, stuffing spilling from the cavity. In her mind she saw Annie Chapman and thought of how she'd pulled out her intestines, piling them over to one side so they would be out of the way. Immediately, her appetite disappeared.

"Any news?" she said.

Doctor Llewellyn looked at her and wrinkled his brow.

"Concerning Whitechapel."

"Just conjecture. No solid leads. I even heard Inspector Abberline came by for a visit with a midwife theory."

"That he did, but I'm sure I redirected him."

"So, you don't think it's possible the killer is a woman?"

Eliza struggled to come up with a response, but then Llewellyn spared her by putting his hand over hers. "I'm in agreement with you." He gently turned her hand palm side up. "No one would think these hands could be used for anything but good." The tiny scabs from where the broach had pricked her were still barely visible, but Doctor Llewellyn made no mention of them.

Lord Covington, seated at the very end of the table, raised his glass and tapped it with a spoon. Eliza slid her hand out of Doctor Llewellyn's. There was something she didn't like about his touch, and now she wished she were sitting next to Henry after all. Her father cleared his throat and made a longwinded holiday toast to his friends and family. He mentioned her upcoming graduation, wedding, and even choked up a bit when he spoke of her leaving for America. There were a few yawns during the speech and more than one couple was distracted whispering to one another, so that when he finally got to the end of it, everyone cheered, and Eliza knew it wasn't because she was moving after the wedding, but she couldn't help feel that way.

* * *

An hour before midnight Eliza sneaked out of the house. The air outside was thick with a cold damp fog. Benches normally visible in the daylight hours had completely vanished. The dense haze made the surrounding gas lamps ineffective. They reminded her of the way a lighthouse appeared from a ship's point of view, dim and feeble.

A few more people were out than usual at the late hour and she assumed it was because of the holiday. Their footsteps tapped on the wet cobblestones, the sounds coming from all directions before anyone would actually physically appear. They walked through the fog and it moved around them like a ghostly smoke dragon. She considered returning home more than once, crawling into her warm bed, and ignoring Catherine's demands. Who did this prostitute think she was that she could blackmail anybody? It angered Eliza to be caught in the middle of such a vile woman's scheme. She shouldn't have to sneak around in bad weather. Her nose was bitter cold, and watery mucous ran from her nostrils, over her lips, leaving a salty taste in her mouth. She wiped it away with her sleeve. Eliza feared the possibility she might become ill and be unable to finish her final exams. These thoughts only fueled her rage as she rushed through Regent's Park wearing a frock coat and hooded cloak, the doctor's bag clutched in her hand.

Eliza followed the louder sounds of hooves clopping; it wasn't long before she was able to get a hansom cab. While inside, she opened her bag and rearranged it, putting the items she'd need on top. The carriage came to a halt and the driver knocked on the roof. Eliza stepped out into a large puddle of murky water, sending up the odor of raw sewage. She clenched her jaw and ground her teeth together, then covered her nose with a scarf she'd stolen from Nanette and paid the man. He pulled away to avoid splashing her, and she was thankful for it.

When he was out of sight, Eliza went toward Mitre Square. There were even more people out on the streets at East End than usual. She knew Catherine would be one of them. Every few minutes, someone would come out of the fog and if it weren't for all the wine she'd had at dinner, she'd probably be a little jumpy.

A block away from the square, she heard a woman shouting slurred obscenities. Eliza walked softly behind where the sounds were coming from. She looked down an alley and saw the shadow figure of Catherine leaning against one of the walls. As Eliza approached, a small group of loud partygoers were walking by. She set her medical bag down and then crept closer, her footfalls silent compared to all the noise. Catherine was drunk and shouting at them about how she would soon be rich.

Eliza's heart sped up as she quietly waited behind the prostitute. After the people had passed, the prostitute took in a deep breath and paused. As she exhaled, Eliza held up the ends of Nanette's scarf, which were tightly wound around each of her hands, leaving some space left in between. Eliza quickly brought the scarf down hard against the prostitute's throat. Catherine tried to scream, but her words were choked off by the pressure against her neck. Eliza dragged the kicking, thrashing woman into the alley. The backward movement and struggle only made the scarf tighten more, and Catherine's choking turned to weak gasps for air.

After about fifteen feet, the prostitute's fight slowed. The fog hid them in the alley. Eliza could no longer see the street at the other end. She continued to pull Catherine by the scarf until the woman's body went limp. When it did, Eliza moved the fabric away and let her body fall to the ground. She came around and kneeled beside the body, took her right glove off and checked for a pulse. The prostitute was still alive, barely, which was what Eliza had wanted. She put her glove back on, and then reached into the medical bag she had placed there earlier. The surgical knife was right on top.

Nanette's scarf had left deep red marks across Catherine's throat. While positioning herself over the unconscious harlot, Eliza lifted up her own skirts, forgetting that they'd been splashed with sewage. When she caught a whiff of the foul stench that soaked the hems it made her even more furious, so she plopped herself down hard onto Catherine's abdomen. The woman groaned underneath her. Eliza leaned forward and stared at the wretched woman's face. Hate filled her with an extreme heat that spread throughout her extremities. Eliza tightened her grip around the knife and gritted her teeth. Catherine opened her eyes and saw Eliza on top of her. With one long stroke of her arm she sliced through Catherine's neck. The prostitute convulsed between Eliza's legs. She moved her lips and tried to talk, but no words could escape. There was only a gurgling sound that came from the open wound as hot blood pulsed out, steam rising from its crimson flows.

Still enraged, Eliza slashed the long, drawn face she hated more than anything in the world. *One V for vile, and one for vulgar!* The carving didn't stop until Catherine's body ceased to twitch. Eliza envisioned the woman's pupils dilating. She wanted to see the woman die and be the last person the whore saw before she did. Eliza exhaled a deep sigh of relief. The torment of being blackmailed was over. It was time to cover up her crime and make it the Whitechapel Murderer's. She got off the body and kneeled down next to it. Eliza pulled up Catherine's skirts and began her work below. She took her time, remembering how she'd cut up Annie Chapman. It had to look the same, but progressively worse. In honor of Professor Huxley humiliating her because she'd confused the kidneys with the ovaries, she excised one for him, as well as the uterus. Eliza thought of what her father had said that night in his study. *"The killer is evolving."*

"Indeed, father," she whispered. "The killer most certainly is."

She finished laying the extracted uterus and kidney onto Nanette's scarf. Eliza was tying up the ends when she heard a police whistle and shouting somewhere in the fog. Uncertain of the direction or distance of the sounds, she hurried the rest of what she was doing. Out of fabric to clean her instruments, she cut off half of Catherine's apron. Small bits of junk came out of the pockets and landed scattered on and around the body. Eliza shoved the cloth into her pocket, then set the organs in her medical bag, and stood up. She pulled the cloak hood over her head and walked quickly into the boggy mist, avoiding any people out on the streets.

After passing a man who nearly bumped into her, then pardoned himself, Eliza ducked into a dark doorway, took the swatch of cloth from her pocket, and quickly wiped off her dirty instruments. She threw the fabric down, placed her tools back into the medical bag and continued walking. Then another police whistle blew. This one seemed much louder. She picked up the pace, her heart racing and pounding in her chest. She rounded a corner and a horse reared up and neighed. Eliza shrieked and jumped to the left. The animal came down, hooves clapping like thunder against the cobblestone. A carriage door swung open with a shadow of a man in its opening. His gloved hand reached out to Eliza.

"Get in, quick."

She took hold and climbed in.

Chapter 14

Eliza sat down in the seat across from the man. Their black leather gloves stuck together for a moment before pulling apart. "Thank you, sir," she said.

He tipped the rim of his top hat forward, which hid his face even more. The only distinguishable feature was his pointy chin. Everything else was veiled in shadows. Eliza examined his attire. It appeared he was a gentleman of some sort based on his fashionable suit. As her stare moved over his clothes, she could feel him watching her in return.

"Where shall I tell my man to take you?" His voice was low and deep.

"Regent's Park, please sir."

He tapped the roof of the carriage with a cane Eliza hadn't noticed before. The handle was made of bronze formed into the shape of a serpent's head. Red rubies were inlaid for the eyes. It was quite elegant.

Eliza sat back and put her hands together in her lap. The gloves stuck to one another. Pulling them apart filled the coach with a muted sound of tearing paper and she wondered why blood had to be such a tacky substance. *Had the gentleman noticed when he took her hand? Then again his glove seemed sticky, too.*

The carriage rode on, and Eliza sat with a small smile on her face and eyed the carriage's interior as an excuse to observe more details about the gentleman. The legs of his pants were as wet as the bottom of her hem. She could make nothing else out about him since he wore nothing but black. If someone were to look upon the pair, they'd think they were either going to, or coming from, a funeral. Then something next to the man's feet caught Eliza's eye. It stopped her breath. A medical bag very much like hers was on the floor of the carriage to his right. A feeling of panic sped up her heart rate. She looked at him and she could tell his eyes were already on her face.

"It is late for a woman of Regent's Park to be out in such a dangerous part of the city," he said.

Eliza took a deep breath to calm herself. "I was visiting friends."

An odor clung to the air between them—the smell of metal and salt—a scent of blood. It couldn't all be emanating from her. She moved forward, closer to the man, then inhaled deeply. The man sat up and grabbed her wrist. "What is it, Miss? Are you faint?"

"No, sir."

He let go of her and this time, it was *his* glove that stuck to hers. They eyed one another. Heart muscles tightened within her chest.

The carriage stopped, and a moment later, the door opened. "Regent's Park," the driver said. Eliza took her medical bag and stepped down.

She turned around and looked up at the man in the carriage. "Who shall I thank, sir?"

The gentleman tipped his hat forward again and smiled, bringing together thin slivers of pink flesh above the pointy chin. "Simply a good Samaritan, Miss."

"Thank you, then."

"Remember not to travel at the East End late at night. For your own safety."

"Yes, sir."

The driver shut the door and Eliza walked into the park as fast as she could. The carriage pulled away, and when the sounds were barely audible, Eliza headed home. For a moment, she wondered if he would have his driver follow her, but then she came to her senses and was sure paranoia must be setting in.

Once more, Eliza came quietly through the servants' entrance.

Then she unfastened her skirts and let them drop to the floor. She rinsed the hems, her cape, and coat with her gloves on, then left everything hanging over a chair for Nanette to wash better the next day. In the kitchen, she opened her medical bag on the cutting block table, took out the wrapped organs, then walked over and placed them on the hearth fire. She listened to them sizzle and crackle for a while, entranced by the orange and yellow flames licking and devouring the pieces of a whore. Before leaving, she added a few more logs and stoked the fire to keep it hot and burning high.

Eliza went upstairs to her room and fell asleep thinking of the good Samaritan.

And wondering whether or not he was truly all that good.

* * *

The next morning, Eliza and her parents arrived home from church and were told by Mr. Sutton that several men were waiting to speak with Lord Covington in his study. After her father went to greet them, Eliza joined her mother in the parlor for tea.

"Why are there so many people here? And who are they?" Lady Covington said.

"Mr. Sutton told me that there's an Inspector Abberline, an Inspector Dew, and a Detective Halse here. Along with two police surgeons, Doctors Sequeira and Brown," Mrs. Sutton said.

"Something more must have happened in Whitechapel. What else do you know?"

"Papers say there were two women murdered last night. *London Star's* calling him Jack the Ripper now. He wrote a letter taunting the police and everything."

"Two?" Eliza said. Her mind went straight to the gentleman in the carriage. The smell inside, how their gloves kept sticking, and his medical bag on the floor. Could he have been The Whitechapel Murderer? This Jack the Ripper? Her mother's voice pulled her away from the idea.

"The world has gone mad, Mrs. Sutton. From now on Eliza, you're to use one of our carriages to get to and from the university. Don't even think of refusing me."

Eliza didn't argue. There was no point in it, and she needed to take the advice of the gentleman Samaritan and stay away from the East End. Only if it was necessary to brush up on the female anatomy to pass her exams would she give it another go; otherwise she'd stay away.

Nearly two hours had passed when her father finally came into the parlor. He told Mrs. Sutton they would need to dine early.

"What on earth for?" her mother said.

"The men would like me to join them later at the station."

"The police station?"

"Well, I can't very well have them at the gentlemen's club now can I?"

"Indeed, you cannot."

Then Eliza wondered if her Samaritan went to clubs. He was certainly dressed for it. Her father turned his attention to her. "Seems I was right, and the murderer has become more vicious. This is why they need my insight."

Her mother turned toward the two talking and listened.

"You must help them, Father. I just wish there was something I could do, too."

"Thomas," said her mother. "I've told your daughter she's not to leave this house without taking one of our carriages. I won't have it."

"Yes, dear," he said. "I'm sure Eliza is well aware of the situation." He looked at his daughter and rolled his eyes.

Eliza smiled and took a sip of tea.

* * *

For the next week, the family's carriage took Eliza everywhere she needed to go. She didn't want to admit it, but riding in the coach with the curtains closed really did make her feel safe. Even though she knew Catherine Eddowes—the *London Star* had revealed the prostitute's surname—was no longer following her, Eliza wondered if her gentlemen Samaritan friend might come looking around. She thought he could have the same curiosities about her that she had for him. And what would he think about her evolving his brutality without his own hand in it? Perhaps he'd be angry with her for bringing so much attention to himself. Maybe he was plotting to kill her, or even worse, expose the truth. The thoughts would drive her mad if she continued this way.

The Samaritan was a gentleman and therefore would be educated. He wouldn't allow himself to be caught under any circumstances. Besides, he'd been killing prostitutes and women of ill-repute in the East End. It was obvious he knew Eliza didn't belong there, had even said as much. She had nothing to worry about. Soon enough she'd be a graduate physician and then married off. Her heart sunk as the last of her thoughts seemed rather dull. What would living with Henry be like compared to saving lives and taking them, blackmail, and riding in a carriage with Jack the Ripper? She knew exactly what it would be like—it would be suffocating.

After breakfast, Nanette, who'd smartly kept quiet about having to wash the filthy skirts, cloak, and frock coat, helped Eliza put on a different coat, hat, and gloves. Then, while Eliza waited for the family carriage to pull up front, an altogether different one raced from up the street and halted at the gate in a peculiar angle. Eliza couldn't help but think it might be Jack the Ripper, her Samaritan gentleman, come to call—or kill. Her heart began to race. The carriage's driver came round and opened the door. To Eliza's surprise, a servant stepped down and was hurriedly walking toward the house. Eliza went out and met the woman at the gate, just as her own carriage pulled up. It was the Williams's maid, her eyes teary and full of fear. "Please, Miss," the maid said. "It's Mrs. Williams. She needs you as fast as you can come."

Eliza told her driver she'd be riding in the Williams's carriage.

He nodded and turned around. Then she followed the Williams's maid into their carriage. "What happened?" Eliza said. The carriage sped up the street, bouncing them around in the back.

"Sir Jon left early. You know he spends Fridays helping the poor at London Hospital."

"Yes, yes, I know." *Although we're both well aware he's doing more than that.*

"I went to help Mrs. Williams dress for breakfast and found her still in bed. She wasn't coming to. I even shook her."

"But why send for me? Doctor Williams is—"

"This fell from her hand." The maid passed a small glass bottle to Eliza. She raised it and took a whiff. The scent was mildly astringent. A label on the outside of the bottle read, *laudanum*. "There was another empty one on her night table next to the bed."

Eliza's heart sank. Laudanum was useful in small doses, but deadly in large amounts. She was about to yell out at the driver to hurry when the carriage pulled up to the Williams's house. The two women opened the door and climbed out on their own, then ran into the house. Ann's body was as the maid had described it, sprawled out across the bed. She was alive, but her breathing was very slow and her pulse faint. "Does anyone else know?" Eliza said.

"No," the maid said. "Not even the driver. I shut the door when I left and told the rest of them to stay out. That Mrs. Williams was feeling ill today."

"Good. Then it would make sense that you called for me—very smart. "What's your name?"

"It's Abigail, Miss."

"All right, Abigail, let's get Mrs. Williams sitting up in bed. We'll need to wash her, change the clothes she has on. Have someone in the kitchen make her some tea. Tell them to knock first, and then you take the tray. I'll also need you to send your driver to the Royal Free Hospital to tell a Professor Huxley I will not be attending classes today."

"Yes, Miss."

"Let's use cool water."

Eliza helped Abigail with every aspect of the care. Ann

urinated on herself and soaked the bed sheets only an hour after they'd got her dressed, so they had to go through the entire routine again, but all the commotion seemed to be causing her to stir. Off and on she'd been opening her eyes. Eliza held a candle near Ann's face to get a better look and noted that her pupils were pinpoints.

The maid gently held her head, while Ann took several sips of tea. After which she lay back against the pillows, then suddenly sat straight up with bulging eyes and opened her mouth. A dark liquid shot across the bed in a steady stream. Eliza and Abigail looked at one another with wide eyes.

Ann groaned and then lay down again. For the next hour, she would rouse, vomit, and then pass out, but she was becoming much more coherent during the times she was awake. Pushing away the cup of tea and shaking her head no.

It was late afternoon when Eliza thought Ann was stable enough for her to leave. She gave Abigail strict instructions to follow, and she was to send for her again if there were any problems. "When does Sir Jon come home?" Eliza said.

"Not 'til very late on Fridays, Miss."

"Good. Try and keep him away from her if you can, for the next day or so."

"That shouldn't be a problem. They've been sleeping in separate rooms for months. Hardly talk to one another at all anymore."

"Has she done this before?"

Abigail lowered her eyes and nodded. "It was never as bad as this, Miss."

Sweltering rage filled Eliza's chest. She took in a deep breath which only compounded the sensation of hate rising beneath her ribcage. Eliza rushed to the bedroom door, swung it open and headed for the foyer.

"Shall I call for the carriage?" the maid said.

"No, thank you. I'll walk."

Stepping out into the cold air felt like a sledgehammer against her chest so full of heat and rage. Eliza couldn't exhale fast enough and began choking on the Williams's porch. She started walking before anyone saw and came to assist her.

How could Sir Jon be so cruel? Her boot heels clacked against the icy street and the sounds resonated from the high treetops. *Were all men this way? Perhaps even her father?* She didn't want to know or even think it. Men were inherently lecherous, it seemed, and there was no way to prevent it—except to perhaps, eliminate the temptation.

Chapter 15

Ann Williams had sent a basket of fresh fruit to the Covington household two days later. "My goodness," Eliza's mother said. "How lovely, and grapes, too. Very decadent for this time of year, she must have special ordered them. Apparently, your visit with her went well, although she was a bit late in sending her regards." She picked up a piece of toast and nibbled at a corner.

"We merely caught up on what had been happening in our lives. Ann is a wonderful person and a dear friend, if a bit awkward in society."

"I only wish she would come out more. It would do her a world of good. It's a shame she can't have children. I've heard rumors of Sir Jon's affairs."

"Mother!"

"Well, I won't give you any details, but Ann should be out showing support for him and not mulling around at home. It only lets everyone know the rumors are true. Maybe you should mention it to her on your next visit. I assume you'll be seeing her again."

"Maybe. I'm busy these next few weeks." Eliza finished her tea.

"Which reminds me, the baker—"

"Mother, you choose. Please, for anything else that comes up, pick what you would have wanted for your own wedding. I trust your tastes and know you'll arrange the wedding of the century. My suggestions will only make it drab and I know how important this is to you."

"Eliza, you can't be serious."

"I am."

"But it's *your* special day."

"And it will be even more special if you arrange everything, Mother."

Tears began to swell in her mother's eyes. She raised a napkin to dab them. Eliza rose from her chair, walked over, and kissed her on the cheek. "I've got to head out now, but promise me you'll take care of all the wedding plans."

"Of course, dear, but you should have eaten something more."

Eliza left the room before her mother burst into tears. It was apparent she was on the verge. What mother doesn't dream of planning her only daughter's wedding? And be fortunate enough to have one like Eliza who wants no part in it.

Soon there would be obligatory dinners to attend at the Osborne's home and holiday gatherings. Time was running out and then she'd be married and have to move. The life she knew and loved was coming to an end, but she had no intention of giving it up quietly.

No. Not quietly at all.

* * *

The Royal Free Hospital on Henrietta Street, associated with The London School of Medicine for Women, was a teaching hospital. The girls would make their rounds and take notes that Professor Huxley would go over the following day. It was busier than usual, so Eliza and her classmates were spread throughout the building, seeing patients on their own. Vagrants were lined up one after the other, waiting behind makeshift partitions of thin sheets used for curtains.

Eliza walked over to an isolated corner and pulled back the linen. A pretty young woman with blonde hair, not nearly as fair or golden as hers, sat at the edge of a table. She looked up when Eliza rifled through her medical papers. Her eyes were a pale blue compared to Eliza's bright ones. "Hello, Miss. Can you tell me when the doctor will be in to see me?"

"I am the doctor."

"Oh, I'm sorry. I just thought that—"

"I was a nurse."

She smiled and nodded.

Eliza continued flipping through the pages, then went back to the first one and froze. Eyes wide, she looked at the woman and then back down at the notes. "Your name?" she said.

"Mary Kelly, just like it says on those papers you've been reading."

A bit uppity for a prostitute. It was an extremely convenient coincidence however, and had to have more meaning than to simply taunt her. Fate was telling her what she had to do. Thinking quick, she brushed off the harlot's snippy remark. "Sometimes the nurses make mistakes and put the wrong papers in the room. I imagine you'd feel better if I made sure this was really you."

"Oh, yes, Miss, I mean, doctor. I'm sorry, just a bit nervous is all, and I'd like to be heading back to East End before dark."

"I understand. How can I help you?" She hoped it was syphilis.

"Well, if I can trust you." Mary spoke with a honeyed voice and looked up with angelic eyes. Eliza could see how this pathetic charm might work on Sir Jon, but she wanted nothing more than to slit this woman's throat right this very moment.

"I assure you. I'm as silent as the grave."

"Well, I suppose. You are a doctor, right?"

"Yes, I am." *Or rather, will be, very soon.*

Mary looked her up and down for a moment, took in a deep breath then spoke softly. "I've been seeing a gentleman as of late, and I mean a *real* gentleman. He's got no children of his own and I'd like to give him one or more."

The rage began to swell within Eliza. Heat erupted from her chest and radiated to her limbs, veins and arteries searing with molten hatred. It needed to be controlled. There was no way to extinguish this despicable woman right here at this very moment.

"Why didn't you go to the London Hospital in East End?" Eliza said. "They could have helped you there." Eliza was sure it was because Mary didn't want Sir Jon to find out what she was up to.

She wondered what he would do, if anything, were he to discover it.

"They know me too well at that place, if you know what I mean. I wanted to keep things private. Like I told you, it's a gentleman I'm seeing. He'd want me to come here anyhow if he knew. A hospital with lots of women ought to know more about having babies."

"So this gentleman, he doesn't know your plan?" Eliza was pleased she could feign concern, when what she really wanted was to stab her pencil into the woman's eye.

"No, I want to surprise him. Don't look down on me doctor, it's not what you think. He loves me, and he'd be overjoyed if I could give him a baby. He wants one more than anything else in the whole world."

"I see. Well, has everything been working properly down there?"

"Yes."

"And your monthly is regular?"

"Yes."

Eliza couldn't help wondering why Mary even bothered coming to the hospital and was certain it showed on her face.

"I know what you're thinking," she said. "My womanly parts are working fine. I just want to know if there's a way I can get pregnant faster, help it along somehow."

"Ah…well, that's all you had to say." Eliza smiled, her rage buried under miles of cool ice. "There's a new elixir some are using to do what it is you want. It promotes health and optimizes the reproductive system."

"Why haven't I heard of it?"

"Scientists and doctors are just now testing it. I shouldn't have said anything. You must swear to secrecy." Eliza squinted and put her index finger over her lips and whispered, "Shhh."

"Yes, of course," Mary said.

"This hospital is where they are testing it."

"Oh, that's good news. Can I have some then?"

"I'm quite sure you understand they are *very* particular about who gets it."

"Saving it for the rich are they?"

"But maybe..."

"What? Tell me."

"No, it's a silly idea."

"It isn't. Please, you've got to help me."

"Well, every now and again I do charity work at the East End. What if I were to take some from here and bring it to you after I was done with my duties?"

"Or I could just meet you here?"

"No, that won't do. It would give me away for sure if someone saw us talking. It will have to be at night, when I've finished my work. I'll understand if you're too eager and want to look for something else, there are plenty others that would—"

"Don't cut me off, yet. I'm willing to wait. About how long you think?"

"In a week, or two at the latest."

"Well, that's not long at all. I'm up for it."

"Since it will be dark soon, you should probably head back to East End. When I come to see you with the elixir, I'll give you a physical exam then as well if you'd like."

Mary hopped off the table edge. "Such service—who am I to get a personal doctor's visit, and a treatment as well?"

"I feel for your needs. You and your gentleman friend seem desperate for a child."

"Yes doctor, very much so."

"Where shall I come when it's all ready?"

"Miller's Court. Number 13."

"Good. You have your own place?"

"Well, yes. I told you I was seeing a *gentleman*."

"Ah," Eliza said. Sir Jon must be paying for this wench's room. The thought sickened her and the anger swelled again. "I have no way of getting a message to you, so I'll be there when I can. It will be later in the evening, though. That I know."

"I'll be ready."

"Good day to you then, Miss Kelly," Eliza said through gritted teeth.

Mary grabbed Eliza's hand and shook it. "Thank you, doctor. Thank you so much." Then she leaned over, brought it up to her lips and kissed it.

Eliza pulled her hand away. "That's not necessary," she said.

Mary Kelly laughed as she walked out of the partitioned room. It was obvious that she knew she'd made Eliza uncomfortable and was taking advantage.

Behind the makeshift curtain, Eliza clenched the medical papers and held her breath. Feeling faint, she reached over and leaned against the table. Several minutes passed until normalcy came again. She folded up the papers, pushed them into her pocket, then moved the curtain to the side and walked down the hall with a smile across her face.

Chapter 16

A few days after her encounter with Mary Kelly, Eliza was deeply focused on a dissection of the human heart when Professor Huxley leaned over her shoulder, the odors of liver and onions on his breath. "What is that pinched between your forceps, Miss Covington?" He moved his spectacles down to the tip of his nose.

"A vein, sir." Somewhat startled by him, her words came out more like a question than an answer.

The professor leaned closer to her ear and whispered. "Why bother coming to exams later in the month, you'll only embarrass the both of us, and you're already guaranteed to pass."

"It is a vein, sir," she said with more confidence.

"For what?" He spoke up and straightened his posture.

"The heart."

"But where do they come from?"

Eliza looked up to see if any of her classmates were watching. They all appeared to be busy with their own dissections. She wondered why he was so particularly hard on her. It seemed brutally unfair.

"Miss Covington," he said.

"Yes."

"Answer the question."

"They're from the body, sir."

"Which part?" He stomped his foot.

Eliza's heart was racing and her cheeks felt warm. She hated Professor Huxley and imagined plunging the forceps into his eyeball then leaving class to the clapping and cheers of the other women.

"The lungs," she said, unsure of her answer.

"Amazing," he said. "And a very lucky guess," he whispered while walking away.

Certain an envious smile was on his face, Eliza wished she could carve a permanent one there. A sense of power surged through her at the thought it was something she could actually make happen. Killing Annie Chapman was an accident, but making it appear as though Jack the Ripper committed the crime was genius—she knew that. Murdering Catherine Eddowes was a choice and she recognized that as well. Eliza had given in to the dark rage she only recently discovered dwelled within her. It was possible to control, but as long as external factors existed triggering the hate, it would need periodic release. Slaying those who hurt her in their roundabout ways as well as those who hurt the ones she loves most, was the only way to liberate the fury.

* * *

Eliza arrived home and was removing her hat and gloves when she noticed the day's post on a table in the foyer. A returned letter from Doctor James Riley was on top. Eliza recognized the envelope. "Mrs. Sutton, isn't this one of my wedding invitations?" Eliza picked up the card and showed it to the maid.

"Yes Miss, I believe it is."

"Do you know why one was sent to Doctor Riley?"

"Your mother did the invitations, miss. You'll have to ask her."

"Where is she?"

"In the parlor."

Eliza tossed her frock coat over to Mrs. Sutton, then stormed off with the invitation in her hand. "Mother, what is the meaning of this?" She held the envelope up in the air and waved it back and forth.

Lady Covington looked up from the embroidery work she was doing. "Calm yourself, and don't speak to me that way, it upsets my nerves."

While crossing the room, Eliza noticed the wool skirts worn for school didn't rustle. Perfect for stalking—if she were to tiptoe, no one would ever hear her approaching. She held the invitation out for Lady Covington to see. "What of it?" her mother said.

"Are you taunting him? You know he suffers from a broken heart. How could you?"

"Your father made me send it."

"Why?"

"You should ask him."

"He's been so busy with work these past few evenings, I haven't even seen him."

Lady Covington laughed.

"What do you find amusing about this, Mother?"

"Your father has been spending his evenings at the gentleman's club, dear. And not the ones our circle of friends frequent. Says those detectives and police surgeons come together and work on solving the Whitechapel murders. What do you think of it?"

Eliza kept quiet. *He couldn't possibly be out doing something else—bad things. Not when I'm so close to graduating, marrying, and leaving.*

"Do you believe that's what those men are really doing into the late hours of night? Should I be worried? Eliza, are you listening?"

"Yes, Mother, I mean no, Mother, you shouldn't worry. Father is—"

"I *know* he is knowledgeable and well-respected, but he's not getting any younger and needs his rest."

"I'm going to try and wait up for him tonight. I really want to know why he would send James an invitation. It seems cruel and very unlike Father to do such a thing."

"All men have their reasons for doing what they do. You should leave it alone."

"That's no excuse, and I want an explanation." Eliza tromped out of the parlor.

Eliza waited in her father's study for a long while after dinner. She sat in his desk chair and looked over clipped news articles of the murders, a feeling of guilt soured in the pit of her stomach. Certainly not because there was any reproach for killing the women, but she was to blame for keeping her father working so late at night these past few weeks. He was busy trying to help solve crimes she had committed. Some brandy would surely help the feeling pass, so she poured herself a glass. While taking the occasional sip, her fingers flipped through the pieces of paper, and she read clipped articles from *The Times* in an album Lord Covington made of the murders.

Behind her, on the bookcase wall, were at least a dozen more similar albums he'd put together since her childhood. Eliza was always curious about his fascination with the macabre, but she eventually grew out of it. He'd even handwritten some notes in his latest, *Jack the Ripper* collection. One in particular stood out. Words that were staggered and scrawled out across a page—"*The Juwes are The men That*

Will not be Blamed for nothing."

What did it mean? The article on the next page said the chalk writing was on a wall near where they found a piece of bloody apron. Eliza didn't remember seeing the words while cleaning her knife and instruments, but neither was it something she'd been looking for. The bloody apron piece she remembered tossing to the ground. Then she wondered if it were possible that Jack the Ripper had been where she was. Could he have been hiding in a dark corner? Watching her? Eliza was sure she'd have noticed, but maybe not. The Samaritan gentleman came to mind, which made her lift the brandy snifter and take a bigger sip. Was there chalk on his gloves? It was hard to remember.

Looking up to think more on the subject, her father entered the study. "Father," she said. "I'm so glad you're home."

"It's late, Eliza. What could be so important? I'm certain it can wait 'til morning."

Something in his manner exuded a hint of guilt, which had her too perplexed to reply. He came up to the desk, leaned over, and closed the album. Rife with heady cigar smoke and alcohol, her father reeked of a gentleman's club. His strong odor made her step back, and what she saw next made her gasp.

"What is it?" he said.

Eliza looked down at his desk where some scattered newspaper clippings still lay. "Seeing all this death, I think it has affected me."

"It never bothered you before. Take another sip of brandy." While he was collecting the pieces of shorn rectangles and squares, she glanced at his shirt collar again. And there it was—a finger-length's smear of red lipstick. Lord Covington looked up and she turned away.

"You're right, what I wanted to say can wait. I'll talk with you tomorrow." He stepped toward her and leaned in. Repulsed to the point of being faint, it took every bit of her will to kiss him on the cheek. "Good night, Father," she whispered through clenched jaws.

"Get some rest," he said. "You look very out of sorts." He gave her a peck on the cheek.

Wanting to run out of the room, out of the house, and down the street screaming, NO! Eliza forced herself to walk calm and slow out of his study. Instead of going upstairs, she went to the kitchen and poured water from the tea kettle into a basin. Eliza washed her face and lips with scalding water and cried.

Chapter 17

Eliza's head was in a fog when she woke. Her face felt raw against the crisp linen of the pillow. Flinging back the covers, she got out of bed and inspected her skin in the mirror above the wash basin. It was slightly pink compared to the bright red capillaries webbed across her sclera. Sleep had come late, as dreadful thoughts of the previous night's discovery lingered in her mind and kept her busy thinking, devising. Nanette entered the room to help her get dressed for the day. Without saying a word, she took some powder from the vanity and dabbed it all over Eliza's face.

Downstairs at breakfast, Lord Covington was reading the paper while Lady Covington sipped tea when she entered the room.

"Good morning," her mother said, as Eliza entered the room.

Eliza nodded and smiled.

"You look ill this morning and your eyes are red."

Her father lowered his paper, looked her up and down. "She seems well enough."

"To be in a hospital perhaps," her mother said.

"And that's where I'll be Mother, so you have nothing to worry about." Eliza pulled out a chair and sat down. Mrs. Sutton came over and poured a cup of tea, then added a splash of milk.

Lady Covington picked up a muffin and tore a piece away with her teeth. After swallowing, she glared at Eliza. "Well, did you talk with your father about the invitation?"

"I—"

"What invitation?" he said.

"The one you had me send James Riley."

"Father, how could you?"

He laughed, shook the newspaper straight and went back to reading.

It was shocking to see this side of him. So heartless and cruel. *An adulterer.* She raised her tea cup between trembling fingers and took a sip. Her mother smirked, and Eliza wondered if she knew and if she did, for how long? *Why hadn't she reacted to it? Had she ever?* It was doubtful. The hate rose, she had to leave. After finishing her last bit of tea, Eliza pushed the plate of uneaten muffin away and stood up.

"Are you leaving?" her mother said. "You've had nothing."

"I'll have something between classes."

Lord Covington didn't say a single word when Eliza left the room.

* * *

During one of many tedious lectures by Professor Huxley that day, Eliza wrote Doctor James Riley a letter. It multiplied a hundred times the love she actually felt for him, but she thought he deserved that after how her father had treated him. The note explained why it was impossible for her to return to London Hospital. There was still too much love in her heart for him and it hurt to be near. James would cherish the words and she wondered how long he would keep the letter—maybe forever.

After classes, Eliza made rounds at the Royal Free Hospital on Henrietta Street, since she'd no longer been permitted to go to the London Hospital at East End. Steady traffic came to and from the small supply room where the linen and medicines were kept. Two hours later, mostly everyone charged off to an emergency on the first floor. Eliza quickly walked into the storage room and closed the door. A strong smell of astringent made her wrinkle her nose. Rows of glass bottles and vials lined the shelves. To the right was a cluster of smaller brown vials with droppers. The paper labels on the outside read *laudanum*. Eliza took three of the bottles, wrapped a strip of gauze around each one, and then slipped them into her apron pockets before walking out.

Over the next three days, a total of seven vials were collected, brought home, and their labels removed. But it wasn't until Thursday next, November 8th to be exact, that Eliza carefully lined them upright in her medical bag before leaving the house for classes.

That morning, she'd handed Mrs. Sutton a note with strict directions not to deliver it until dinner. "I won't be dining here tonight," she told the maid, "and I don't want to explain why to

Mother just yet."

Mrs. Sutton nodded and took the envelope.

Eliza also left separate instructions with Nanette. "Let them know you saw me in my room and helped me change my clothes. I told you I was dining out with friends and to expect me home late."

"Yes, Miss," Nanette said. When the young maid went back to work, Eliza snuck into the girl's room and stole a black hat from her clothing chest. It was time to give the servant a bit of extra pay for her hard work and to replenish the supply.

With her bag stuffed so full she had to lay her cloak across the top to conceal its contents, Eliza climbed into her family's carriage.

* * *

Sitting in class, struggling to stay awake while Professor Huxley lectured on and on about the heart, Eliza thought about graduation exams taking place next week. Feeling confident she would do well—regardless of his hateful remarks about her knowledge or lack thereof—her mind drifted off.

Mary Kelly would be the final victim she'd contribute to the evolution and legacy of Jack the Ripper. Knowing she'd assisted in making the gentleman Samaritan infamous made her smile. Only two days after meeting him, it was resolved in her mind he was most certainly the Whitechapel Murderer—Jack the Ripper as the papers were now calling him. From one killer to another she felt it, the camaraderie of simply knowing the darkness in someone like oneself. Eliza was sure he suspected her as well. He seemed almost protective by telling her not to travel the East End after dark.

By the time she finished classes and rounds at the Royal Free Hospital on Henrietta Street, a dense fog had rolled in on the streets of London. Riding in the hansom made her feel like a normal person again—alive—as though she was going somewhere with a purpose. And what a purpose it was!

After exiting the cab, she put on Nanette's hat. Most of the working girls at East End knew her as Jane by the dark hooded cloak she wore, and she had no want of anyone approaching her for services this evening.

First stop was the London Hospital on Whitechapel Road. Before walking in, she took the letter for James out of her medical bag. Lowering the brim of the hat down over her face, Eliza entered the building. The receptionist was talking to a young couple at her desk. Then she got up from her station and led them somewhere down the hall. Eliza walked over and set the envelope down in plain sight next to some papers, then left. It was time she let James go and moved on with her life. Eliza had familial and social obligations she could not deny. He'd played an important part when she was young and naïve, but that innocence had long since passed.

It was evening and her hunger required some nourishment. In the dark corner of a pub, Eliza sat and ordered a meat pie. Patrons were busy drinking their pints and hardly noticed her. Their conversations revolved around Jack the Ripper, what the police were doing, and that they were a bunch of bumbling idiots.

Darkness blanketed the East End when Eliza walked out of the pub. Intensifying the sinister mood, the fog had gotten much worse. On cold nights as these, thick, black smoke from chimney stacks filled the streets and appeared green against the dim, yellow lamplights. It was an all-encompassing murky haze that included the odor of a bog. She held her gloved hand out and couldn't see it. She smiled, thankful for the perfect situation and felt even more forthright in her plan. It was as if some unknown force was aiding her, making it easier to commit the crime and escape unseen.

Her boots tapped against the cobblestone as she walked. A flat echo of the same sound bounced off a nearby rooftop. It would be difficult to know who or what was coming or going from where. The tapping grew more rapid as she picked up her pace, and soon she would be at Miller's Court knocking on the door of number 13.

This would be a night to remember.

Chapter 18

Alleys lined Dorset Street and all the surrounding buildings of Miller's Court. There were almost too many places to choose from for hiding, but Eliza settled on a dark corner across the way from Mary's room. Wanting to be sure the harlot was alone, she watched and waited.

An hour had passed and nothing happened. What if Nanette forgot to tell her mother she was dining with friends? Although, ever since the reigns were handed over for making her wedding arrangements, Lady Covington seemed less worried about where Eliza was or her activities. Lord Covington was out late most nights now. The lipstick on his collar came to mind again and her chest tightened. If it weren't for the detectives and police surgeons dragging him to gentleman's clubs with the excuse of working on the Whitechapel case, he never would have been tempted with adultery. His infidelity was their fault, and she would give those men something to keep them all busy for a while.

Some commotion was taking place outside Miss Kelly's room. The thick haze made it difficult to see. Eliza focused and saw a dark-haired woman with a gaudy red shawl wrapped around her shoulders leaving. Fortunately, it wasn't Miss Kelly. A man was approaching her. "Barnett," she said to him. "What are you doing here?"

"None of your bloody business, now out of my way."

The woman stepped aside and allowed the man access to Mary's room. He opened the door, went in then slammed it behind him. Eliza took in a deep breath and sighed while she watched the woman walk away. It would be a long night. *This particular prostitute stays rather busy.* It was tiring but made her angry enough to continue waiting.

Concealed by the fog, she left the confines of her hiding space and approached Mary's room, crouching down close to a small grimy window. One of the glass panes was broken out and she peeked in. The man, Barnett, had a large build. His physique reminded her of someone who might be a dock worker, and the cap next to his wool trousers with suspenders still attached on the floor reaffirmed it. His wide rear was contracting and relaxing between the whore's legs while he grunted like a pig. Eliza could see nothing else past his mass, and what she was able to observe made her nauseous, so she crept back to her secret hiding place across the way.

It was over two hours later when the man finally left Miss Kelly alone. After waiting another hour to be sure no one else would be coming, Eliza adjusted her hat, picked up her medical bag and approached the building, leery but thankful for the thick vapors that obscured everything.

After pounding on the door with her gloved fist, she took a step back and waited, hoping she gave Mary enough time after her last visitor to wash up. Miss Kelly opened the door wearing a sheer linen chemise and had an expression of curiosity on her face. "Oh yes," she said. "You're the doctor from the Royal Free Hospital. Come in."

Eliza nodded, stepped into the room and waited for Mary to close the door before she spoke. The room was the smallest one she'd ever seen, dark and void of any life or color except for a copy of a famous painting depicting a grieving widow in front of a grave. It was dreadful but felt appropriate. A rank odor of a salty sea hung in the air, along with smoke, and alcohol. It reminded her of what her father smelled like when he came home from the gentleman's club that night.

A small table sat in the corner next to a feeble wooden bed. Centered in the room against the far wall was the fireplace, the surrounding bricks stained by the black of burnt cinder and ash. An old table and two chairs were positioned in front of it. "Are you expecting anyone?" Eliza said, biting her tongue and stopping short of a longer question. She nearly added the word *else* at the end which might have triggered some suspicion.

Walking toward the fire, really only five steps into the room, she noticed Mary's undergarment hanging over the back of a seat. Eliza took off her hat and hung it on the chair's wooden post, inadvertently concealing most of the shoddy clothing. Not wanting to put her bag on the table, she placed it on the same chair as her hat, and then opened it. One by one, she took out the unmarked vials of laudanum. Mary joined her at the table with her eyes wide and a smile on her face at the sight of the small glass bottles. "You really came through, miss," the harlot said. "When should I take it? Shall I have some now?"

"Yes, yes, I'm getting to that."

"You still doing a bodily exam?"

"I think it would be a good idea, don't you?"

"Let me just wash up a bit."

Acidic bile rose up Eliza's throat and burned the back of her palate and tonsils. She quickly swallowed hard to make it go back down. Mary went over to the wash basin on the table next to the bed and dropped a piece of fabric into the water. Lifting up her chemise with one hand, she then took the wet cloth with the other and squeezed the excess liquid, then began vigorously wiping between her legs. Eliza swallowed another wave of rising stomach acid, then turned away and looked deep into her medical bag. The metallic blade of the surgical knife reflected the orange glow from the fire. She reached in, grabbed hold of the handle, and lifted the instrument so that it was resting at the very top of the bag. Ignoring what Mary was still doing, Eliza walked over to the bed and set the bag down at the foot of it and off to the right.

Mary had finished cleaning herself and followed behind Eliza as they both walked over to the table. The liquid in the brown glass vials appeared to dance with the flames of the fire behind them, captivating and hypnotizing the prostitute. Eliza smiled, thinking this would be too easy. "You'll want to drink one whole bottle a day until they're all gone," she said. "Then in the next week or so, your body should be primed for reproduction."

Mary snatched one of the bottles off the table and removed the stopper. Then she circled the vial's opening under her nose. "Smells awful strong, almost like—"

"Drink it," Eliza said. Her heart began to race as she watched the prostitute put the glass to her lips, tip the entire bottle of laudanum into her mouth, then swallow it all in one gulp.

"Ack!" The prostitute gagged.

"Quick, put your head back," Eliza shouted. "Don't you dare spit that up!"

Mary coughed, then caught her breath and calmed. "It's a worse bitter than laudanum that." She stared at the bottle before setting it back down on the table.

"Nothing of the sort, stop exaggerating. Do you want to get pregnant or not?"

"Aye, miss."

"Besides, it's only for a week. Can you do it, or shall I leave this minute and take it with me?"

Mary slowly nodded her head with a ridiculous smile across her face. Eliza wondered if the opium was already at work.

"Have you eaten recently?" she asked Mary.

"Not since breakfast." She laughed and swooned a little to the left.

"Excellent, then let's get on with that exam."

As the prostitute stumbled over to the bed, a hint of sympathy touched Eliza to see such a pathetic creature. Mary was a pretty girl with blue eyes almost like her own. They were both young and already set on their paths by unseen hands that forced them along an invisible board, like game pieces. There was no changing who would win; in the end she knew it would be the men. In that moment, Eliza decided she wouldn't kill the poor wretch. Simply do the world a favor and make having children for her impossible.

Mary sat on the side of the bed just in time, a second later, and she might have hit the floor. Eliza picked her legs up by the ankles and swung them around onto the bed. The rest of her body fell back against the flimsy mattress of straw and fabric. She lay there and began laughing.

"You'll need to stop moving for the exam," Eliza said.

The prostitute nodded, then put her hands over her mouth, but continued to giggle. A candle stuck into a broken wine bottle was situated on the bedside table. Shaking off the nonsense, Eliza stepped over and got it, then brought the light closer to where she would be working. She rolled the sleeves of her cloak and frock coat then raised Mary's chemise over her hips, exposing the pale skin around the pink flesh of her vaginal opening. A small triangular patch of fine blonde-reddish pubic hair was right above it, reminding Eliza of Greco-Roman paintings depicting beautiful nude women.

Mary instinctively spread her legs apart and Eliza was not repulsed by what she saw. It was one of the lovelier specimens she'd ever seen. Finding it hard to concentrate, she could do nothing but stare.

"Well," Mary said. Taking Eliza's eyes away from the piece of heaven so many men adored.

"I don't see anything significant on the outside."

"That's good isn't it?"

"Yes, but I need to get a look within." Eliza put her hands on Mary's legs and gently pushed them back. "Hold them like that," she told the girl. Then Eliza positioned herself on her knees at the end of the small bed. Leaning forward didn't take much, and then she was right between Mary's legs. Despite the nasty dock worker who had recently been there, the scent that wafted up onto Eliza's face was clean and almost sweet. It was apparent why this girl in particular was so busy and had a gentleman keeping her. Then she remembered why she was there. The man Mary spoke of didn't deserve to be trapped, not that way anyhow, and as busy as this whore was selling her beautiful wares, Eliza would never have to worry about her needing any backstreet abortion services when she was through with her.

"You'll feel some pressure." She plunged her index and middle finger inside Mary as far back as they would go. With her other hand on top of the prostitute's abdomen she simultaneously pushed down and pushed up her fingers, feeling the organs in between.

Mary groaned a little, but it wasn't a sound of discomfort. Eliza thought the woman might actually be enjoying it. She looked down at her face and her eyes were closed, but her lips made a slight smile. Through her sheer chemise, Eliza saw her erect nipples along with her firm round breasts, which were nearly as perfect as what was between her legs. She adjusted her fingers inside a little and watched a kind of ecstasy veil Mary's face. The woman moved her rear end up in circles and Eliza felt her vaginal walls clench. Moisture that was warm and soft filled the cavity. Eliza slid her fingers out and observed the clear glistening substance. Mary's eyes were still closed. She was heavy under the influence of the laudanum and Eliza knew she could do anything to her with little protest.

After wiping the glazed fingers on the bed, she reached back into her bag and fished for the long curette. Mary started giggling again.

"Stop moving," Eliza said.

Eyes still closed, she sighed softly. "You did that nearly as well as my gentleman friend."

"Don't try and turn a simple exam into a loathsome act." Eliza was flushed with anger and embarrassment, so she spoke her mind, assuming the prostitute probably wouldn't remember the conversation. "Sir Jon should be spending his time with his wife. Not with the likes of you."

The prostitute's laughter intensified, shaking the entire bed. Eliza's heart began to race and pound. The high pitch made her head throb. "Stop laughing," she shouted. "There's nothing funny about it."

Mary paused for a moment, a huge drug-induced smile across her face. Then she said, "Sir Jon isn't my *particular* gentleman, Miss Doctor." More laughing came and then panting for air in between. "He's one of my favorites, but no, it's Lord Covington I'm all about."

Eliza stopped breathing. Her vision blackened from the periphery inward. With one hand still in the medical bag fumbling for the curette, a sudden sharp sting and then an itch came from her pinky finger. The pain kept the darkness from blinding her completely. It was the surgical knife. She carefully slid her fingers along the flat of the blade until she reached the handle. Then she pulled it from the bag.

The drugged whore's eyes were still closed when Eliza turned toward her. The laughing had become taunting cackling. With the instrument in her hand, Eliza moved over Mary's spread legs, which the prostitute still held back with her hands. Before losing her sight to the blackness that was quickly closing in, Eliza thought of a backhand stroke. She threw an imaginary ball up into the air, and moved her arm back. Mary opened her eyes and Eliza swung.

* * *

It was the hardest game of lawn tennis she'd ever played, and it all happened in the dark. A heart-pumping frenzy of swinging and striking that required all her energy, and hate was the fuel. Her vision came back in flashes—images of blue eyes staring up at her, blood, and gore.

Eliza wasn't quite finished with the game. She continued to play until her sight had fully returned. What she saw was annihilation, but to her, still incomplete, not done. Mary's lifeless head turned toward the wall. "Don't you look away, Miss Kelly," Eliza said to the mutilated corpse. She took a large piece of flesh she'd cut away and what looked to be an organ and propped them under the body's head to keep it straight. Mary appeared to be watching what Eliza was doing which was what she wanted.

"You desired to have a baby with my father. Here, right?" She cleared out the rest of the young woman's innards and then put her lifeless hand in the empty cavity. "It may be a little difficult for you now. And to think I was going to let you live. You have no heart, Mary Kelly. No heart at all." Eliza gripped the knife handle with both hands, raised it up in the air and plunged it down into the middle of the body's chest. Then she moved the blade back and forth to pry the sternum apart. When there was a large enough opening she pulled the rest of the ribcage apart with her bare hands. Bone shards cut into her palms, but she hardly noticed.

The heart was still warm when Eliza extracted it, wrapped it in a swatch of fabric, then placed it down into her bag. Sitting up on her knees, she realized her clothing was drenched in blood and bits of bone, flesh, and hair. Piece by piece, she removed her clothing and placed them into the fire. Because the wool was damp, it was necessary to stoke up the flames and add a log or two to get it nice and hot and keep it that way until every blood-stained garment was ash. In her frenzy, she'd sliced her arms and thighs. Fortunately, her skirts had taken most of the slashes to her legs. The ones on her forearms were a little deeper but wouldn't need stitches.

Another piece of bed linen was torn away to wipe her knife off before putting it away. Careful not get any more blood on herself, she went over to the water basin, dipped one end of a clean piece of linen into the bowl then quickly yanked it out, assuring her no blood would get in the water.

The hearth was ablaze and lit up the room even better than daylight. Eliza noticed the broken window pane as she looked around. There was an extra piece of linen she crumpled up in her hand and set into the open frame. Just in case someone walking by did the same thing she'd done earlier and peeked in.

All that was left clean was her chemise and a layer of underskirt. Eliza picked up the broken wine bottle that held the burning candle and looked around the dark corners of the room for clothes. Mary's green bodice and brown skirt were what she found and quickly put on. There was also a shawl Eliza picked up and wrapped around her head and shoulders to partially cover her face. One more time, she went around the room and gathered up what was hers. About to walk out the door with her medical bag discreetly tucked under her arm and hidden by the shawl, she saw the hat. Eliza walked over, picked it up and put it on top of the blazing fire. She looked back at Mary's body, whose head had turned to face the wall again.

Not only had Jack the Ripper evolved.
He had become the perfect killer.

Chapter 19

The following day was the Lord Mayor's Show, complete with a parade and multiple celebrations to honor the newly-elected Sir James Whitehead. The festivities were in full procession by noon. Eliza slept in, knowing her family never attended the parade. Lady Covington refused to stand out in the dreary November weather for anyone. The Covingtons would honor this year's elected official by attending the dinner held by the Royal Courts later in the evening.

Before sitting down to breakfast, Eliza stepped over to the window above the sideboard, pulled a curtain open and looked outdoors. A befitting air of gloom came from the sea in the guise of dark ashen clouds. Even cold, wet weather wouldn't keep the throngs of people desperate for something to celebrate in their warm homes, and soon the news of another murder would be spreading through London streets faster than the plague.

Eliza knew they would not be making the Royal Dinner this year. She visualized her father in his study with his head hung low, emptying his brandy decanter, asking for another, while grieving over his dead whore. He would get over it soon enough. Eliza had done a great service for all those whom she cared deeply about.

Now Mary Kelly's heart was nothing but ash settled at the bottom of her family's kitchen's hearth. Soon to be shoveled out by Mr. Sutton and put into the trash, which will eventually make its way into the Thames, and once more end up at the East End where she belonged.

* * *

Life in the Covington house during the next three weeks played out exactly as Eliza had imagined. Throughout the rest of November, her father spent most evenings alone in his study. Lady Covington carried on as though nothing had happened, although she did seem somewhat merrier than she had been before.

Just as Professor Huxley had confidentially told her, Eliza graduated from the London School of Medicine for Women. No honors were given, of course, but she hardly cared anymore. What she'd learned about herself and the human body elevated her status above and beyond the classical education.

Inspector Abberline congratulated Eliza at the graduation dinner her parents hosted at the end of the month. "And thank you for your past advice with…Whitechapel," he said.

"Have you any new leads?" she inquired.

The inspector looked over at Lord Covington who was standing across the room near the punch bowl with his head hung low. "No miss, none whatsoever—nothing for you to worry about, though. Best of luck with your nuptials next month and then off to America, I hear?"

"Yes, sir," Eliza said. Henry was standing by her side smiling from ear to ear.

"Blessings to you both." Inspector Abberline nodded then walked off toward Lord Covington and the two men spoke quietly to one another, looking around the room for anyone who might be watching. Eliza wasn't concerned. She knew they were proud, educated men, chasing their tails. As she'd overheard once in the East End pub, 'they were bumbling idiots.'

Then it was a great surprise to all the guests when Ann Williams and her husband entered the room. Eliza quickly walked up and shook hands with her. While Henry spoke to Sir Jon, Eliza led Ann over to the table covered in seasonal sweets and delights.

"I never thanked you," Ann said softly.

"Please, there's no need. You would've done the same for me. Things are better for you at home, I think." Eliza looked deep into

Ann's eyes.

"Yes, much, thank you again."

"And how was the eating chocolate? All these glorious treats spread out as far as the eye can see and not a single chocolate. I've yet to convince Father it isn't an evil thing."

"Speaking of evil things," Ann swallowed and looked down at the floor. "You don't know anything about the latest Whitechapel murder, do you?"

"Nothing at all, but what luck, right?"

"Eliza," Ann whispered as if to shush her.

"What is it, Ann? You can't tell me you're not happy with the news. You look absolutely beautiful this evening."

Ann was about to say something more, but Eliza waved Henry and Sir Jon over.

"What is it dear?" Henry said. He handed her a glass full of bubbling champagne.

"I was just telling Ann how absolutely beautiful she looks this evening. Don't you think so, Henry?"

"Yes, of course." He smiled at her, raised his champagne glass and took a sip.

"Wouldn't you agree as well, Sir Jon? Ann's beauty this evening rivals anything else that ever came out of Wales."

Sir Jon coughed and cleared his throat. His face turned red and Henry patted him on the back. "Are you all right?" he asked him.

"Yes, I'm fine. I'm fine."

"Well, I suppose," Henry said. "If you were to become ill, a room full of doctors would be the place to do it."

Sir Jon agreed and everyone laughed except for Ann. She stared at Eliza with squinted eyes. Once more she was about to speak, when Sir Jon took her by the arm, excused their leaving, then led her over to Lady Covington.

Henry turned to face Eliza, leaned in, and kissed her on the cheek. "Ah my dear, I'm so proud you've succeeded in this accomplishment I know you've been wanting."

"I am so happy."

"I'm sure our joy will only continue with the wedding and our move."

"Henry?" Eliza stepped back so that she could look him in the eyes.

"What is it? You upset about leaving? I know—"

"America's such a big country, Henry. Must we be always confined to New York City?"

Henry smirked. "Of course not, dear. Father has plans to open banks across the entire country. We'll be traveling from one coast to the other and you shall see *all* of America. And I'm almost certain every place we reside will be in need of an educated doctor."

Sudden images of Henry between the legs of American whores flashed through her mind, and she immediately tightened her grip around the glass. Before it shattered in her hand, Eliza remembered the way she'd left Mary Kelly. The prostitute's helpless, dead stare with those pale blue eyes in an unrecognizable face released the tension in her hold.

Eliza smiled and raised the glass to him.

"To new beginnings."

Author's Note

From August to November in 1888, five women were brutally murdered in London's East End that were attributed to Jack the Ripper because of their MO. There were also two murders that some speculate could have been his "starter kills." One occurred in the spring of 1888, and the other in the summer of the same year. Mary Kelly was his last victim and most vicious murder in London.

Many people believe that he came to America and began butchering women in a similar style to the ones in Whitechapel. Reports came from New York City beginning in the spring of 1889. The bodies of women being found murdered in very much the same way Jack's victims had been. These reports continued across the United States all the way to San Francisco for over more than a decade.

Since then, there have been hundreds of books written about Jack the Ripper—Who he was, why he murdered those women and then seemingly stopped, if it was possible he was a *she*, and even that he was an alien from another planet. Could it have been Royalty? Perhaps a conspiracy? The point is, regardless of all the theories, these murders remain some of the most memorable and written about crimes in history.

Rena Mason is a registered nurse and worked in the operating room for over 12 years. A longtime horror fan, she currently lives in Las Vegas, Nevada, is a member of the Pacific Northwest Writers Association, and a member of the Horror Writers Association. Her short story, "The Eyes Have It," is in the anthology, *Horror For Good: A Charitable Anthology* from Cutting Block Press. Her debut novel, *The Evolutionist*, will be out March 2013 from Nightscape Press. To learn more about Rena and her upcoming projects, visit her website www.renamasonwrites.com.